A
WEDDING GONE
TO THE DOGS

a Samantha Davies mystery

S.A. Kazlo

For Mandy and Mike Jr. who make my life complete.

WINGS FALLS

A. SWEETIE PIE'S CAFÉ
B. THE CLOTHES HORSE
C. THE SMILING PIG
D. THE SOUND MACHINE
E. THE TOY BOX
F. SAINT ANTHONY'S CATHOLIC CHURCH
G. CIVIL WAR MONUMENT
H. THE EWE AND ME WOOLERY
I. MOMMA MIA'S
J. THE NUT HOUSE
K. WINGS FALLS LIBRARY
L. WINGS FALLS PARK
M. AL'S FLY SHOP
N. TOP DRAWER CONSIGNMENTS
O. CANDIE PARKER- HOGAN'S HOME
P. WINGS FALLS SENIOR CENTER
Q. WINGS FALLS POLICE STATION
R. WINGS FALL COMMUNITY COLLEGE
S. SHOP AND SAVE
T. SAMANTHA DAVIES' HOME
U. WINGS FALLS ANIMAL HOSPITAL

Acknowledgements

Many thanks to my two critique groups:
The GFWG—Zackary Richards, Robin Inwald, Sandy Buxton, Kay Hafner, Billy Neary, Sarah Vanderzyden
The Storyboaders—Candie Moonshower, Roxyanne Young, Lisa Rondinelli Alberts
I'm forever grateful for my publisher, Gemma Halliday, for making my dream of Sam, Candie and Porkchop a reality, thank you.
Thank you, Jennifer Rarden, for your fabulous editing.
And for my biggest cheerleader, my husband Michael. I love you.
My readers, thank you from the bottom of my heart for taking the time to enter my little world of Wings Falls and its characters.

CHAPTER ONE

———

"Gladys, where did you buy this?" My Southern Belle cousin, Candie Parker, blushed down to the roots of her auburn curls. As a writer of steamy romance novels, it took a lot to fluster her, but the filmy negligee she held up in her hands had her creamy complexion turning the color of a ripe tomato.

We were gathered at The Ewe and Me Woolery. By we, I meant me, Samantha Davies, and my fellow Loopy Lady hookers. And no, I didn't mean that kind of hooker. We were a group of rug hookers who gathered every Monday morning to gab, get caught up on the local gossip, and hopefully get some rug hooking done, but today was Saturday morning and a special occasion—a bridal shower for Candie. She sat at the head of the table gushing over a *very* revealing negligee that the oldest member of our group, Gladys O'Malley, had gifted her. The negligee was a confection of filmy lace and satin ribbons, but a spider web would cover more. Gladys is somewhere in her eighties. Exactly where? No one knew. It was a well-guarded secret. Tin cans would turn to gold before Gladys revealed her true age.

I looked around the front room of The Ewe. We rug hookers had affectionately shortened the name of our happy place. Lucy Foster owned the rug hooking studio, along with her husband Ralph. She had let us use her shop for this surprise wedding shower for Candie. We Loopy Ladies had a blast decorating for the shower. It helped that a few mimosas flowed while we hung lavender and white streamers from the shelves and cubbies lining the walls of the studio. They overflowed with the lengths of fabric needed to satisfy our wool addiction for the rugs we created. Twelve of us, plus Flossie Garner and Valerie Fisherman—campaign workers for Mark— gathered around an old oak table to *ooh* and *ahh* over Candie's presents.

Candie was getting married in two weeks to the love of her life and a real nice guy, Mark Hogan. He held the title of Mayor in our little hometown of Wings Falls and was running for reelection this November. The primary election was a week from Tuesday, so it would be a really busy two weeks for Candie and Mark.

Wings Falls was a sleepy little town in upstate New York where we all lived. I grew up and had lived there all my life, except when I'd shuffled off to Cornell for my college years. Not much happened there, which was fine by me. Oh, unless you counted the two murders that had occurred there last year, but that could have happened anywhere, right?

Candie had met this love of her life about five years ago when Mark had hired her as his part-time secretary. Since Wings Falls' budget didn't support a full-time secretary, this worked out fine for Candie. It gave her the time she needed to work on her romance novels and a little added income, too. She felt the reading public was too fickle to depend on them for her livelihood.

On the floor next to Candie's feet rested a large black trash bag filled with discarded wrapping paper and ribbon. A pile of gifts was stacked on the table in front of her. Besides the gossamer negligee she'd received from Gladys, the ladies had gifted her with the wants from her wedding register—place settings of china, crystal goblets, towels, and much more. I'd saved my presents for last. I reached under the table and grabbed one out of a large canvas tote resting on the floor next to my feet. I handed it to her. Porkchop, my reddish-brown dachshund, snuggled next to the tote. He was my constant companion and the unofficial shop dog of The Ewe. He accompanied me on Monday mornings to the Loopy Ladies' gatherings.

Candie held up the sausage-shaped package I had handed to her. It was wrapped in violet paper and tied on each end with matching ribbon. Violet was the color theme for her wedding. It matched the shade of her eyes perfectly. I was her maid of honor and more than thrilled to wear a gorgeous knee-length dress in a lavender silk, which flattered my curves. Hank, my main squeeze and Mark's best man, would wear a violet-colored vest to match my dress. She'd even included Porkchop in her wedding entourage. He would be the ring bearer. I had already ordered a tux for him to wear as he pranced down the aisle with a lavender pillow tied to his back and Mark's and Candie's rings attached.

"I wonder what this is?" She squeezed the package and gave it a good shake.

A big smile spread across my face. I knew she'd love my present, as it came from my heart with a ton of love.

Candie ripped off the wrapping. The rug I'd spent hours hooking unrolled in her hands. Tears sprang to her eyes. I must admit my eyes misted up, too. The ladies clapped, and words of praise floated around the table. The rug was what we hookers called a "wedding rug." It would commemorate her and Mark's wedding day. Traditionally, the couple to be married stands on it while exchanging their wedding vows. The rug I hooked featured entwined red hearts with Candie's and Mark's initials in the center. Their wedding date was hooked across the bottom in light-green wool. I hooked the background in the same shade of lavender as my dress. Lucy spent hours over her dye pots perfecting the correct shade from a swatch of material of my dress I gave her.

Candie clutched the rug to her chest. "I love it. When did you find the time to hook it?" she asked as she wiped her eyes with the sleeve of her rhinestone-studded blouse. My cousin never met a rhinestone she didn't love.

I laughed. "Believe me, it wasn't easy, what with you bopping in and out of my house at all hours. You nearly gave me a heart attack a few times when I heard you and Precious pull into my drive." Precious was Candie's '73, baby blue Mustang convertible. "More than once I needed to quick hide it in a closet so you wouldn't spoil my surprise."

Laughter filled the room when my cousin, a perfect Southern lady, stuck her tongue out at me.

"I have one more present for you." From the shopping bag sitting at my feet, I pulled out a narrow box wrapped in the same lavender paper as the rug. My hands trembled as I handed it to her.

Candie's eyes widened with curiosity. She tore off the wrapping and lifted the lid of the box. If she was crying before, tears streamed down her face now. She stared at the box and sucked in a breath.

Gladys shook her head. The purple curls hugging her head bobbled. She dyed her hair according to whatever struck her fancy. It might be orange for the fall or red, white, and blue for the fourth of July, but the purple I felt for sure was in honor of Candie's wedding. "What's in the box that's got you bawling like a baby?" she asked.

Candie drew a knife out of the package. Its sterling silver handle, embossed with roses, gleamed under The Ewe's lights. The stainless-steel blade measured eight inches. Candie looked at the knife then at me. "But Memaw gave this to you," she said between tear-clogged breaths. Memaw was our grandmother, Memaw Parker. She'd raised Candie since the age of five years old when Candie's parents had been killed in an automobile accident. Because I was an only child, my parents would send me off to their farm in Hainted Holler, Tennessee, every June to enjoy the summer playing with Candie. I'd looked forward all year to the days of summer spent running through the farm's fields with her.

I sniffled away my tears. "Memaw would want you to use it on your wedding day, like she did on hers and your momma and mine did on theirs."

Candie wiped the tears from her eyes and cradled the delicately crafted knife in her hands.

"Your grandmom used this on her wedding day?" Susan Mayfield asked.

Candie nodded. Soft curls floated about her face. "Yes, they got married right before Grandpa Parker was sent off to war in 1942. It was a small wedding because Grandpa shipped out a few days later. But Memaw's momma gave them this beautiful knife to cut their cake. Great-Grandma used it to slice her wedding cake, and so did both our mommas."

"Woo wee, that knife sure has some history. Did you use it when you married George?" Helen Garber asked me.

I closed my eyes and silently groaned. As the most outspoken of our group's members, Helen's tongue knew no restraint. Leave it up to her to bring up my ill-fated marriage to George. We'd divorced about six years ago. George and I still co-own a funeral home together, The Do Drop Inn Funeral Parlor. Apparently, his late-night body pick-ups had involved more live bodies than dead. Well, at least one very live body. He'd been doing the horizontal mambo with our secretary. I nodded. "Yes, I did, Helen, but I'm sure Candie will have a long and loving marriage to Mark, like my parents and grandparents and our great-grandparents before them."

Helen harrumphed, folded her arms across her sizable breasts, and sank back in her chair.

Lucy stood and clapped her hands. This dispelled the tension filling the room moments before from Helen's comments. "Okay ladies, it's time for some fun and games."

Giggles erupted around the table, fueled, I was sure, by more mimosas.

Jane Burrows bounced in her chair. "Oh, goodie, I love games."

Who knew? Jane was our town librarian, a mousy sort of woman who always wore khaki slacks and sweater sets that mirrored her mother's fashion sense. At fifty-eight, she was still single and lived with her mother.

"Follow me into the dye room," Lucy said.

Like rodents following the Pied Piper, we got up and followed our leader into the space where she created her magic, brewing up fabulous colors in her dye pots for us rug hookers. A stove sat against the wall, next to a stainless-steel sink. On the large wooden table occupying the middle of the room rested bowls filled with ring-shaped candy, one bowl for each of us shower attendees. Next to each bowl sat a narrow wooden shish-kabob-type stick about a foot long.

Lucy clapped her hands once again to get the attention of the giggling and chatting ladies. "Listen up please, while I explain to you how to play this game. You all will clench a stick between your teeth. Then lean over the bowl of candy in front of you and try to slide a piece of candy up your stick. The person who, in three minutes, places the most rings of candy on their stick, wins. Ready, set—go!"

After much laughing, dropping of sticks, and candy rolling across the table, Flossie Garner, one of Mark's most loyal campaign workers, was declared the winner.

"Congratulations," I said to Flossie after she claimed her prize—a bottle of Riesling wine. I wouldn't have minded winning that prize either. Riesling was my favorite. "What will you do after Mark wins the election in November?" Although five months away, I was channeling only positive thoughts. The primary election for mayor was a week from Tuesday. Unlike Mark's previous campaigns for mayor, this time he had a challenger, Bret Hargrove. "You've been such a dedicated worker on Mark's campaign, you and Valerie both." I nodded towards the other campaign worker sitting across the table from us. "You've worked so hard and devoted a lot of time to help reelect Mark."

All of my spare time was spent at Mark's campaign headquarters, too. I wanted to contribute whatever I could to help with his reelection. As outgoing as Flossie acted, Valerie was shy. She hadn't been easy to get to know, but she was committed to Mark and his campaign. For one so young, she wore outfits that added years to her young age of thirty. Polyester skirts and blouses were a favorite of hers, along with serviceable brown oxfords as her choice of shoes. Valerie never brightened up her complexion with make-up, either.

Flossie was younger than me. If I ventured a guess, I'd say she was in her late thirties. She was petite, about five feet tall, with heavily frosted brown hair skimming her shoulders in an attractive bob. Pretty in a pixyish sort of way. Don't say a bad thing about Mark in her presence, though. She'd bare her claws and a tiger would emerge. You'd receive quite an earful. Ever since Mark announced his bid for reelection, she'd been in the forefront of his campaign, manning phones at his headquarters, handing out flyers, composing press releases. Anything that needed to be done, Flossie was up for it.

Flossie rolled her eyes. "Valerie, oh puh-lease. She has a major crush on Mark. That's the only reason she hangs around the headquarters. She practically drools when Mark is there. But I'm sure Mark will find something for me to do in the mayor's office. Mark said that after he and Candie are married, she will probably want to quit her job. She'll stay home to take care of him. I'm sure he'll hire me to fill the secretary position when she does."

I didn't know if my mouth was scraping the floor of The Ewe, but this was the first I'd heard of Candie leaving her job as Mark's secretary. And in all the time that I spent at the headquarters, I never suspected that Valerie carried such a major crush for Mark. At least, I'd never witnessed anything when I worked at his headquarters. Candie never mentioned it, and I knew Mark would not encourage Valerie's feelings, either. He was a straight-as-an-arrow kind of guy and up to his eyeballs in love with Candie.

The bell over the door to The Ewe jingled. The sign on the door was turned to *Closed*, but apparently someone ignored the message.

A female voice called out from the front room. "Yoo-hoo, are y'all still celebrating my Markie's upcoming nuptials?"

Candie was the first to leave the dye room and greet the person who had entered The Ewe. I trailed right behind her, curious as to the identity of the newcomer.

Candie stood in the middle of the room with her hands on her hips and a frown on her face. "That hussy," she whispered to me. "What nerve she has to show up here—and look at her dress. It's so short I can see her religion."

CHAPTER TWO

———

The sun backlit the woman standing in the doorway of The Ewe. A shiver snaked down my spine. My hand flew to my throat. The vision before me looked like Vampira, but a much older version. Would she want a taste of my blood? She wore four-inch red hooker heels, and this time I *was* referring to *that* kind of hooker. The ones who made their living selling their, um how should I phrase it, their assets. My feet ached looking at her heels. A very short red dress clung to her body. The neckline plunged so low I wondered why her puppies didn't fall out.

"What brings you here, Babs?" Candie said between gritted teeth.

Startled, I looked wide-eyed at my cousin. "You know her?" I asked.

"Never met her, but Mark showed me her picture a while ago. She's his ex," Candie whispered back to me out of the corner of her mouth.

This certainly was a day for surprises, and not only the wedding shower kind. "His ex? Ex-what?"

"Ex-wife. Long story. I'll tell you about it later. Let me see what this witch wants first. Believe me, it can't be anything good." Candie turned to Babs/Vampira.

Babs flicked a strand of long, jet-black hair over shoulder. She closed the door behind her and walked farther into The Ewe. "Oh, my Markie has told you who I am? Isn't that sweet of him? I knew he'd never forget me."

"Yeah, like food poisoning," Candie said under her breath.

I coughed to stifle the laugh bubbling up my throat.

"I recently heard from a dear friend of Markie and mine that he was running for reelection as mayor of this cute little town again, and since I was in the area, I had to stop by and give him all my support." Babs placed a slender manicured hand on Candie's arm. I swear her blood red fingernails were two inches long. How did women manage with nails so long? I mean, I wouldn't be able to button my jeans or pick up a pencil. I guess they would be great for scratching the love of my life's back—my dog, Porkchop. Oops. That was before Detective Hank Johnson entered it and who now ranks right up there next to my dog.

Lucy edged her way in front of Candie and me. Good thing too, because if Candie clenched her jaw any tighter, it would snap. I didn't think that a bride with a broken jaw would be the best look for her wedding pictures. "I'm sorry, but my store is closed today. We're having a private party. If you come back tomorrow, I'll be happy to see to your needs."

God bless Lucy, the ultimate smoother-over of tense situations.

Babs waved a hand. The ring on her finger flashed in the sunlight streaming into the store. Out of the side of my mouth I said to Candie, "Her rock would rival the Hope diamond."

"It's a fake like her hair and the rest of her body, or my Dixie is in love with your Porkchop," Candie answered back.

I laughed in spite of the tense situation. I couldn't help myself. Dixie was Candie's calico cat. It would be a hot day at the North Pole before my beloved dachshund, Porkchop, and Candie's Dixie would be besties.

Babs didn't seem to hear Lucy, or she chose to ignore her. She walked past her and over to the table where Candie's gifts were displayed. Babs picked up the negligee Gladys had gifted Candie and let it slide through her fingers. "Is this for your wedding night, Candie? I'm sure you'll be able to give Mark a few pointers. My friend told me you had a few engagements before you snapped up my Markie." Babs let out a laugh that sounded more like a cackle. Vampira was emerging again.

Candie grabbed the negligee out of Babs's hand. I could feel her Southern temper about to explode. Sure, she had been engaged eleven times before, but that didn't make her some kind of floozie. During those engagements, she was devoted to every one of her fiancés and never cheated on one of them. In fact, she remained friends with each of them. Case in fact, her very first fiancé, Tommy Ray Clements, was now rehabbing her large Victorian home. Mark was going to move out of his bachelor pad apartment and into Candie's home once they were married. She felt it needed a little sprucing up and had heard that Tommy Ray was unemployed.

Kindhearted as she was, she invited him north to do the work needed on her house—painting the outside trim of her lavender and white Victorian-style house and fixing a loose railing on the balcony off her bedroom. "Babs, how did you know Mark and I are getting married?" she asked, interrupting my thoughts.

Babs toyed with the earrings skimming her shoulders. I'd bet my next designer purse—and I loved my purses—the large red stones reflecting the light streaming in from the window were as fake as Babs's boobs. "Honey, I have my sources. I've kept track of my Markie ever since our unfortunate break-up."

"Unfortunate break-up!" My cousin's voice almost broke the sound barrier. "You cheated on him with his law partner, something he knows I would never do."

Babs flicked her claws to dismiss Candie's remark. "Oh, sweetheart, it was a little misunderstanding. Now aren't those the cutest little scissors?" She picked up a pair of scissors from the table. The blade was four inches long, and a beaded fob spelling out the word "love" hung from the thumb hole. Lucy gave each of us one as a shower favor. Even Flossie and Valerie loved theirs. They might not be rug hookers, but they were both involved in crafts where the scissors could come in handy. Then her eyes lit on Memaw's cake knife. "Well, would you look at that," she said, her red claws reaching out to trail along the engraved silver blade. "How charming."

"Take my scissors and go. Like Lucy said, this is a private party." I moved between her and Memaw's knife, practically pushing her back with my pair of scissors. I hoped my offer would usher Babs out the door.

Babs grabbed the scissors from my hand. "Well, I certainly don't want to stay where I'm not welcome." She huffed then turned and left The Ewe.

The other women watched from the dye room's doorway. Now Helen Garber slipped her orange-rimmed glasses, dangling from a beaded chain around her neck, onto her nose. The color of her glasses matched her floral-printed blouse. Most days her outfit choices screamed at each other. Today her scarlet red pants shouted at the top of its lungs. "She certainly was an unexpected visitor. Who is she, anyway?" Helen peered out the front window of The Ewe, watching Babs cross the street and climb into a dark-blue Honda.

Candie flopped in her seat at the oak table we had gathered around while she opened her presents. The gifts were neatly stacked before her. "She's Mark's ex-wife."

Gasps of surprise filled the room.

"He was married before?" The weathered skin on Gladys's face turned down into a frown.

Valerie clenched her fists so tight they started to turn white. "That can't be. You must be mistaken. Surely, he would have told me."

I turned a curious look towards Valerie. "Why would he have told you?"

Valerie's face flushed. She stammered, "I mean, those of us who are closest to him in the campaign. A woman like that in his past could cause problems with his campaign."

Maybe there was something to what Flossie said about Valerie having a crush on Mark. Why was she so upset about Candie's announcement that Mark had been married before? Heck, if anyone should be upset, it should be me. Candie had never even breathed a word about it to me, and we were as close as sisters.

Candie heaved a deep breath. "As you all now know, Mark was married to Babs once upon a time. His first job after law school was with a firm in Pennsylvania. Babs worked as a paralegal with the firm. I guess she was quite a looker back then, and Mark fell hard for her."

"You mean she didn't always look like Vampira?" I was acting catty, but I couldn't resist.

My remark drew laughs from the ladies.

Gladys slapped the table, causing us all to jump. "You're right, Sam. I knew she reminded me of someone, but I couldn't put my finger on it. She's got the seductress look right down to her eye makeup. Were those bat wings she drew on her eyelids?"

"So, what broke them up?" Jane asked from the far end of the table.

"I guess Mark's star wasn't rising fast enough to suit her. She cheated on him with one of the other young lawyers in the firm. Someone who was more cutthroat. But one conquest wasn't good enough for her, either. After Mark, she found four more gullible men," Candie said.

My curiosity piqued, I asked, "She's been married five times? I wonder why those marriages didn't work out?"

"As you saw, Babs is a lot of show on the outside, but when men get to really know her, she's all about their assets. Money assets," Candie said.

"Men," Gladys huffed out. "They think only with their pants."

The laughter at Gladys's statement lightened the gloom hanging over the room caused by Babs's appearance.

Lucy shook her head. Her white bob skimmed her shoulders. "There are a few exceptions, Gladys. My Ralph, and your Frank and Mark. Oh, and Sam, I'd add Hank to that list. Wouldn't you all agree?"

We all nodded our heads in agreement.

I knew it really wasn't any of my business, but I was still a little stung by the fact Candie hadn't told me about Mark's former wife. "So why the big secret about Babs? I mean, it was decades ago."

Candie nodded. "I know, but he's still embarrassed about the big mistake he made marrying her. It was a hit to his ego, her cheating on him…and with someone he thought was a friend."

I could relate. When I'd found out George had been busy belly-bopping with the secretary of our funeral parlor, and in a town as small as Wings Falls where everyone knew everyone, I'd imagined us to be the main topic of the gossip mill.

I blew out a ragged breath. The tension in the room was so thick I could have cut it with the wedding cake knife. "Umm, ladies, how about we keep the party going tonight at The Round Up?" The Round Up was a local restaurant/bar that was known for its hot wings and barbeque.

Groans resounded from around the table.

"Stick a fork in me. I'm done. What with all the mimosas and food I've had today, I'm about to bust," Gladys said.

Heads nodded around the table in agreement with her.

"I'll join you, if you don't mind," Flossie said.

"You can count me in, too," Valerie added.

Youth. I loved how they didn't have to count calories like the rest of us who had approached middle age.

Candie balled her hands into fists and pounded them on the table. "All I know is if she causes any trouble for Mark and his reelection, she'll be sorry."

My gaze snapped back to Candie. She stared off into space, completely unaware of the conversation that had just taken place. She was still wrapped up in Babs crashing her shower.

CHAPTER THREE

———

"What can I get for you folks tonight?" A waitress in her twenties, with a pen poised over her order pad, stood next to our table behind Candie's chair.

"Honey, a Diet 7-Up for me." Candie turned to me. "I'm stuffed from all the food you ladies served at my shower earlier today. I'll have to watch what I eat so I can fit into my wedding dress."

Mark, Hank, Candie, and I sat at a large round table in The Round Up. The Sundowners, a favorite country band, tuned up on a small stage next to the dance floor.

I glanced around the room. The décor had remained unchanged since it opened in the sixties. The same wagon wheel chandeliers hung from the wooden ceiling, only with a lot more dust. Framed pictures of the stars who had performed here in the past— Crystal, Hank, Reba, and Willie to name a few—decorated the paneled walls. The Round Up had been a regular stop for their tour buses. I especially liked the signs on the restroom doors asking whether you were a "cowboy" or a "cowgirl." If you were really brave, when the band took a break, you could attempt to ride the mechanical bull sitting in the rear of the restaurant. It was rumored that the owner, Bill Collins, a robust man in his sixties, wanted to retire and hand the business over to his two sons, Chris and David. I'd hate to see that happen. Bill *was* The Round Up. Dressed in his western-style shirts, with their pearl snap buttons, jeans, and cowboy boots, he loved walking amongst his diners, welcoming them to his restaurant and shooting the breeze with them. His sons—not so much. They were more interested in the bottom dollar that the customers brought in than mingling with the customers.

I nodded at the waitress. The name tag on her western-style blouse read Jennifer. "I'd better stick to a diet ginger ale."

As she turned to take Mark's and Hank's order, I leaned towards Candie so she could hear me over the din of the restaurant's patrons. "We have our final dress fittings on Monday, right? I don't want to embarrass everyone and split a seam in my gorgeous dress when I walk down the aisle at Saint Anthony's." The slender design of my bridesmaid's dress didn't allow for all the chips, dip, and cake I had eaten at the shower this afternoon. I was sure the mimosas added a few calories, too. The barbeque sandwich I lusted after tonight wouldn't help the waistline either. I knew I'd have to hit the gym sometime tomorrow and every day for the next two weeks until the wedding.

"Hi, everyone. Hope I'm not late?"

I looked up. Flossie stood by the table. There hadn't been any time to ask Candie about Flossie taking over her secretarial job after she married Mark.

Since the shower this morning, Flossie had changed into snug-fitting jeans and a figure-hugging black T-shirt. She stood holding hands with a tall slim fellow. "This is Dan Brewer. Do you mind if he joins us tonight?"

Dan sported a neatly trimmed beard streaked with a few strands of gray. Thick red hair skimmed the collar of a blue knit shirt that he'd paired with well-worn jeans.

"Hi, Dan," we all said in unison.

Dan pulled out the chair next to me for Flossie to sit.

"Good manners," Candie said out of the side of her mouth. Manners were huge to Candie. Our Memaw Parker drilled them into us when we were very young.

Flossie went around the table introducing us all individually to Dan. Hank and Mark stood and shook his hand. She explained that Dan was a friend in town visiting for the weekend.

"Have you heard from Valerie?" I asked. After the shower both Valerie and Flossie said they were going back to the campaign headquarters. Since the election was a week from this coming Tuesday, they wanted to work the phones some more. Should the rest of us have been there, too? I guess, but it had been a hard race and we all needed a break.

"We saw her on our way in. She's parking her car," Flossie said. She picked up one of The Round Up's laminated menus and began to scan it.

I glanced towards the door to try to spot her. I wanted to motion her over to our table when she entered the restaurant. "Isn't that Valerie at the bar?" I asked. "And look." I nudged Candie in the ribs. "Is she talking to your ex, Tommy Ray?" I groaned. "Rob Anderson is here tonight, too." Rob worked as a reporter for our local newspaper, the *Tribune*. He fancied himself an investigative reporter, with hopes of being discovered by one of the big papers in New York City. From the articles of his I'd read, I was afraid his wish would be a long time coming.

Valerie had come into The Round Up alone. Was she hoping to spend time with Mark? Maybe there was something to what Flossie had said about Valerie having a crush on Mark, or maybe she was only a loyal member of Mark's campaign team. There were dozens of us who wanted to see him reelected. We had witnessed what he had accomplished in the past four years for Wings Falls. He made it a better city to live and work in, unlike his opponent, Bret Hargrove. Bret promised the voters the moon and with no way to deliver it unless there was a major tax increase to help Wings Falls' budget. But some people were gullible and would vote for anyone who gave them something for nothing. Mark waged a clean campaign, but I couldn't say the same for Mark's opponent. Mark spent a major portion of his time combating the lies Bret spread. Hopefully, the citizens of Wings Falls would remember all of Mark's accomplishments when they went to vote. But tonight, Mark wanted to relax and spend time with the love of his life and soon-to-be bride and his good friends.

"You folks set to order yet?" Jennifer returned with Mark and Hank's beers and Candie's and my sodas. "I see you have a couple of newcomers." She dug her order pad out of her apron and pointed her pen towards Flossie and Dan. "You two want to order any drinks?"

Flossie and Dan nodded and ordered beers.

"Anyone want to share some loaded nacho platters to go with your beers?" Even after all I'd eaten today. I was still hungry. Go figure. I thought we could all enjoy some munchies while we waited for Valerie to join us. The cheese nachos might mean more hours on the treadmill, but it would kill time while enjoying our drinks. Heads around the table nodded at my suggestion. "Add three orders of your super cheesy nachos," I said then added, "We could share an order with our partner, if that's all right with everyone."

Flossie hugged Dan's arm. I got the impression he was more than a friend visiting from out of town. "That sounds great." She motioned towards the band warming up on the small stage. "I hear they are really good and can't wait until they start. My feet are itching to dance tonight. Have to work off some of those goodies we ate at your shower today, Candie." Flossie laughed. "Although, I don't think I'll start my diet tonight."

Candie joined in the laughter. "I have to agree. If I want to fit into my wedding dress, I'm going to have to do some serious watching of what I eat for the next two weeks. I want to float down the aisle, not waddle."

Mark pulled Candie to his side. "You look perfect to me."

She reached up and kissed him on the cheek. "Y'all see what a prize I have? He's not only the best mayor Wings Falls ever elected, but he'll be the best hubby, too."

Mark leaned down and kissed Candie on the lips. A kiss much more than the one she had planted on his cheek.

Candie sat up and waved her hand in front of her face. "Phew weee! That was a real barn burner."

We all laughed.

Hank reached over and squeezed my hand. He bent down and said in a voice low enough that only I could hear, "Wait until later, and I'll top his kiss."

Heat rushed up my neck, and my cheeks burned.

"What did Hank say to you?" Candie asked. "Your face is redder than Grandpa Parker's long johns."

I willed my body to cool down. "Ummm, he said he was hungry and wondered when the nachos would arrive."

Candie shook her head. "He's hungry all right, but I don't think for nachos."

This conversation was getting a little too personal. I wanted to steer it away from me. I pointed towards the bar. "I see Valerie is having quite a conversation with Tommy Ray. I wonder what they're talking about. He looks to be showing her something."

Candie glanced in their direction. "Rob Anderson is seated next to Tommy Ray. He seems mighty interested in what Tommy Ray and Valerie are looking at, too. Isn't he the reporter who took pictures of Porkchop?"

I nodded. "Yes, he came to my house to do a calendar shoot. It will be released at the same time as my book." I smiled, remembering how cute Porkchop looked in all the outfits he wore for the different months—a Santa's hat for December, swimsuit and goggles for August, Uncle Sam's beard and top hat for July, and my personal favorite, bunny ears for April. He was such a ham and loved every minute of the shoot. "Oh, and did I tell you that Bob Spellman called yesterday—you know, my editor at Rolling Brook Press? They want to push up the release date so *Porkchop, the Wonder Dog* will be out for the Christmas season."

Candie clapped her hands. The rhinestones on her blouse bounced with her excitement. "How exciting!"

Hank leaned over and kissed me again. "We'll have to have a proper celebration later," he whispered in my ear.

The thoughts of what that celebration might entail curled my toes.

Dan piped up. "You've written a book? I'm thinking about writing one, too." It was the first time he'd contributed to the conversation. He had sat quietly next to Flossie, enjoying his beer.

"Yes," I said. "A children's book about the adventures of my dog, Porkchop."

A look of disdain crossed Dan's face. "Oh, a children's book. I thought you meant a real book."

My hackles rose, along with my dander and anything else that could rise up in anger. Dan sank ten points in my likeability book. The idiot didn't know that children's picture books were the hardest to get published. Through gritted teeth, I informed him of such.

Luckily, Jennifer arrived with our nachos, which helped disperse the tension hanging over the table.

"So, Candie, how are the renovations on your house coming? Will Tommy Ray be finished before the wedding?" Hank knew how to lighten the moment. I guess it came from his years as a police detective. No wonder Wings Falls Police Department lured him away from Albany PD.

"He says he only has a little more to do, and then he's done. He needs to replace some molding around the door leading out onto the balcony off my bedroom. It has some rot. I want everything to be perfect when my Mark moves in." Candie gazed up into Mark's eyes.

From the look in their eyes, I'd say everything was perfect right now. You could cut their love with a knife. Speaking of knives, I said, "Memaw would be so tickled if she knew you were going to use her bridal knife to cut your wedding cake."

"It certainly is a beautiful knife. I love those kinds of family traditions." Flossie grabbed a handful of nachos from the platter she shared with Dan.

"Southerners are big on family tradition and loyalty. Aren't we, Sam?" Candie asked. She licked some cheese off her fingers from the nacho dip. The look in Mark's eyes said he'd love to be the one doing the licking.

I nodded in agreement. "I may be only half-Southern, but I'd say you are right. You don't mess with one Parker and not have a whole clan of Parkers breathing down your neck."

I glanced up to see Valerie behind Candie's chair, holding her phone out to Candie. I was so absorbed in Mark mooning over Candie, I hadn't seen her approach our table. "Candie, look at this. When I saw Rob Anderson at the bar, I stopped to see if he could write an article on Mark's campaign. You know, get Mark some good publicity. Tommy Ray was there, sobbing into his beer over at the bar. I was able to snap a picture with my phone when he got up to go to the men's room. He left it sitting on the bar."

"Let me see." Candie reached into her purse and pulled out a pair of rhinestone-studded glasses. As I'd mentioned before, there wasn't a rhinestone Candie hadn't met she didn't love. She adjusted her glasses up her freckled nose then looked at the picture on Valerie's phone. She gasped. "Well, I… I'll wring his scrawny neck. We were kids then. What's he doing with that now? And on his phone?"

Mark looked over Candie's shoulder. The blood drained out of his face. Red flushed up his neck. "Umm," he stuttered, clearly shocked at what he was seeing.

CHAPTER FOUR

———

Candie grabbed Mark's hand. "Honey, Tommy Ray and I were youngsters when we snapped this picture. You know how young people in love do crazy things." Desperation filled her voice. Tears rolled down her porcelain cheeks and stained her blouse.

"Candie, what's the matter? Can I do anything?" My heart broke watching my cousin suffer so.

She handed me Valerie's phone. Heat flushed up my neck, too. I could feel Hank leaning in to see the image as well. His intake of breath and the way his body stiffened when he saw the picture gave me a big hint that he was surprised by the image, too. The picture, taken when Candie was in her early twenties, showed her and Tommy Ray engaged in a very sexy pose. She was dressed as Little Red Riding Hood and Tommy Ray as the Big Bad Wolf.

"Umm, well, I'd say it is a different take on the fairy tale." *Was that ever an understatement.* "Oh, and I see you liked rhinestones way back then, too."

Her costume featured some very strategically placed rhinestones. It certainly was a very different version of the Little Red Riding Hood fairy tale than my mother read to me.

A weak smile crossed Candie's lips. She reached over and gave my shoulder a one-armed hug. "I love you, too, cousin."

Shock still mirrored on Mark's face. Was he rethinking his engagement to Candie? Did thoughts of what Babs had done to him years ago flit through his brain? I shook my head. No, he had to know that Candie would never betray him like Babs had. This was a silly, although very sexy, picture from Candie's past. It had nothing to do with the present. I could wring Tommy Ray's neck for not having destroyed it years ago. I knew Mark's and Candie's love would weather any storm or, in this case, a sexy picture from the past.

Valerie sat next to Flossie and Dan. She cleared her throat. All eyes turned to her. "I'm afraid the picture's not the only problem. Did you notice Rob Anderson, the reporter from the *Tribune,* sitting at the bar, too? When Tommy Ray got up to go to the men's room to do his business, Rob leaned over to look at the photo. I tried to grab it before he could see what it was, but he snapped a picture of it with his phone before I could snatch it off the bar. He mumbled something about using it as the hot headline for tomorrow's paper."

Valerie looked hard at Candie. "This is going to be really bad for the campaign if it gets out."

Candie jutted out her chin and brushed the tears from her cheeks. "When our engagement ended, Tommy Ray told me he destroyed all copies of this picture. It's obvious he lied to me. He won't get away with besmirching my good name. He'll be sorry he ever tangled with this Parker."

Mark sat up straighter in his chair and cleared his throat. His love for Candie knew no bounds, and it showed as he tenderly stroked Candie's hand. "Candie, sweetie, now don't go getting your blood pressure up. We'll handle this together."

Candie shook her head then looked up at Mark. Pain shown in her violet eyes. "But what will this do to your campaign? What if Rob goes through with his threat and publishes it in tomorrow's paper? It could ruin your chances of being reelected mayor. Oh, Mark, maybe we should call off the wedding."

Mark slammed his fist down. Drink glasses and beer bottles jumped on the wooden tabletop. Nachos spilled out of the bowls we shared with our partners. "No. Absolutely no. It's taken me five years to get you to the altar, and you're not backing out now. We've all done some stupid things in our youth. Heaven knows I have. The only thing that counts is the here and now. Come on. The band has started to play our song. I want to dance with my beautiful bride-to-be." Mark stood and reached out his hand to Candie. Mark may only stand five-foot-six and be balding, but to me, at this moment, he was Superman. I couldn't have felt prouder of my soon-to-be cousin-in-law.

The Sundowners played "I Will Always Love You," a favorite of mine, by Dolly Parton.

Hank pulled me close to him and kissed me. I saw a flash out of the corner of my eye. Flossie sat with her phone poised in her hands. "I couldn't help myself. You two look so cute and in love."

I blushed. Hank had never said the "L" word, so I didn't know if his feelings ran as deep as mine. I could only hope.

"I'll email you a copy of the picture," Flossie said. She turned her phone towards us so we could see the image of us kissing on her phone.

Still holding me close, Hank whispered, "Do you want to join them?" His breath tickled my ear and shot a shiver down my spine.

I nodded. We followed Candie and Mark onto the dance floor. Hank folded me into his arms. I laid my head on his shoulder and closed my eyes, lost in the words of the song and the feel of his muscled body close to mine. Couples dressed in cowboy boots and jeans crowded the dance floor around us swaying to the music, but I was lost in a world of only Hank and me.

"Why, Markie, I stopped by your campaign headquarters, and they told me you'd be here."

My eyes snapped open. *No, it couldn't be. Could this evening become any more disastrous?* I twisted in Hank's arms. Was I dreaming and had drifted off into nightmare land? No, Babs stood there in all her vamping glory. She'd traded in the red bandage she wore to The Ewe for an equally short and clinging black number. Sequins ringed the plunging neckline and the cuffs of the sleeves. It would have given Memaw Parker a case of the vapors. Babs still wore the red stilettos she had donned this morning. What did she want?

"Candie, dear, you don't mind if I cut in and have this dance with Markie? I always thought of this as our song when we were, you know, together. Remember, Markie?" Babs tugged on Mark's arm. She blinked her batwing eyelashes and ran her two-inch-long blood-red fingernails down his cheek.

Couples around us had stopped dancing and stared at Babs and Mark.

Mark looked from Candie to Babs. "Babs, all I remember is the disaster of a marriage we had. As you can see, I'm enjoying a dance with my fiancée."

Candie stepped out of his arms. "It's okay. I think you have some unfinished business with Babs. Sam and Hank will see me home. Sam, do you mind if we leave now? I feel a headache coming on. I think there's been too much excitement for me today." Candie bit her Passion Pink-covered lower lip. I could tell she was trying to hold back a river of tears. No way would she break down in front of that she-devil Babs. Her Parker pride was too strong for that to happen.

"Hey, folks, smile for the camera."

We all turned in time to see Rob Anderson with his phone aimed at the five of us. Babs clung to Mark with her arms draped around his neck, her ruby red lips curved into a smile.

Candie marched back to our table. With trembling hands, she snatched up her purse. Now the tears she'd kept at bay streamed down her face.

Flossie and Valerie looked up from their plates of nachos, shocked expressions on both of their faces. Dan was too engrossed with his beer to pay us any attention.

Valerie nodded towards the dance floor. "What happened out there?"

Flossie swiped at a glob of cheese clinging to her pinkie finger. "Yeah. How come Mark is dancing with Babs?"

Candie hiccupped and said, "Mark needed to set that woman straight on where she stands in his life. Sam, I want to go home, *now*, before I kill the witch."

This was the second time today Candie had threatened doom on Babs. I thought it best to get her out of The Round Up before she did something she'd regret. I put my arm around her shoulders and looked up at Hank. "Please, Hank?"

He nodded and tossed some money on the table to cover our share of the bill as I reached for my purse.

I placed my hand on Candie's elbow to steer her towards the door. I looked back over my shoulder and said to Valerie and Flossie, "Candie's not feeling well. I need to get her home."

Both the ladies sat with their mouths open, but that was all the explanation they were going to get from me tonight.

Rob Anderson sidled up to Candie as we walked away from our table. With a pen poised over a pad of paper, he said, "Miss Parker, I heard your comment to the woman dancing with the mayor. Can I quote you for tomorrow's paper?"

Candie looked up from trying to shove her arms into the tangled sleeves of the light denim jacket she had worn tonight to ward off the evening's chill. With a quizzical look on her face, she asked, "What are you talking about?"

A smug grin spread across Rob's narrow face. "You threatened the woman who cut in on you while dancing with the mayor."

"You hear me, Rob Anderson. There's no story here. Why don't you go find an ambulance to chase?" I tugged on Candie's arm. "Come on, Candie. You're upset and don't owe him an explanation." I pulled her towards the exit, weaving through tables of Saturday night revelers trying to talk over the band. It might be June, but summer evenings in the Adirondacks often cooled off the heat of the day. I hoped the night air lowered her temperature.

On the way to the exit, we passed the bar. Tommy Ray was back from his trip to the cowboy's room. He sat nursing another beer. Candie yanked out of my grasp on her sleeve and marched up to him.

"Candie," I called after her, but she ignored me and kept on walking, her back stiff as a board. She was a woman on a mission. I turned to Hank, desperate for help. He nodded and followed me over to the bar.

When I caught up with Candie, she was standing in front of Tommy Ray, her spine straight and her head held high. "Tommy Ray, you lied to me. You said you destroyed every copy of that photo. I thought I could trust you. Obviously, you've proved me wrong." She paused long enough to hold out her hand, palm up. "Now hand it over to me, right now."

Tommy Ray looked up at Candie with red-rimmed eyes. Tears etched his craggy checks and trailed into a day's growth of whiskers. "Candie-kins, I'm sorry. I couldn't help myself. Our time together. Why, I'll treasure those as the best days of my life. It's not the same with Darlene. She doesn't understand me. Not like you did."

Candie stomped her foot twice on the scarred wooden floor of The Round Up. Peanut shells crunched under her feet. Her hand was still outstretched in front of him. "Tommy Ray, that was thirty years ago. You can't live in the past. You and your girlfriend have been a couple for a long time now. Go back to her, talk to her, straighten things out. Time moves on, and so does life. Now, give me the picture. I want you to finish up the job you're doing for me then go back to her. I'm marrying Mark Hogan—at least I hope I am—and I don't want you around messing things up with your foolishness."

My heart almost broke from the hang-dog look Tommy Ray gave Candie as he handed the infamous picture over to her.

Candie crumpled the photo in her ring-studded fingers and turned to Hank and me. "Come on. I want to go home. I have a headache."

"I'll bring the car around," Hank said and walked towards the door.

I smiled to myself. I think my big, tough, cop felt uneasy in this love mix-up. Give him a murder to handle, and he'd feel right at home.

"Candie, stay please, or at least let me see you home." We turned to see Mark standing behind us.

I looked back at our table and saw Babs chatting away with Valerie, who must have said something funny, since she started to laugh hysterically. Her dyed black hair bounced around her shoulders.

Candie shook her head. "Hank and Sam will see me home. I can't stay. It would only give that reporter more gossip for his newspaper. We'll talk later." She reached up and placed a kiss on his cheek. A kiss far different from the passionate one they shared earlier in the evening.

CHAPTER FIVE

————

"I thought Father Pete's sermon on love and forgiveness was very appropriate. Didn't you?" Candie and I sat in our usual booth in Sweetie Pie's Cafe, next to the window looking out on Main Street. We came here every Sunday after the ten am Mass at Saint Anthony's. I wondered if we still would after Candie and Mark were married. Mark was an Episcopalian, so he didn't attend Mass with Candie. I always enjoyed this quiet time with my cousin. True, we gabbed every day on the phone, but this was a special time for the two of us.

Candie looked up from the menu she was studying, not that she didn't know it by heart. I always ordered a bowl of grits with a pat of butter melting on top plus a side of bacon. Candie, a plate of ham and eggs. But there were times we were tempted to veer off our Sunday regular and go crazy with, say, an order of Franny's fluffy pancakes. Sometimes during the week we'd stop in for a bite to eat, too.

"Yeah, I guess so," Candie said with little enthusiasm.

I studied the forlorn look on her face. "Didn't Mark call last night?"

"Oh, yes, he called. My phone rang almost as soon as I stepped in the door."

I frowned. "So, what's the big deal? Everything's all right, isn't it? He understands the photo is a part of your past and has nothing to do with today, doesn't he?"

Candie sighed. The wisps of auburn hair surrounding her face fluttered. "Oh, the sweetheart couldn't be any more understanding, but I don't think he realizes the consequences."

I raised an eyebrow at her concern. "What's there to understand? He loves you, you love him. You two live happily ever after. Period. End of story."

"Oh, Sam, you are so naïve. If only things were that simple. Don't you see? If Rob Anderson carries out his threat and publishes the picture he snapped of Tommy Ray and me in the *Tribune*, not only is Mark's bid for reelection in jeopardy, but his whole career is finished. It would ruin him. I couldn't live with myself. I don't see how we can possibly get married now."

I was tempted to smack Candie upside her head with one of the plastic-coated menus tucked next to the metal napkin holder. Luckily, my parents and Memaw Parker frowned on public displays of violence and outlawed them in my childhood.

"Candie, you are talking pure nonsense. I don't think there's a person alive in Wings Falls who hasn't done something foolish in their youth." Where was a cup of caffeine when you needed it? Not that I could indulge. Due to a rise in my blood pressure, my doctor had banished caffeine from my diet—only decaf for me.

Candie's eyes bored into me. She placed her menu on the faded red Formica tabletop. "Name me one crazy thing you did in your twenties."

I ran my fingers through my curls then smoothed them back in place, afraid I'd given myself a rooster-do. My forehead furrowed in concentration. I'd really stepped in it this time. The harder I thought, the deeper my forehead folded into wrinkles.

Candie waggled her bejeweled fingers at me. "I'm waiting. If you concentrate too long, your face will freeze that way."

"What way?"

"Like Old Lady Splotz."

Candie had referred to the old woman who lived next to her. She reminded me of the dried apple head dolls my mother used to craft when I was in grade school. It would creep me out when I came home from school and saw a row of wrinkled, shrunken heads lined up on our kitchen counter. Mrs. Splotz could have modeled for them.

I shook my head and brushed a hand over my forehead to make sure not a wrinkle remained. I shook my head. "I guess I did live a pretty dull life."

Candie sighed and pointed a finger at me. "See what I mean? Nothing in your past will ever come back to embarrass you or anyone you love."

"Candie, Mark loves you. The whole you. Your past and present. I'd say especially the present, since he is a part of it." I waved a waitress over to our table. Even though I couldn't enjoy it, I knew my cousin could use a shot of caffeine.

"Thanks, Joy," I said. Joy, the niece of Franny Goodway who owned Sweetie Pie's, waited on us most Sunday mornings. Joy had moved north to attend college. She waitressed part-time at her aunt's cafe to help pay for books and other school necessities.

"Franny back in the kitchen this morning?" I glanced towards the kitchen that resided behind the counter area. There was an elongated window opening cut into the wall where customers could watch Franny cook up her magic.

Joy nodded. Her afro nodded along with her. A smile split her dark skin. "Yes, Sam. She's whipping up some of her fabulous cinnamon buns. Would you and Candie like one?"

I groaned. "Joy, we have to fit into our gowns for Candie's wedding. After what we ate yesterday, I'm afraid we are back on the diet wagon. A bowl of grits for me with skim milk. Oh, and a mug of decaf, please." I figured it best to skip my usual side order of bacon. Every calorie saved meant I could take a deep breath in that gown. I looked at Candie to place her order.

"I guess I'll have the same, but please none of that decaf stuff. The stronger the better for me."

Joy laughed and slipped her order pad in the pocket of her pink uniform then left to place our order. Sweetie Pie's was fashioned after a fifties diner. Booths hugged the glossy white walls. A counter with five stools lined the kitchen wall. Black and white tiles covered the floor. The waitresses all wore pink uniforms with a lace-rimmed handkerchief flowing out of the breast pocket.

When Joy walked away, I pointed to Candie's violet-colored blouse. The main color theme in her wardrobe was violet, as it matched her eyes. "You have a rhinestone missing at your neckline."

She glanced down and fingered the empty spot in the line of rhinestones. "Oh, drat. This is one of my favorite blouses, too. I wonder what happened to it. I'll have to search for it when I get home."

The diner seemed overly noisy. Customers sat head-to-head reading and gossiping over the morning paper. As I scanned the room, I noticed people looking at the paper then pointing to Candie. My heart sank.

"Here's your coffee." Joy stood next to our table holding a tray with two ceramic mugs. Steam floated over the rims.

I jerked up in the booth. I was so involved looking around the room, I hadn't noticed her. She placed the mugs on the table before us. "Oh, sorry, Joy. What's got everyone buzzing this morning? Seems like everyone has their nose stuck in the newspaper."

Red flushed up Joy's cheeks. She fiddled with the tray she'd used to bring out coffees. "I don't really like to say what's on people's minds, but they are awful interested in the pictures in this morning's *Tribune.*"

If it were possible, Candie's porcelain skin paled even whiter. The freckles dotting her nose stood out.

The door to Sweetie Pie's burst open. Warm air rushed in. The temperature was already rising, foreshadowing another hot summer day. "Morning, everyone. I've got free newspapers. Hot off the press."

I dropped my head into my hands and groaned. Mark's opponent, Bret Hargrove, stood framed in the doorway, a stack of newspapers clutched under his arm. The morning's sun back-lit his blond surfer-boy good looks. His year-round tan had to be courtesy of a tanning booth, especially up here in the North Country.

"Here you go. Have a newspaper on me," Bret said as he circulated the diner, shaking hands with the breakfast crowd and handing out the morning's *Tribune.*

If I wasn't afraid of insulting snake-oil salesmen, I'd compare him to one.

"Be sure to vote for me in ten days. If we want this town to grow, new leadership is needed to do that. Right folks?" A chorus of "yesses" bounced off the diner's walls. "You want a picture of me? Sure." Bret pressed his face against an elderly woman's cheek.

I swear I almost needed to drag out my sunglasses or be blinded by the glare sparkling from his enhanced white teeth as he grinned. Handsome he was, I'd give him that. In his midforties, he still sported a rock-hard body. He must keep in shape at the local gym, along with making use of the tanning beds.

Candie slid to the end of the booth. "Why, that weasel. This town has grown like never before under Mark's leadership."

I placed a hand on her arm. "Where are you going?" I was afraid the mad on my cousin's face gave me the answer to my question.

Candie pulled her arm away from me and started to stand. "I'm going to give him a piece of my mind."

"Why, look who's eating breakfast in this fine diner—Little Red Riding Hood." Bret glanced from the front page of the newspaper to Candie and then back again. "I will say you haven't aged too badly." Laughter floated around the diner. Bret sauntered over to our table and slapped a newspaper on the Formica top in front of Candie.

Candie and I both gasped at the same time. Candie sank back into the booth's seat. True to his statement from the night before, Rob Anderson's snapshot of Candie dressed up as Little Red Riding Hood to Tommy Ray's Big Bad Wolf was spread across the paper's front page. And below it, a picture of Babs Wilcox cuddled up against Mark on the dance floor at The Round Up. Printed in a two-inch bold headline above the pictures: "Trouble In Paradise."

I grabbed my purse, rooted a twenty-dollar bill out of my wallet, and tucked it under my coffee mug. "Come on," I said to Candie. Tears streamed down her face. "Let's get out of here. The diner's air has turned rancid. I can't eat a thing."

Candie nodded and followed me to the door, her head bent like a scolded child.

Joy rounded the counter carrying a tray ladened with our two bowls of grits. "Sam, something wrong?" Apparently, the commotion in the dining room hadn't reached the kitchen.

I shook my head. "No, Candie, isn't feeling too well."

Joy smiled. "Pre-wedding jitters?"

"Yeah, something like that. I left the money for our meal on the table." Just because Bret ruined our meal didn't mean I would stiff Joy. I held the door open for Candie.

Bret's booming voice followed us out of Sweetie Pie's.

* * *

"Sam, what am I going to do? I don't want to damage Mark's career."

We sat in my Volkswagen Bug parked in front of Candie's Victorian-style house. Following her favorite color scheme, it was a vision of lavender with the gingerbread painted white.

"Stop thinking like that. You haven't done a thing wrong. People have short memories. This will all blow over in a day or two, and then they will be on to the next piece of gossip. Here, let me help you take some of these shower gifts into your house." Not all of Candie's presents fit into Precious—her baby blue Mustang— yesterday, so I'd packed what I could into my egg-yolk yellow VW

Bug convertible. The rest we would grab from The Ewe tomorrow morning.

I pointed to the pick-up truck in her driveway. "I see Tommy Ray's here. Working on a Sunday? I guess he took what you told him last night about finishing up, and soon, seriously."

"He better have. I wish I could have fired him, but he's almost finished and it's so close to the wedding. He's lucky Mark didn't boot him out last night." Tommy Ray bunked in Mark's two-bedroom apartment while he worked on Candie's house. He gave her a good price on the rehab since she threw in the living accommodations.

Candie and I piled our arms with the presents and made our way up to her house. She opened the front door and leaned in. "Tommy Ray, you hound dog, you'd better be getting your work done right quick," she shouted into the house. "Tommy Ray, do you hear me?"

I bent and gave Dixie, her calico cat, some loving while Candie climbed the winding oak staircase to her second floor. The banister was a work of art—leaves and grapes cascaded down the newel post—hand-carved by a craftsman over a hundred years ago.

A crash sounded from the second floor. "Oh my God, oh my God, oh my God!"

CHAPTER SIX

———

As I stumbled up the massive staircase, I shouted, "Candie! Candie!"

Out of breath, I rushed into her bedroom. My gaze darted around the room as I looked for her. Her massive turn-of-the-century Victorian bed stood against one wall, covered with a lavender and lace duvet. A mound of pillows rested against the headboard. On the far wall hung a five-foot-tall ornately carved mirror. An oak dresser, cluttered with Candie's perfumes and jewelry, stood proudly on the opposite wall.

The doorway leading out to the balcony off her bedroom framed a trembling Candie. A warm summer breeze floated into the room. I ran towards her, tripping on an orange extension cord coiled over the Persian rug on the floor. "Oomph," I said, catching myself before I tumbled to my knees. "Candie, what is the matter?" I asked, rushing to her side.

My cousin pointed a shaking bejeweled finger toward the balcony floor.

I screeched to a halt next to her. "Sweetie, what is the matter?" I asked, then my gaze followed her finger to a lump stretched out on the floor. "Oh," I breathed out, grasping onto the back of a wrought-iron chair sitting on the balcony next to the door.

Tommy Ray lay sprawled on the floor of the balcony. A nail gun rested next to his still, lanky body. Blood pooled next to his head. A nail resided in his skull.

I glanced over to Candie. She started to shiver. I touched her hand. It felt cold and clammy. I feared she would go into shock. "Come on, sweetie. Let's go inside. I'll call for help."

Candie nodded and let me lead her back into the bedroom.

I steered her towards the bed and gently pushed on her shoulders for her to sit on the edge.

"I'm going to call 9-1-1 now," I said.

Candie stared off into space and meekly nodded. "Oh, Tommy Ray, I couldn't have stayed mad at you. You really were special to me. After all, you were my first love, and a person never forgets that."

I blinked. Did Candie think Tommy Ray killed himself because she got mad at him about the picture? Maybe he became distraught after he saw Candie and Mark together at the bar last night and realized he'd never win her back. *What a waste of life.*

I pulled my flip phone out of the back pocket of my slacks. Yes, I still had a flip phone, and by that I didn't mean one of the newer smart phone versions. Technology and I were not the best of friends. But as my finger poised over the nine button, I heard sirens blaring outside the house.

I frowned. How could they know what happened here already? "Candie, will you be all right? I'm going downstairs to let the police in."

She nodded. Tears trickled down her cheeks. I knew she was already mourning the loss of a dear friend.

Banging shook the front door. I scrambled down the stairs as fast as I could.

"Police, open up," a voice shouted from the other side of the door.

I groaned. I'd recognize the voice shouting on the other side of the door anywhere. I opened the door, and Sergeant Joe Peters, with his gun drawn, charged into Candie's living room. Two uniformed officers followed behind him. They entered the house at a slower pace.

"I should have known you'd be here," Sergeant Peters said, aiming his gun at me.

I pointed to his gun. "You can put the gun away, Joe. You know Candie and I haven't committed any crime."

Joe puffed out his chest. The buttons on his gray uniform shirt strained to their limits. "I'll be the judge of that."

Joe and I had a long history, reaching all the way back to kindergarten. It wasn't my fault he'd peed in the school's sandbox. So I'd told the teacher. Big deal. I mean, would you want to play in pee-soaked sand? But I guess kids have a long memories, and all through school, the nickname "Sandy" had stuck to him for his playground exploit.

Joe's head swiveled around the living room. "Where is the victim?"

I turned and pointed to the stairs. "On the balcony off Candie's bedroom. Tommy Ray is dead."

"Sam, who's there?"

My eyes traveled to the top of the stairs. My cousin clung to the top banister for support, face ashen. Her auburn curls tangled about her head.

Afraid that she would collapse, I raced up the stairs. Joe Peters and the two officers ran up behind me.

"It's Sandy Peters and two officers. You remember Joe."

In a faint voice, she replied, "Oh, yes. The boy who relieved himself in the school's sandbox when you were in kindergarten."

The officers couldn't contain themselves and laughed out loud. Joe twirled around on the steps and glared at them. The officers promptly choked back their laughter but couldn't hide the grins that tugged at their lips.

I took Candie by the hand and led her back into the bedroom. "Candie, lie down on the bed. I can take care of any questions Joe might have."

She meekly nodded and did as I suggested.

"Where's the body?" Joe asked in a demanding voice.

I pointed to the balcony. "Out there."

Joe tramped out onto the balcony with the two policemen. "Geez, the sucker certainly chose a nasty way to kill himself."

Candie gasped and let out a loud cry.

I marched over to the balcony door and shook a finger at Joe. "Sandy." I didn't care if he didn't like that nickname. "Do you have to be so crass?"

Joe looked up at me and furrowed his unibrow. "Sorry to hurt your sensibilities, Miss Samantha. Death isn't pretty."

I certainly knew about death from my years as co-owner of the Do Drop Inn Funeral Parlor with my ex, George. I dug my nails into the palms of my hands so I wouldn't smack Joe and be arrested for assaulting an officer of the law. "No kidding, but can you show the departed some respect?"

More sirens sounded below the balcony. "Reed, go down and show the EMTs where to go," Sergeant Peters said, directing the tall, young African American officer.

Officer Reed edged past me and ran down the staircase to the living room.

EMTs rushed into the house. They carried a gurney between them up the stairs. This was no mean feat since the stairs curved halfway up to the second floor.

Sergeant Peters walked off the balcony and approached Candie and me. "So, what's your connection to the deceased this time?"

Candie and I both gasped. "None," I said.

Joe raised his unibrow. "None? Oh, come on. You expect me to believe you? A fellow decides to nail his brains. You don't know anything about him?"

My stomach did somersaults. "I mean, I know him—or rather knew him. He's been working on Candie's house. Getting it ready for the wedding. I'd say hi to him whenever I saw him and make small talk. But that's about all."

Sergeant Peters tipped his uniform hat farther up his head and looked over at Candie. Her color appeared a little better, but not much. "That's right. You're marrying our mayor in two weeks, aren't you, Miss Parker? I see you made the headlines in this morning's paper."

Anger flashed through me. "What does the morning paper have to do with Candie getting married, Sandy?"

Sergeant Peters gritted his teeth and mumbled, "I hope the mayor knows what he's getting into."

The second officer, whose name tag read March, had remained on the balcony when Officer Reed went downstairs to let the EMTs in. Now he stepped into the room and motioned to Sergeant Peters. "Sergeant, can you come out here?"

Joe looked at both Candie and me. "Don't go anywhere."

"Where would we go?" I said under my breath.

Candie stood next to me, twisting her hands together. A hysterical laugh escaped her lips. I feared the thin emotional thread that held her together was about to snap.

Joe returned to the bedroom and held his plastic-gloved hand out to Candie. He uncurled his beefy fist and asked, "Does this belong to you?" A large purple rhinestone rested in the palm of his hand.

Both Candie's and my gaze flew to the front of her blouse. Candie fingered the gauzy neckline where a rhinestone was missing. "I must have lost it this morning. Before I left for church, I stepped out on the balcony to enjoy the morning and a cup of coffee. Where did you find it?"

"Not that I should be telling you, but the deceased held it clenched in his hand. Seems mighty strange to me he should be holding it. Did you and he struggle out on the balcony? Maybe, he got fresh with you, and you shot him with the nail gun?"

"Nooo!" Candie wailed then collapsed onto her bedroom floor.

CHAPTER SEVEN

A sharp voice resounded from the bedroom's doorway. "That's enough, Sergeant Peters. Detective Johnson can take over the questioning."

Candie's hand flew to her mouth. She turned towards Mark. "What are you doing here? You can't be involved in this. You have your primary to think about."

Mark walked over to Candie and drew her into his arms. "Sweetheart, the heck with the election. You are more important to me than any old election. You are my life. When will you get that into your pretty little Southern head? Without you, nothing else matters."

Hank stood behind Mark. Why was I always at the scene of dead bodies? That was how we'd first met last summer, when I'd tried to do a good deed and donated a bag of dog food that Porkchop had turned his nose up at to the local animal shelter. Porkie and I had stumbled onto the dead body of the shelter's owner. Hank was newly transferred to Wings Falls Police Department from Albany PD, and he was the investigating officer in the murder.

A faint smile crossed his handsome face, and did I see his left eyebrow arch a wee bit? I could feel the blush creeping up my cheeks. I swear the look in his crystal blue eyes said, *"Not again."* I wanted to cross the room and smooth back the lock of wavy brown hair that insisted on falling across his forehead.

Officer March walked to the door of the balcony. Plastic gloves covered his hands. He held what looked like a fluffy paint brush in one. Black powder smudged his gloves. "Detective Johnson, I think you might want to see this."

Hank reached out and squeezed my hand as he walked past me. Sergeant Peters followed him onto the balcony. Mark remained behind and cradled a weeping Candie in his arms. Between the police and the EMTs, I hoped the balcony was shored up to support all the people gathered on it. The balcony was one of the areas on Tommy Ray's to-do list to fix. Candie's home was over one hundred years old, and some areas, like the balcony, were showing their age. As if reading my thoughts, the EMTs backed into the bedroom to make room for the police.

I heard low murmuring but couldn't make out any definite words as to what was taking place on the balcony.

Hank came back into the bedroom and motioned Mark over to him. "Mark, can I have a word with you?"

I walked over to Candie and put my arm around her trembling body. Mark and Hank spoke in hushed tones in a corner of the bedroom.

Officer Reed entered the bedroom, followed by Mrs. Splotz. The wrinkle-faced woman strode behind him with her scrawny chest puffed out. She clutched a yipping dog of indeterminate breed to her chest. Dixie, Candie's cat, hissed from the bedroom door. I hadn't noticed her before now, but she must have sensed a canine intruder in her domain and wasn't rolling out the welcome mat.

I scooped Dixie up in my arms. "I'll put her out of the room so a battle doesn't break out," I said.

Candie nodded, her eyes dull to all the commotion.

Mark and Hank walked back over to Candie. "Honey, did you see Tommy Ray at any time this morning?"

"No, he wasn't here when I left for church this morning. The first time I saw him was…was out there." Candie sobbed and pointed towards the balcony. "When Sam dropped me off after we stopped for breakfast at Sweetie Pie's."

Hank turned to me. "Sam, did you see Tommy Ray this morning?"

I shook my head. "No, like Candie said, his truck wasn't here when I picked her up."

"What time did you pick her up?" Hank asked.

I gazed into his troubled blue eyes. "Hank, what is this all about? I picked Candie up at nine thirty. Like I do every Sunday for the ten o'clock mass at Saint Anthony's. Then afterwards we drove to Sweetie Pie's for breakfast."

"And what time did you leave there?" Hank drew a notepad and pen from the inside pocket of his tweed sport coat. He flipped it open and jotted down our answers.

I furrowed my brow. I didn't like the questions he was asking. What was he trying to imply? What had Officer March discovered? "Well, we didn't stay for our usual breakfast. We left a little early."

"How come?" Hank asked. "Did something happen to cut your breakfast short?"

Had Hank heard about our encounter with Bret Hargrove? That wouldn't surprise me. In a town as small as Wings Falls, gossip spread like wildfire.

"Bret Hargrove walked into Sweetie Pie's with a stack of newspapers. He handed them out to any customer who wanted one. He made sure to point out the lead article written by Rob Anderson." I wrung my hands. Anger still boiled in me at Hargrove's antics this morning.

Hank looked up from his notepad. "And what was it about?"

I hesitated. I didn't want to even think of what he wrote, let alone the picture he plastered on the front page. "The picture of Candie dressed as Little Red Riding Hood with a story to go with it."

Mark stepped next to Hank. "Why, the rat! I'll sue him for libel."

Candie placed a slender hand on his arm. "It's okay, sweetie. He can't do anything to me. I let it roll off my back." She gave a weak laugh. Now Candie was trying to comfort Mark.

Nothing better happen to prevent their wedding. They were the perfect couple and truly in love. I dared anyone who tried to stop it. *Whoa.* I shook myself. Here I was, wishing dire consequences on Rob.

While Hank was questioning me, Sergeant Peters talked to Mrs. Splotz. He turned from her and asked, "Miss Parker, are you sure you weren't here with Tommy Ray?"

Candie gave Peters a firm nod of her head. "Absolutely."

"Mrs. Splotz, will you please tell Detective Johnson what you told me?"

Mrs. Splotz stuttered then said, "Well, about ten o'clock, I was taking my Spunky, here, for a walk. He's such a good boy, not like her cat, who terrorizes the neighborhood."

Candie's back went rigid. "My Dixie does not terrorize your dog. If you kept him on a leash and in your own backyard, there wouldn't be any problems."

"Ladies. Please continue, Mrs. Splotz," Peters urged.

Mrs. Splotz shifted Spunky in her arms and patted her gray curls. "Like I was saying, while I was walking my Spunky, we heard shouting coming from her balcony. Isn't Mommy right, my Spunky Wunky?" She nuzzled her face into her dog's neck.

"Did you see Miss Parker? Was she arguing with the deceased?" Peters asked.

Mrs. Splotz looked up from her dog's neck. "Her back was to me, but I'd know those auburn curls of hers and the way she wears her hair anywhere."

True, Candie did have a distinctive shade of reddish hair and she always wore it up off her neck in a loose bun, except for today. She wore her soft curls around her shoulders.

"Thank you, Mrs. Splotz. I'll have Officer Reed take your statement."

"Young man, I'm only doing my civic duty." She followed the officer, who guided her out of the room. When she reached the door, she said, "Oh, I forgot. The woman arguing spoke with a strong Southern accent."

I grabbed on to the back of the tufted chair next to Candie's dresser. The one thing my cousin couldn't hide—her accent.

Candie clutched on to Mark's arm. "But I swear it wasn't me."

"Sergeant and Detective Johnson, may I see you for a second?" Officer Reed called from the balcony.

With their heads together, they looked at the nail gun. Officer Reed pointed to the handle. Both Joe Peters and Hank nodded. Reed and Hank turned and walked back into the room. Joe strutted behind them.

Joe stood in front of Candie and pulled the handcuffs from his utility belt. "Miss Parker, I'm taking you to the station for questioning in the murder of Tommy Ray Clements."

Candie's hand flew to her mouth. "What? What are you talking about? I didn't even see him today." She turned to Mark. "Please, Mark, you have to believe me. I'm innocent. Sure, I was mad at Tommy Ray last night, but you know me. I could never hurt him."

Mark pulled Candie into his arms. "I know, sweetie. I'll call Jason Nugent. He's the best criminal attorney north of Albany."

I touched Hank's arm. "Criminal attorney? Why would she need a criminal attorney if Tommy Ray committed suicide?"

"It may not be suicide," Hank said.

"I don't understand. He was dead when Candie and I came home from Sweetie Pie's. The medical examiner will determine his time of death and can tell if we were in church or at the diner when he was killed. Right?"

Hank shook his head. "Those times are only approximate."

"What evidence has Sandy come up with?" I said it loud enough so Bozo Peters could hear me. I didn't care if I riled him up.

"There weren't any fingerprints on the handle of the nail gun," Hank said.

The blood drained out of Candie's face. She started to shake. "No fingerprints?" she repeated. "Then he couldn't have committed suicide." She swayed towards Mark but collapsed on the floor before he could catch her.

CHAPTER EIGHT

—————

Mark gently picked Candie off the floor and placed her on the bed. I plucked one of the lace pillows from the head of the bed and tucked it under her feet.

"I'll see if she has any smelling salts in her medicine cabinet." I ran to the bathroom attached to her bedroom.

I flicked on the light and opened the white metal cabinet hanging over the porcelain sink. I shoved aside bottles of lotions and potions and smiled to myself. I guess even my cousin's creamy skin needed a little help to maintain its youthful glow. There it was—the bottle containing capsules of smelling salts, tucked behind a jar of Youth Dew cream.

I grabbed it and ran back to the bedroom. By then, Candie had started to stir. I handed a small vial to Mark. He snapped it and waved it under her nose.

Mark sat on the bed and cradled Candie's head in his arm. She looked up at him with watery eyes. "Please, Mark, believe me. I didn't harm Tommy Ray."

He nodded his head and pulled her closer to him. "I do, sweetheart. I do. We'll find whoever did this to Tommy Ray."

Sergeant Peters walked over to the bed and stood next to Mark, his handcuffs still dangling from his fingers. "I need to take her to the station for questioning."

Mark stood and ran a hand through his thinning hair. "Not without her lawyer."

"Why would she need a lawyer if she's innocent? It's Sunday, and what lawyer will come out today?" Joe Peters frowned then clamped his lips shut.

Mark held his ground. "You know the law, Peters. She won't be questioned without her lawyer present. I don't care how long it takes for one to get to the station."

Joe shoved his handcuffs back into their case. He didn't like his authority questioned. Mark was the mayor of Wings Falls and could pull rank on him. He jutted out his chin. He wasn't about to back down yet. "Fine, I'll take her to the station, and her lawyer can meet us there."

"No, I'll take her to the station, and we'll meet you there." Mark might have been inches shorter than Joe, but he stood his ground.

Candie pushed herself up on her elbows from the pile of pillows mounded at the head of her bed. "Absolutely not, Mark. You can't be involved in this. Not with the election coming up."

Mark bent and put a finger to Candie's trembling lips. "Hush. We'll have no more talk about the election." He reached out his hand and helped Candie off the bed.

Mark walked to a far corner of the bedroom and pulled his phone out of an inner pocket of his sport coat. He punched in a number and stood talking quietly for a few minutes. He nodded then ended the conversation.

He walked back over to Candie. "I just talked to Jason Nugent. He'll meet us at the station in a half an hour." He turned to Joe and said, "We'll meet you there."

Joe grimaced at Mark's statement but knew better than push it any further. He went back onto the balcony and spoke to the officers gathered there in a hushed voice.

I looked up at Hank. "You know Candie didn't do anything, don't you?"

He didn't answer.

My heart squeezed in my chest. "Hank?"

He shook his head. "Sam, I can't say anything right now. I only know I have a possible murder victim on Candie's balcony and it's my job to find out who did it." He turned and joined the others on the balcony.

As Mark led Candie out of the bedroom, she looked at me over her shoulder and said, "Sam, please take care of Dixie."

I couldn't hold back my tears any longer. They streamed down my cheeks. I ran to her and pulled her into my arms for a big hug. "Don't worry, Candie. I'll take care of her, and remember, we're Parkers. We stick together."

Candie jutted out her chin, grabbed Mark's hand, and said, "You're right. We're Parkers. We'll find out who did this and nail their hide to an outhouse wall."

A faint smile curved my lips. I marveled at my cousin's spunk, not to mention her apropos wording, even as Mark, with his arm around the lady he loved, walked them out of Candie's bedroom. I nodded and silently agreed with her clever play on words. *Yep, we'll nail their hide to an outhouse wall.*

* * *

"Well, I'll be. I knew something must have been up when I heard the call over my scanner." Gladys O'Malley's main form of entertainment was her police scanner. Being a wee bit hard of hearing, she usually cranked the volume up to full blast. She listened to it way into the night. In the winter when the windows were closed, it wasn't so bad, but now that it was summer—and my windows were thrown open to invite the cool evening breezes into my bedroom— many a night I woke up to the squawk of her scanner. "He was done in with a nail gun." Gladys poked her rug hook in the air. "I bet it was a real sight."

"Gladys, must you be so, so… Oh, I don't know, gross?" Jane Burrows looked a little pale as she hunched over her rug hooking frame.

It was Monday morning, and we Loopy Ladies were gathered at The Ewe for our weekly hook-in. Of course, the topic of conversation was the murder of Tommy Ray. Candie wasn't with us this morning. Her afternoon of being grilled at the station had left her exhausted, both physically and emotionally. She called when she got home. Joe didn't have enough to hold her. Now it was up to Hank to find the murderer. I hoped sooner rather than later. After all, there was a wedding to be held.

"Candie called me when she got home. She said Joe raked her over the coals. Apparently, someone told him about the incident at The Roundup on Saturday night." I looked up from my rug of a smiling pumpkin. I was getting ready for fall, even though we still had a few months of summer warmth and sunshine left to enjoy before our harsh winter weather descended on us. Porkchop sat at my feet. He chewed quietly on a rawhide bone Lucy gave him when he entered The Ewe. He was the unofficial shop dog and majorly spoiled by The Ewe's owner. She said he added a coziness to the shop. I guess that meant we hookers were chopped liver.

"What happened Saturday night?" asked Helen Garber. Today her outfit shouted, a bright-yellow top with gold mums dancing across it. She wore a matching pair of polyester yellow pants.

"Candie wasn't really pleased with Tommy Ray on Saturday night." While I pulled orange strips of wool for the pumpkin, I related what had happened at The Round Up on Saturday night.

Helen poked at her glasses sliding down her nose. "I can't say I blame Candie for being mad. If my ex-fiancé pulled such a stunt, I'd have him drawn and quartered."

"Me, too" and "You've got that right" came from the other Loopy Ladies sitting around the oak table in Lucy Foster's front room.

Jane Burrows, our quiet librarian, laid down her hook. She tugged on the front of the navy twin set she'd worn this morning and cleared her throat. In the summer, she switched out her long-sleeved twin sets for short-sleeved ones. All eyes swung to her. "I say we help prove Candie innocent."

"What?" I asked, astonished that the meek and mild Jane would say such a thing but proud my friends believed in Candie's innocence.

"You heard her," Patsy Ikeda said. "Remember how you tried to pin a murder on me last year when Calvin Perkins was murdered? And then Hilda Pratt was poisoned at Lucy's hook-in. You have the skills to prove her innocent. After all, you solved those two murders."

I gulped. It was apparent Patsy still held a grudge because I suspected her in the murder of a local animal shelter owner. It wasn't my fault he blackmailed her because he helped to illegally import a rare breed of dog for her from her ancestral homeland of Japan.

"Patsy's right. You solved two murders, and you do have a connection with the police department," said Roberta Holden. Roberta was three years older than Candie and me, but at fifty-eight, she was full of energy. She often taught classes here at The Ewe and was a reporter for the *Senior Chatter,* a newsletter published by our local Senior Center. "With my reporting skills and your 'in' with the Wings Falls PD, we'll catch Tommy Ray's killer before you know it."

"I hear a lot of talk from the people who come into the restaurant. I'll keep my ears open for any gossip about Tommy Ray's murder," Susan Mayfield said. She and her husband owned the Momma Mia Restaurant on Glen Street. The best Italian restaurant in the North Country. Mark and Candie planned on holding their wedding reception there.

Marybeth Higgins had sat quietly throughout all of this. She timidly raised her hand.

"Yes?" I asked, like a teacher calling on her student.

"I'm really good with the computer. I can do any research you might need done," she said.

I nodded. "Great and thank you, Marybeth, No one can hide in today's world of the internet. The killer may have left some info on the web."

Lucy Foster smiled. "I may not be able to offer much, but you can always meet here to report on your findings."

"Wonderful." I couldn't help the smile spreading across my face. My heart burst with pride. The Loopy Ladies may be an odd assortment of women but they stuck together, even when things got tough.

I raised my thermos filled with decaf coffee. "Ladies, here's to proving Candie innocent."

"Here, here," they shouted, raising an assortment of coffee mugs and thermoses.

CHAPTER NINE

———

"They said what?"

Candie and I sat on a tufted loveseat in the fitting area of Sylvia's Bridal Salon, waiting for the salesgirl to bring out our gowns for their final alterations. I glanced around the room and smiled at the gilded cupid poised on a white column in the corner of the room. Pictures of happy brides decked out in their gowns filled the walls.

Candie blinked her eyes. Moisture clung to her lashes. She was trying to hold back tears after I'd told her about yesterday's Loopy Lady gathering and how everyone wanted to help find Tommy Ray's killer.

"Yes, even Marybeth offered to use her computer skills to find out anything she could on the internet. Who knows what kind of trail that person may have left?" I reached into my Chanel handbag. Today was special and deserved Coco. I pulled out a tissue for Candie to dab her eyes. She wouldn't want mascara staining her wedding gown.

The door to the fitting room opened, and in walked Valerie Fisherman. I blinked then turned on the sofa to Candie. *Valerie?* I mouthed to my cousin.

Candie shrugged her shoulders. She was as unaware of Valerie working at Sylvia's as I was. In all our trips to the bridal salon for gown fittings, we had never encountered her.

Valerie cradled a plastic garment bag in her arms. She hooked it on a brass stand and zipped down the front of the bag. A confection of violet lace and silk puffed out of the bag.

I pushed myself off the sofa and walked over to the gown. "Hi, Valerie. I didn't know you worked here. We never ran into you when we were here for our fittings before."

Valerie shrugged. "I've been here for almost six months, but I work mostly evenings."

I fingered the violet lace of Candie's gown. "That's probably why we haven't seen you. Our appointments have all been during the day. It must be so much fun, surrounded by all these beautiful dresses and all the happy brides and prom goers."

Candie joined me by her dress. "Yes, and working for Sylvia, she is such a peach. She can find the perfect dress for every bride and girl going to the prom."

Her shop was the go-to place for all things bridal and prom in the North Country. She'd been in business for over twenty years and knew the perfect dress for each of her customers. She'd never married. Supposedly, her one true love had been killed in an automobile accident two weeks before her own wedding. She'd made it her life's mission to make every woman who set foot in her shop the most beautiful bride to walk down the aisle.

Sylvia strode into the dressing room. The sweet scent of gardenias floated in with her. A long garment bag rested over her thin arm. "Hi ladies. Candie, your big day is only around the corner." She pushed aside the curtain to a dressing room and hung the garment bag on a hook on the far wall. She unzipped the front of the bag and pulled out my gown. It was a deeper shade of violet silk than Candie's but with none of the lace that made up the bride's dress.

Sylvia then lifted Candie's dress off the brass hook and out of its bag. Lavender lace and silk billowed out.

My hands flew to my chest. "Oh my, Candie. That is so beautiful."

I heard a gasp behind me. I turned to see Valerie smiling at Candie. "You are right, Sam. She will be such a beautiful bride walking down the aisle."

Flossie had to be wrong about Valerie having a crush on Mark. She was just a devoted campaign worker.

"Candie, let me place it in the dressing room." Sylvia pulled back the heavy damask curtain of a large cubicle set against the wall of the fitting room.

Candie slid her hands down her hips. "I hope I can still squeeze into it. It's time to see if my Saturday night binging at The Round Up did any damage to the fit of my dress."

I returned to the love seat while Candie sashayed into the dressing room and pulled the curtain closed.

"*Umph, umph.* Drat those cheesy nachos."

"Candie, are you all right?" I called from the loveseat.

The curtain of the dressing room slid open. Before me stood a princess all decked out in her finery.

Tears misted my eyes. "Oh, Candie, I wish Memaw Parker could see you. She would have busted her buttons with pride. You look like an angel."

Candie swept out of the dressing room. The slim-fitting dress clung to her curves in all the right places. The neckline did a modest scoop over her breasts and ended in cap sleeves. A lace train flowed behind her.

"Turn around, and I'll button you up," Sylvia said. She reached up to her sleek black hair and pulled her glasses off the top of her head. With the glasses firmly on her nose, she began to tackle the row of about fifty tiny buttons that trailed down the back of Candie's dress. A tomato-shaped pincushion was attached to her wrist by an elastic band, and a yellow tape measure was draped around her neck. She was ready for any needed adjustments to the gown.

Buttons fastened, Candie turned back to face me. "Sam, hand me my shoes. I need to try them on to make sure the length of my dress is perfect. I don't want to trip as I walk down the aisle."

I opened the shoe box resting at my feet and handed her the low-heeled shoes dyed to match her dress. Mark was about the same height as Candie. She didn't want to tower over him when they stood at the altar.

After she slipped the shoes on, Candie preened in front of a gilt-edged mirror hanging on the wall of the fitting room. She turned one way and then another to get the full effect of her gown.

"So, what do you think? Okay?" she asked.

"Perfect," Sylvia, Valerie, and I said in unison.

The four of us laughed. The cheesy nachos hadn't done any damage. Sylvia poked and pulled at the gown to make sure the fit was perfect. She sat on the floral-patterned rug covering the floor of the fitting room to pin the dress's hem to the correct length.

* * *

A few minutes later, Sylvia gave a grunt and pushed herself up off the floor. "My bones are getting a little too old for sitting on this floor." She stood and arched her back. "Let Valerie help you out of the gown. I'll have it steamed and the hem adjusted. It will be ready for pick up the day before your wedding."

Candie returned to the dressing room. With Valerie's help, she shimmied out of her gown. Back in her street clothes, she parted the room's curtain and handed her dress to Sylvia. Sylvia zipped the dress back into its plastic garment bag for safekeeping.

She turned to me and smiled. "Now, for your gown."

I groaned. I didn't think I'd get off as lucky as Candie. Even the stretchy yoga pants I pulled on this morning seemed a little snugger. But if I wanted to walk down the aisle as Candie's maid of honor, there was no avoiding trying my gown on.

* * *

An hour later, we said our goodbyes to a smiling Sylvia and Valerie. Now we were making our way to Sweetie Pie's for a light lunch.

"We certainly lucked out with our gowns," Candie said, scooting into a booth by the window.

"You're right. I felt sure you'd have to shoehorn me into my dress. Maybe the extra twenty minutes I spent on my exercise bicycle last night burnt off all those calories from this past weekend." I reached over to the juke box sitting on the end of the table and flipped through the selection cards. I felt like a little Elvis to go with our lunch. Even my cousin didn't mind my playing him. She felt it her duty to like a fellow Southern boy. Although she did draw the line when I selected Donnie O.

Candie, who was occupied digging into her purse for a quarter, shot a look at me. "I thought you and Hank planned a hot date."

I shook my head. "Well, last night got canceled, for obvious reasons."

Candie looked down at her hands. They rested on the booth's table. "Sorry," she said in a hushed voice.

I grabbed hold of them. "Don't even give it a moment's thought. You're innocent, and we're going to prove it. Hank and I will have plenty of nights to spend together." In my mind, I secretly hoped for a lifetime of them. "I called him after the Loopy Ladies meeting."

Candie looked up at me. A faint smile curved her full lips. "What did he have to say? Are you going out tonight? I certainly hope so."

"Yesterday, I kind of mentioned that the Loopy Ladies are going to help prove you innocent. I don't think he liked the idea." His tone of voice had hardened when I mentioned that. "He said tonight wasn't a good night for him, too, when I asked if he wanted to come over and watch a movie. You know, cuddle up on the sofa with a glass of wine."

Candie tapped her ruby red–polished fingernails on the scratched Formica top of our booth's table. "*Humph.*"

"He was a little distant. Said he was tired and thought he'd spend the night in with Nina."

Candie puffed up with righteous indignation. "Nina? Who's she? Is he two-timing you? I'll scratch her eyes out. Who does Hank think he is? He can't string you along then dump you for another woman. I'll bet she's some hussy."

I couldn't contain my laughter. "Candie, calm down. It's okay. Don't you remember? Nina is his bulldog."

Candie puffed out a breath of air. "Oh, that's right. What with all that's going on, it slipped my memory. *Humph.* What's gotten into him?"

I wondered the same thing, although my Porkchop was better company than some humans I knew. "He's tired. I did invite Nina, too, but he said another night would be better."

"The man needs his red blood cells checked. What red-blooded man wouldn't want to spend an evening with a sexy woman like you instead of his dog?"

I agreed with Candie. Was Hank having second thoughts about our relationship? My heart sank at the thought of him not being a part of my life.

"You ladies ready to order?" Franny stood next to our table, an order pad poised in her hand.

I looked up at Franny. "A Caesar salad and a glass of water with a slice of lemon will be fine for me."

The curls on Candie's head bobbed in agreement. "I guess I'll have the same."

Franny raised an eyebrow at us. "You ladies feeling all right?" she asked while jotting down our orders.

"We're fine," I said, "but we just came from Sylvia's Bridal Salon for our final fittings, and I dare not gain an ounce before the wedding."

Franny laughed. "I understand. I'll be back in a sec with your water. Do you want the dressing for your salad on the side?"

I nodded. "Maybe you better. Then I can control what I dump on it."

"Gotcha." Franny turned to go.

I scanned the diner as she walked back to the kitchen. The room was packed with lunchtime patrons, all busy enjoying their meals of various sandwiches and burgers or pulled pork, a favorite on Franny's menu. She'd brought the recipe with her when she moved north like so many other items on her menu. She and Clint, Marybeth Higgins' brother and the owner of the Smiling Pig Barbeque, could be rivals for the best pulled pork in Wings Falls.

"Look at that." Candie ogled the hamburger and mound of fries on the plate a waitress delivered to the table next to us.

My stomach rumbled and my mouth watered. "It does look delicious, but we don't want to be stuffed into our gowns on your wedding day."

"Love Me Tender" chimed from my purse. I dug my phone out. I looked at the caller ID and groaned.

CHAPTER TEN

———

Candie pointed at my phone. "Who is it?"

"George," I said in a flat voice, devoid of all enthusiasm.

"Don't answer it. I'm getting indigestion thinking about him." Candie rolled her eyes and placed a hand on her stomach.

"He knows not to call unless it is a dire emergency. I'd better answer it."

Candie slapped the table. Our silverware jumped on the table. "Then he'd better be lying in a ditch at the side of the road inhaling his last breath."

I laughed. There certainly was no love lost between my cousin and my ex. I knew I needed to answer. I was still part owner of the Do Drop Inn Funeral Parlor. Since it was an uncle who willed me the money to buy the funeral parlor when George and I were first married, I had a vested interest in it. It did help support my designer purse habit.

I flipped open my phone. "What do you want, George?"

George's voice was edged with panic. "Sam, you have to help me out. Nancy needs to take a leave of absence. I'm slammed at the funeral parlor. Summer colds have really taken a toll on the good folks of Wings Falls."

I furrowed up my forehead. "Nancy. Who's Nancy?"

"She's the new secretary we hired."

I didn't keep up with the day-to-day running of the Do Drop. I left that up to George. He may have acted like a toad in our marriage, but I trusted him not to cheat me on my monthly checks from the funeral parlor. Besides, our accountant was a good friend of mine, and if a penny was misplaced, he'd let me know.

"She just started working there and has to take a leave already?" I asked.

"Yeah, something to do with her mother falling and breaking her hip."

"I'm really busy right now. What about Anna? She was the secretary before you and she danced in the sheets," I couldn't help adding. For some reason, I wouldn't let his betrayal of me go, even though I'd moved on to my hunky Hank. Or at least I thought he was mine. His recent absence from my life since Saturday had me a wee bit worried, or maybe I was just being paranoid. After all, he was busy with Tommy Ray's murder investigation.

A hysterical laugh came through the line. "Anna? You've got to be kidding me. She's so wrapped up with the twins, she hardly even notices me."

A smile crept across my lips. *Was there trouble in paradise?*

"Sam, please, you know how the office works. You took care of everything when we were first married. Please, I need you."

Why did I feel happy at his desperation? It felt good right down to my toes. "All right, I can spare you a couple of days, but call a temp agency to get a replacement for Nancy until she returns. I'm busy right now with Candie's wedding and my book launch."

George thanked me profusely. I agreed to stop by the funeral parlor after my lunch with Candie and see what I could do. It wasn't as if I didn't know the routine. I had worked at the funeral parlor during the early years of our marriage before I decided to sprout my writing wings and we hired Anna.

"So, what does the creep want?" Candie asked as soon as I hung up from George.

I related the conversation and told her of George's predicament. Candie laughed out loud. People at the nearby tables turned their heads to see what the commotion was all about. "Anna doesn't have the time for him." Candie laughed so hard tears ran down her face.

"Shh," I put a finger to my lips, but a smile spread across my face, anyway. The Cheshire cat had nothing on me.

Candie couldn't hide her smile and laughed. "I guess Anna's found out he's about as useful as a steering wheel on a mule with those boys of theirs."

I nodded and couldn't agree more. In fact, I should thank Anna. She did me a favor. Since leaving George, I now would have a hopefully soon-to-be-successful career as a children's author. Also, fingers crossed, a very loving and caring man was in my life. Yes, I couldn't be happier without George, and I could handle a few days dealing with him.

We finished our salads. Valerie's reaction earlier this morning at Sylvia's niggled at my brain. "Candie, did you notice how Valerie reacted when you tried on your wedding dress?"

Candie pulled a tube of lipstick out of her purse and swiped some Passion Pink across her lips. She recapped the lipstick tube and looked up at me with a blank stare. "Honey, I didn't notice anything this morning but the gorgeous gown I'm going to wear down the aisle when I become Mark's wife. Why? Was she out of sorts?"

Maybe I was reading too much into Valerie's reaction to Candie's bridal gown. Then again, maybe Flossie was jealous of all Valerie did at Mark's campaign headquarters and wanted to make her look bad. I shrugged. "No, she looked really happy when you tried on your wedding dress. If she has a crush on Mark, like Flossie says, do you think she'd be so excited about seeing you in the gown you're going to wear walking down the aisle to be Mark's bride?" I motioned Franny over to ask for the check.

Candie opened her purse and slipped her lipstick inside. "Who knows what those two are thinking. All I know is that Mark is mine and we're about to get married, assuming I'm not the prime murder suspect. They will have to work out their own issues. Whatever they are. I don't have time to deal with them."

"Salads to your liking, ladies?" Franny ripped our check off her pad and placed it on the table.

Candie wrinkled up her nose. "If I was into rabbit food, I'd say it was delicious."

Franny and I laughed.

Franny smiled. "Your big day will be here before you know it. Then you can get back to some real Southern cooking."

"I can't wait. I hope I'm not too weak to walk down the aisle by then." Candie fluttered her eyelashes and heaved a deep sigh.

I grabbed my purse and scooted to the end of the booth. "Come on, cousin. I need to get home and see to Porkchop. Then I guess I better get over to the funeral parlor and see what I can do there."

* * *

I took in my surroundings. A ten-foot-long oak bar hugged the wall on my left. A large urn filled with pink and white roses sat where mugs of frosty beer used to hold court. Their scent filled the room. I could never appreciate those beautiful flowers like other women. The Do Drop was once a bar, a favorite hangout for the locals, but after working at the funeral home for so many years, the flowers reminded me of death. Twenty-five years ago, when George and I bought the building—well, really, I did with that inheritance from a bachelor uncle—we wanted to rename it Davies Funeral Parlor, but the locals couldn't seem to give up the name Do Drop Inn. So, we renamed it the Do Drop Inn Funeral Parlor, and it stuck. A large wooden chandelier hung over what was once the main dining area of the room. We had covered the oak floor, scarred by chairs and tables, with Persian area rugs. I shook my head. Okay, so much for a walk down memory lane when I was foolish and in love with George. At least the Do Drop furnished me with an income while I tried to make a success of my writing career.

A frowning George strode out of the secretary's office and walked towards Porkchop and me.

"Okay, George, what do you want?" Porkchop trotted next to me. I'd neglected him the last few days, what with the shower and all the goings on yesterday at Candie's. When I stopped home, I couldn't resist his sad brown eyes looking up at me and decided to bring him to the funeral parlor. Porkchop trotted before me back into the office and jumped up on the wing chair sitting in a corner. He tried to fluff up the cushion with his paws, turned in a circle three times, then settled himself down and closed his eyes.

For fifty-five, George still looked handsome. Today, he wore a tailored navy suit. A red and blue–striped tie lay against his pristine white shirt. He always was a stickler for wearing the right clothes. Unlike me, who usually wore jeans or yoga pants. My choice of clothes rankled him on more than one occasion during our marriage. I didn't quite live up to his preppy image. He still sported a full head of brown hair, which was now streaked with gray, giving him a very distinguished look.

I looked around the office. Years had passed since I sat behind the desk and helped George with our fledgling business. He upgraded the room's décor when Anna became the secretary. I should have taken that as a hint something was going on with those two. Gone was the old military surplus metal desk and chair I'd used. A large cherry desk sat in the middle of the room. A plush gray rug lay on the floor. The room was painted in shades of mauve and gray. Floral prints hung on the wall, replacing the gas station calendar I had stared at. Money was sparse when we first started the business, but a cushioned chair would have been nice. George had always nixed my ideas. He'd insisted money was too tight for such luxuries. Apparently not for Anna, however.

"Take a seat, and I'll show you what orders have to be filled and the accounts that need attention." George pulled out the desk chair for me. Surprise registered on my face. He'd never been gallant when we were married. He leaned over me as I booted up the computer. I noticed he still wore his favorite expensive cologne.

A growl rumbled out of Porkchop's throat. He jumped off the chair and ran to the front of the desk. His body shook as he barked.

"It's okay, Porkie. George only wants to show me something," I said, trying to soothe my dog.

George straightened. "Call him off. Your mutt never did like me. Why did you have to bring him, anyway?"

"He was smarter than me where you were concerned," I mumbled under my breath. "If you want me to help you out, he's coming with me. He's been left alone enough lately."

George straightened his tie. "Okay, okay, But keep him away from me."

After spending an hour with George showing me what invoices needed to be paid and the supplies he wanted ordered for the funeral parlor—caskets, embalming supplies, urns for ashes, the usual necessities for dealing with the dearly departed—he left to attend to what I figured was other Do Drop Inn business.

* * *

Porkchop started to whine. I looked up from the computer and rubbed my eyes. I placed my hands on the small of my back and stretched. "Porkchop, you're right. It's time to go home." I got up from my chair and walked over to Porkchop. I bent and rubbed between his ears. "I'm surprised you didn't get my attention earlier."

I grabbed my purse from the bottom drawer of the desk where I had stowed it earlier, snapped on Porkchop's leash, then turned off the room's lights. "George, I'm leaving," I shouted down the hallway. I wasn't sure where he was, but I felt he'd hear me. Nothing, nada. Not a response from him. I checked his office then looked out a window and saw his car was missing from the parking lot. I looked down at Porkchop. "The creep left before us. Can you believe it, Porkie?" Porkchop tilted his head and looked at me with his chocolate-brown eyes. "He left us slaving away while he was off doing who knows what. I might not come in tomorrow. It would do him good if I leave him to deal with everything until this Nancy returns." With a determined nod, Porkchop and I marched to my car. I had better things to do with my time—like helping find Tommy Ray's killer so Candie didn't spend her honeymoon as a guest of the Wings Falls jail. Oh, and maybe discover why Hank had become so distant.

CHAPTER ELEVEN

———

"Porkchop, are you ready for dinner?" Silly question. He was always ready for a bowl of his favorite kibble.

His tail wagged as he followed me into the kitchen, I glanced around the small room. On those popular TV home decorating shows, the couple would walk into the room and say, "Complete gut job." I shook my head and wondered how these young couples could afford all the renovations they proposed. My gaze took in my humble kitchen. Yes, it was out of the 1980s, but this was where I grew up. I flashed back to visions of me doing my homework at the kitchen table while my mom prepared dinner. I remembered the chocolate chip cookies I dunked into a cold glass of milk when I came home from school. Yes, the room still sported a faux marble Formica countertop and knotty pine cabinets, but I don't know that I'd want to erase all those memories, even if I could afford a remodel, which I couldn't. Maybe I was too sentimental. After all, I'd always have the memories.

I poured kibble into Porkchop's bone-shaped bowl. "What do you think, Porkie? If our book is a bestseller, should we do a remodel?"

He didn't have an opinion on the subject one way or another. He was too busy chowing down on his food.

The brass door knocker rapped against my living room door. I frowned. Who could it be? I wasn't expecting anyone. I hadn't heard from Hank since Sunday.

I wandered back into the living room. My guard dog was too busy satisfying his hunger to accompany me. I peered through the peephole on my door and saw a weary Hank leaning against the door. My heart squeezed in my chest.

I gently opened the door so Hank wouldn't fall into the room. "Hi, handsome."

He straightened and gave me one of his sexy lopsided grins. "Hi yourself, beautiful."

Heat flushed up my neck. I didn't consider myself beautiful. Cute maybe, but beautiful? George never said such things to me, not even in the early days of our romance. I could certainly get used to Hank's compliments.

I opened the door wider and pointed to my chintz-covered sofa. "Come in and sit down."

Hank followed me into the living room. He sank into the sofa and let out a weary sigh. "I better not close my eyes, or I don't think you'll ever get me up."

He closed his eyes anyway and loosened his Rug Rats-decorated tie. I could see the tiredness seep out of his body.

I sat next to him and pushed back the brown curl of his hair with a mind of its own that fell onto his forehead. "You've been a stranger."

He turned his head towards me and opened his eyes. "I've been putting in long hours with Tommy Ray's murder case."

I nodded. I should have known. He was the lead detective in the Wings Falls PD, after all.

Porkchop finished his meal and trotted into the living room. He jumped up on the sofa and crawled onto Hank's lap. The two had become best buddies from the first time they met last year. "How you doing, good buddy? Nina misses you." I think Porkchop had fallen in love with Hank's Nina. The few times she spent the night, along with her owner, Porkchop wouldn't leave her side. He followed her everywhere she went in the house and even shared his squeaky warthog toy with her. If that wasn't true love, I didn't know what was. Hank scratched behind Porkchop's ears. He knew the way to my dog's heart, and mine, too. Even if he didn't scratch behind my ears.

"You want a bite to eat? I was going to throw a pizza in the oven. How about a beer? I have a Trails Head in the fridge, chilling."

Hank nodded. He looked too tired to even talk. I left my two favorite men on the sofa and went into the kitchen to throw a pepperoni and sausage pizza in the oven and grab a beer for Hank. I set the timer on the stove and walked back into the living room.

Hank had kicked off his shoes and shed his sport coat. His tie was tucked into the breast pocket of the jacket. He had laid it over a wing chair sitting next to the fireplace. A fire would be relaxing and romantic. Even though it was summer, tonight was on the cool side. If I opened all the windows in the living room, it would cool down enough to make having a fire acceptable. I flipped open the windows then walked over to the fireplace and bent to place a piece of wood onto the grate.

"Here, let me help."

I jumped. I hadn't heard Hank come up behind me. He reached for the log in my hand and placed it on the grate. "Thanks, I've never been good at building a fire. I even flunked the fire-building badge when I was a Girl Scout."

Hank chuckled. "Then let me show you my Boy Scout skills."

I returned to the sofa and settled in the corner as he continued to stack wood on the fire grate then struck a match to it. A warm glow soon filled the fireplace. He certainly did have great skills, and not all of the Boy Scout kind.

With the fire roaring, Hank came back to the sofa and sat next to me. I cuddled up to his lean body. The smell of the fire mixed with the scent of his musky cologne brought a smile to my lips.

Hank placed a finger under my chin and raised it up so I could look at him. "What's got you smiling?"

"I was admiring your skills as a Boy Scout."

"I have all kinds of skills I can show you." He leaned down and placed a kiss on my lips.

We'd been snuggling on the sofa and gazing at the flames in the fireplace for about thirty minutes when the stove timer buzzed. I groaned and broke off a kiss. "I need to see to the pizza, or we'll have more than one fire in the house to contend with."

He let out an unsteady breath and nodded. "There's already more than one fire to contend with."

If I didn't want to serve him charred pizza, I would have ignored the timer. I reluctantly pushed off the sofa and went into the kitchen.

I came back a few minutes later juggling a beer and two plates filled with pizza slices. "Here. Do you want to grab this?"

Hank rose from the sofa and morphed into a handsome waiter serving me dinner.

I motioned for Porkchop to hop off the sofa. "You've eaten your dinner." I knew he'd sit there staring at us with his chocolate-brown eyes while we ate.

"How was your day?" Hank asked after taking a sip of his beer.

I related to him about how George asked me to fill in while his secretary was home tending to her mother. "Porkchop wasn't too thrilled. He growled at George. He and George never did get along."

Hank looked down at Porkchop. "Smart boy." Hank tossed him a piece of his pizza crust.

I swatted at Hank's hand. "You'll spoil him, and he'll gain weight if you feed him too much pizza." I was guilty of spoiling Porkchop with my pizza crusts, too.

"I have to reward him for looking after my girl." Hank leaned down and patted Porkchop's head.

My body tingled right down to my toes hearing Hank refer to me as his girl.

I swallowed a bite of pizza. "Can you tell me how things are going with Tommy Ray's murder?"

Hank rolled his beer bottle between his hands. "Right now, we don't have any real leads."

My eyes widened. "You don't still think Candie murdered him, do you?"

Hank glanced at me. "We can't eliminate anyone as a suspect."

My back stiffened. "Hank, you know Candie. She wouldn't hurt a flea, let alone murder someone."

"Sam, I have to be impartial. She had motive. Tommy Ray could have ruined her chance at happiness. If Mark took the picture the wrong way, he could have called off the wedding. She also had means. She lives in the house where Tommy Ray was murdered. Mrs. Splotz said she saw a woman fitting Candie's description arguing with him."

I reached down and scratched Porkchop's back. He still sat staring up at us, probably hoping for another bite of pizza. "But Candie was with me Sunday morning. I picked her up for church. Then afterwards we went for breakfast at Sweetie Pie's. I was with her the whole time."

"I know, but I can't discount Mrs. Splotz's testimony."

I pounded my fist on the arm of the sofa. "Mrs. Splotz, that old busybody. She has nothing better to do with her time than spy on people. She needs a hobby, like—oh I don't know—maybe hang gliding."

Hank choked on a swallow of beer. "Hang gliding?"

"Well, maybe not hang gliding, but something to keep her from snooping around Candie."

"You Ain't Nothing But a Hound Dog" rang from my phone sitting on the wooden trunk in front of the sofa. Hank's eyebrow rose in question. I shrugged my shoulders. "I felt in the mood for a different Elvis tune." The caller ID flashed Gladys O'Malley's name on the screen.

I frowned and flipped my phone open. "Hi, Gladys. Everything okay?" She rarely called me on the phone. Usually, if she wanted to tell me something, she came knocking on my door.

I listened to what Gladys related then said, "Do you want to call the rest of the Loopy Ladies, or do you want me to? Yes, I'll call Lucy to make sure we can meet tomorrow morning at The Ewe. We'll make it early before anyone needs to go to work. Eight thirty sound good to you?" We agreed on the time, and then I flipped my phone closed.

Hank raised an eyebrow. "What did my aunt Gladys want?"

I hesitated to answer. I knew he wasn't crazy about me getting involved in murder investigations, but this was about Candie. I couldn't sit idly by, no matter what he thought.

I twisted a curl around my finger. "Ummm, that was your aunt Gladys."

Hank nodded. "I know. What are you ladies up to?"

"Well, I guess you'd say we kind of formed a team to see what we could find out about Tommy Ray's murder. Gladys says she's got some info to share with us."

Hank's jaw clenched. "Sam, isn't it enough you go snooping around? Do you have to involve my aunt and a bunch of crazy ladies to join you?" Gladys had tried to matchmake us when he first arrived in town from Albany. Who knew a murder would draw us together as a couple?

I jumped off the sofa and stood with my fists on my hips. "Crazy ladies? You better not let your aunt know you called her a crazy lady. And Candie is a friend to all of them. They don't believe she killed Tommy Ray any more than…than Porkchop there." I pointed a shaking finger at my dog, who jumped onto the sofa and cuddled up to Hank.

Hank repositioned Porkchop and stood. "I think I'll call it a night. I'm exhausted." He grabbed the sport coat he had shed when he first came inside and walked to the door. He placed his hand on the doorknob, but before twisting it, he turned back to me. A worried look filled his eyes. "Sam, I can't stop you, but please be careful. My heart has suffered too many losses already." He turned the knob and walked out into the night.

CHAPTER TWELVE

―――――

I slumped against my living room door and looked down at my pup. "Porkchop, what was that all about?" His head cocked as he listened to me. I peeked out the peephole in my front door and watched as the taillights of Hank's Jeep got swallowed up in the darkness of the night. I turned from the door and scooped my dog up into my arms. I held his warm body close to me and walked back into the living room. I sat on the same cushion Hank had vacated moments before, still warm from his body heat. "I swear having a root canal would be easier than trying to figure out Hank's and my relationship. If we still have one." Tears started to trickle down my face.

Porkchop whined and licked my hand as I swiped at my tears. "Sweetie, that's enough of a pity party for tonight." I settled my sympathetic pup on the cushion beside me and reached for the hooking I was working on before Hank's unexpected visit. He snuggled into the pile of wool strips scattered beside me.

"You know I can't abandon Candie. How could I ever live with myself if I didn't do everything I could to help prove her innocent?" I plucked a wool strip out from under Porkchop's belly. "Why can't he realize I have to do everything I can to help her? If he doesn't understand my loyalty to Candie, I don't know if we have any future." Porkchop looked at me and started to whine again. "Yeah, and I thought we'd finally found Mr. Right. And maybe Nina would be your forever friend." Sad eyes gazed up at me. "Sorry, Porkie. I guess it's only you and me against the world from now on." I jabbed my hook into the pattern on my frame and pulled through a loop.

The mindless pulling of wool strips, which usually calmed my soul, wasn't working tonight. Images of Tommy Ray's body spread out on Candie's balcony crowded out all other thoughts. Why was the rhinestone from Candie's blouse clutched in his hand? Most of all, why was Hank so upset with me trying to find Tommy Ray's killer? Was his pride hurt that I had solved a murder last summer that had stumped the Wings Falls Police? No, I couldn't believe that his self-esteem was so fragile. Not Hank. I placed my frame on the floor and got up from the sofa.

"I think we'll make it an early night, honey. They always say things will look better in the morning. What do you think?" Porkchop didn't answer me. "Yeah, what I thought, too. The wise old person who spouted those words of wisdom didn't know Hank Johnson or the Parker girls. Right now, things look a tad bleak for Team Parker." I swiped away my tears with the sleeve of my blouse and jutted out my chin. I tamped down the remaining embers of the fire and turned off the living room light then patted my leg for Porkchop to follow me. "But you know what Memaw always said— you should never count a Parker out. When we are down, we will rise up stronger than before." Hank Johnson did not know what a force he was dealing with.

* * *

Porkchop and I arrived at The Ewe promptly at eight thirty. Most of the Loopy Ladies were already there. Gladys's news must have really sparked their curiosity. She sat at the head of the table. Helen Garber, Marybeth Higgins, Susan Mayfield, Roberta Holden, Jane Burrows, and Patsy Ikeda sat in wooden chairs circling the table. Marybeth clutched a take-out paper coffee cup in her hands from the local convenience store.

Lucy popped her head out of the dye room. "I'm going to put a pot of coffee on. Anyone want some?"

Marybeth held up her paper cup. "I could use a refill."

Hands raised around the table sent a signal to Lucy to plug the pot in.

I settled Porkchop on the cushioned bed Lucy kept for him tucked into a corner of the room then pulled a rawhide bone out of my purse and laid it next to him. It should keep him busy while we listened to Gladys's news. Before I could turn around to go back to my seat, he was chewing on the bone. "So, Gladys…" I pulled out my chair. "What did you learn?"

Gladys looked around the table, taking us all in. She was basking in the attention her anticipated news was bringing her. "I want to wait until Candie gets here."

As if on cue, the bell over the shop's door jingled and Candie rushed in. Tendrils of hair escaped the loose bun at the nape of her neck. "Morning, everyone. I can't tell y'all how thrilled I am you're helping me with this nasty murder business. I half expect the police to put me in jail any minute! My nerves jump higher than a cricket on a hot plate every time I see a police car cruise past my house. I swear that Joe Peters is circling my block."

I pushed out the chair next to me, and Candie sat down, arranging herself so that she could look around the table at the women gathered there. Her eyes were glistening.

Helen Garber slipped her neon orange glasses up her nose. She tugged down the front of her lemon-yellow polyester shirt. Deep-red cabbage roses danced across the front. "Candie, we have enough ears and eyes at this table to be able to pick up on all the gossip floating around Wings Falls. Someone will have loose lips. We only have to be in the right spot to listen to them."

Roberta Holden tapped her fingers on the table. "You all know how Clyde hears a ton of dirt about the goings on in Wings Falls when he's cutting hair. I swear men are worse than women when it comes to gossip." Roberta's husband owned the town's most popular barber shop.

Candie looked hopefully at Roberta.

Roberta demurred. "I mean, he hasn't shared anything with me yet. Nothing about Tommy Ray, at any rate, but if he hears anything, anything at all…" Her voice drifted off.

Heads nodded around the table in agreement with her. Lucy came out of the dye room with a pastry box, small paper plates, and napkins. "Coffee will be out in a minute. I sent Ralph over to Sweetie Pie's early this morning with instructions to get a couple dozen of Franny's fabulous powdered doughnuts for us." She set the open pastry box on the table and handed half the plates and napkins to Jane and half to Roberta to start sharing them around the table.

Roberta's eyes almost bugged out of her head as she reached for a handful of powdery goodness with just a hint of raspberry jelly peeking out from the end. Powdered doughnuts were her favorite. I couldn't say I blamed her. I needed to catch myself from licking my lips. I limited myself to three a week, or I'd never fit into my clothes.

As the plates, napkins, and doughnuts made their way around the circle, Gladys rapped her coffee mug on the oak table. "Ladies, it's time to discuss the reason I called this meeting."

All heads turned to her.

"I stopped into the Wings Falls Senior Center yesterday, and who was there sitting with a bunch of other ladies, crocheting on an afghan, but Stella Splotz. I swear I don't know what those ladies do with all those afghans they crochet. I mean, how many can a body use? At least I have my pookie bear to keep me warm on chilly nights."

I felt like shaking Gladys. I wanted her to get to what Mrs. Splotz said that Gladys thought was so important. But I knew there was no hurrying her. She'd tell a story in her own time.

Helen wasn't so patient. "Gladys, for heaven's sake, get to the point. What was so earth-shattering you dragged us all out of bed so early in the morning?"

Gladys turned to Helen and gave her the stink-eye. Helen just cocked her head and arched one eyebrow. She did have an edge to her, which often bordered on being rude, but this morning I agreed with her. Gladys needed to get to the point. Proving Candie innocent was more important than a bunch of old ladies crocheting afghans at the Senior Center.

Gladys puffed up her scrawny chest. "Well," she harrumphed out. "When I got to the Senior Center, I thought I'd ask Stella about what she saw Sunday morning. It seems she witnessed quite a bit. And didn't report it all to the police."

Lucy got up from her chair. "Hold that thought for a minute. I'll be right back with the coffee."

It was all I could do to keep from screaming out loud. Would we ever hear what Gladys had to say? My patience was about to snap, but Lucy was back with the pot of coffee within a few minutes, and after she filled everyone's coffee cup, we settled down to hear Gladys's story. I scooted forward to the edge of my chair. "What exactly did she see, and why didn't she tell Hank or Joe Peters?"

Gladys's purple curls bounced as she shook her head. "Can you believe it? She said she didn't want to be a gossip. That old biddy not wanting to tell all of Wings Falls what she saw? *Humph.* I mean, she lives and breathes on gossip!"

"Gladys, what did she say?" Candie said through gritted teeth. My cousin was losing her patience, and I couldn't say I blamed her. Her future might hinge on what Mrs. Splotz told Gladys.

"Sweetie Pie's donates any day-old pastries and goodies they have left over from the night before to the Senior Center," Gladys continued, and heads nodded around the table. "Well, while Stella was loading a take-home bag with doughnuts and bagels. I asked her about the happenings at Candie's house on Sunday. You know, about Tommy Ray's murder and if she saw anything. She looked around the room and then whispered to me that before the police came, Candie's house was busier than Grand Central Station."

Jane Burrows looked up from sipping her coffee. "What did she mean?"

I nodded. That exact question was on the tip of my tongue.

"She said she was in her backyard playing with her dog when she saw Bret Hargrove walk out onto the balcony with Tommy Ray. They were arguing about something, but Tommy Ray was playing that hillbilly music he likes so loud she couldn't quite make out what they said. But she did see Bret give Tommy Ray a shove. It landed him up against the railing of the balcony."

Candie gasped. Her hand flew to her mouth. "That railing is rotten. It was on his list of things to repair. Tommy Ray could have crashed right through it."

Helen's glasses flew off her nose as she shook her head. They landed on her generous bosom. Lucky for the pearl chain connected to the earpieces, or they would have flown across the room. "Either way, he wound up dead at Candie's."

"Helen!" our quiet Marybeth scolded.

Helen shrugged her shoulders. The giant red roses on her blouse bounced up and down. "I'm only stating the obvious."

Gladys continued, "Next thing she saw was Bret and Tommy Ray going back into the house. A few minutes later, Bret pulled out in a hurry in that fancy sports car of his. Then, not long afterward, she saw a woman join Tommy Ray out on the balcony. She seemed to be having a heated conversation with him, too. She said the woman wore a tight-fitting fancy dress and heels high enough to make your nose bleed. She thinks she heard Tommy Ray and her talking about Mark, but she's not quite sure. It could have been the music he was playing. Then she said it was about an hour later, Candie and a fellow pulled up and walked into the house. She thought it kind of strange Candie would be keeping company with another fellow since she's getting married soon. But she said from what she'd heard about Candie, she does have quite a reputation with the men. Not long after they left, a lady she's seen at Mark's campaign rallies showed up on the balcony."

Candie's mouth dropped open. "What is that old biddy talking about? I was at Mass, and afterward Sam and I ate breakfast—or tried to—at Sweetie Pie's. She's mistaken. It couldn't have been me."

Gladys glanced around the table. "I'm only repeating what Stella said. I asked her why she didn't tell this all to the police, but Stella said she didn't want to get too involved because she has some unpaid parking tickets. She also mentioned that the fellow with you talked strange."

Candie turned to me. "Y'all talk strange to me."

"Well, ladies, I think we have our work cut out for us," Helen said.

Patsy Ikeda wiped doughnut crumbs off her fingers with her napkin. "We'll keep our ears and eyes open. I know what it's like being falsely accused of murdering someone." She looked pointedly at me. Geez, it wasn't my fault that she was a suspect in the murder of a local animal shelter owner last year. She wasn't going to forgive me for placing her on my suspect list.

"Wings Falls isn't that big of a town. We'll keep an eye out for this woman Mrs. Splotz says is your look alike," Susan Mayfield said.

Jane Burrows nodded in agreement. "Absolutely. Plenty of people use the library. I'll tell my staff to be on the alert for her. You never know. She might stop in."

My heart warmed at all the support the Loopy Ladies were giving Candie.

Candie glanced at me. "When you see Hank today, fill him in on everything Gladys said. Her information proves I wasn't the only one traipsing around my house. It sounds like Tommy Ray was practically having a party when I was gone."

I shook my head. "I think it would be better if you told him. I don't know if we're a couple anymore."

CHAPTER THIRTEEN

"Sorry ladies, I need to talk to Sam in private." Candie grabbed my hand and dragged me into the dye room.

The Loopy Ladies nodded, wide-eyed, but nobody questioned our sudden departure as Candie weaved us past the chairs surrounding the table in the hooking room.

Once in the dye room, she pointed to a stool next to the large table where Lucy drew out her rug hooking patterns. "Sit," she said. She stood in front of me with her arms crossed over her generous bosom, smothering the rhinestones that pranced along the front of her blouse. I felt like a child about to be reprimanded by her mother.

"Okay, now what is this nonsense about you and Hank not being a couple anymore? Did an earthquake erupt in Wings Falls and I didn't hear about it?"

With a forlorn look on my face, I shook my head. "I only wish it were that simple. No, last night when Hank stopped over, I told him the Loopy Ladies were going to try to help us find Tommy Ray's killer."

Candie leaned her hip against the counter running the length of the room. "So, what's the big deal? You'd think he'd want all the help he can get. Especially when bumbling Joe Peters is on the case with him. After all, if I'm going to marry Mark like he insists, we have to find Tommy Ray's killer sooner than later."

I couldn't agree with her more. "Hank let me know he didn't like me poking around in his investigation, we argued, and he left. Went home I imagine, but I haven't heard from him since."

Candie stomped her foot on the scarred wooden floor. "We know he wasn't thrilled when we got involved in his last two murder investigations, but can't he see this is different? I mean, it's my life we're talking about."

I looked at my cousin in dismay. "Right now, I don't know what he sees, but I do know I'm not going to stop helping prove you're innocent. If we can work things out, fine. If not, Porkchop and I will survive." *With a big broken heart, but we will survive. Parkers don't give up that easy.*

Candie reached over and hugged me. "I love you," she whispered in my ear.

"I love you, too," I answered back.

I scooted off the stool and threw back my shoulders. "Okay, let's get this murder solved. After I leave here, even if we're not a couple anymore, I'll stop by the station and tell Hank what Gladys heard from Mrs. Splotz."

Candie gave my shoulder a hardy squeeze.

We walked back into the hooking room to be greeted by quizzical faces.

"So, what's our plan of attack?" Gladys asked.

Candie and I both looked at each other. She elbowed me in the ribs. "I'm going to stop by the Wings Falls Police Station in a few minutes and try to see Hank. I'll let him know everything you told us, Gladys. But that doesn't mean we can't do some sleuthing on our own."

Gladys's curls bobbled as she nodded. "Great. He may be my grown nephew, but his old aunt can still teach him a thing or two."

We all laughed. It was good to hear some laughter after the horrifying events of the past few days.

* * *

"Hi, Wanda." I stood in the lobby of the Wings Falls Police Station speaking into the small hole in the bulletproof glass that separated the general public from the rest of the building. Wanda Thurston was the PCO—the Public Communications Officer—on duty and monitoring the front desk. A headphone nestled into the black wavy hair crowning her head. She flashed me a smile that stood out against her dark skin.

"Hi, Sam. Here to see Hank?" It was commonly known around the station that Hank and I were a couple. At least, I hoped he hadn't told anyone that wasn't the situation anymore.

I shoved the turquoise and white–patterned Vera Bradley purse that had slid off my shoulder back into place. "Yes. If you could buzz him, I would appreciate it."

I took a seat on one of the metal chairs that lined the wall of the lobby. Comfortable they were not. A portrait of our governor hung on the wall opposite me. His piercing blue eyes stared down at me, causing me to squirm in my seat.

A buzzer sounded, unlocking the metal door guarding the inner workings of the police station. I glanced up, and my breath caught in my throat. Hank stood framed in the doorway, all six-foot lusciousness of him. My mouth went dry. A smile spread across my face at his tie choice of the day—Popeye, flexing his bicep.

Hank followed the direction of my eyes, and a smile curved his lips. Could he possibly be glad to see me? My heart sped up, hoping he was. "Yeah, I was in a Popeye mood this morning. What brought you here?"

I got up from my chair and joined him at the door. "Gladys told us at Loopy Ladies this morning about some interesting information that Stella Splotz relayed to her at the Senior Center."

By the way Hank's jaw tightened, I could tell he was not happy with what I was about to tell him or, more precisely, that I was the one about to impart the info. So much for his happy mood at seeing me.

We passed through the patrol room on the way back to Hank's office. Like the previous times I'd been in the inner sanctum of the station, it was a hub of activity. Officers sat at standard-issue metal desks typing on computers or talking into phones.

"Do you think your cousin will be joining these mug shots on the wall?"

I groaned. Why couldn't Joe Peters be on a doughnut break or something? I turned and plastered a smile on my face. "Joe, if you're a competent police officer, you'll find the real killer."

Chuckles floated around the room. I swear I heard an "Oh, snap!" and a few "You go, girl!" too.

Joe's face reddened. He busied himself flipping through the wanted posters hanging on the wall.

Hank opened the door to his office and motioned for me to go in before him. "You really shouldn't rile Joe so much. He has his faults, but he is a good cop."

I sat in a metal chair like the ones lining the walls in the lobby. Wings Falls certainly didn't spring on luxurious furnishings for its police station. I hung my purse on the back of my chair and waited for Hank to settle himself behind his desk. I guess this was going to be strictly an "official" visit.

"I like your tie," I said, trying to lessen the tension hanging over the room.

Hank looked down at Popeye. "Popeye. Yeah, a great guy to have on your side when you're in a crunch."

I smiled. "Like you?"

My heart tripped into warp speed when he returned my smile. "I try my best, but I can't say I'm a spinach fan. So, what is it you want to tell me? What did my aunt hear at the Senior Center? Do I need to send a car to bring her in? I'm assuming it has to do with Tommy Ray's murder."

Heat rushed up my neck. I stiffened my spine. There was nothing, and I mean nothing, to be embarrassed or upset about. I jutted out my chin. "Gladys got to talking to Mrs. Splotz at the Senior Center. Mrs. Splotz saw a whole lot more than she told your officer."

Hank sat upright in his chair. "Why didn't she tell me?"

I shrugged. "How should I know? She's your aunt and walks to the beat of a different drummer. I mean, she has the ashes of her dead husband sitting at the helm of his fishing boat in her backyard."

A smile curved Hank's lip. His fingers poised over the computer resting on his desk. "Yeah, she does. So, what is this info you have?"

Hank typed as I proceeded to tell him about the parade of visitors Tommy Ray had on Sunday morning. He certainly typed faster than the hunt-and-peck method I used. You'd think as a freelance writer and the author of a soon-to-be-published children's book, I'd be more accomplished in my typing skills.

* * *

After about twenty minutes of my relaying to him all I'd heard of Tommy Ray's guests and Hank questioning me on these facts, he straightened up from his computer and stretched. "Would you like a cup of coffee?"

As much as I would have liked a cup after the intense questioning Hank gave me, I shook my head. I'd had the misfortune of tasting the brew the station served up. Let's say it fell way short of Sweetie Pie's java. I think even a prisoner would rather do time than drink it. "No thanks, I'll pass."

Hank smiled. There was that brown curl falling on his forehead. My fingers itched to smooth it back, but somehow after last night, I felt it better to sit on my hands than to give in to my urges. I glanced at my watch. "I guess I'd better get over to the Do Drop."

Hank's smile quickly faded. "Why do you have to go there again?"

"George says his secretary will be out for a while because of her mom's broken hip."

Hank's mouth curved into a frown. "Right. The secretary's mother broke her hip. Can't he call a temp agency? Why do you have to go?"

My heart did a happy dance. Had Hank's little green monster raised its head?

CHAPTER FOURTEEN

———

I sat in the parking lot of the Do Drop and rested my head on the steering wheel of my Bug. "Okay, I can do this. It's only for a few more days." I'd always left the running of the business up to George, but I was going to tell him to get a temp until the new secretary returned. I had more important things to do—like help prove Candie innocent of Tommy Ray's murder.

I grabbed my purse from the passenger seat then flung open the car door. I stepped out of my car and straightened the black-and-gray-plaid blouse I'd paired with my black slacks this morning. I reached back into the Bug for a sweater. The weatherman had predicted a drop in temperature for this evening. A gust of wind blew across the parking lot, scattering petals from the flowering trees that lined it. I threw back my shoulders and headed towards the front door of the funeral parlor. I pulled open the door and was blasted by hot air—the George Davies kind, not a furnace.

"Sam, it's about time you showed up. The phone has been ringing off the hook."

I turned to see a frazzled George coming down the gray-carpeted hallway leading off the former dining room of the Do Drop.

I mentally shook myself. Yes, I was very foolish and young when I married George. I should have looked past his good looks and slick manner. He was still a handsome man, although I did detect a few crow's-feet by his eyes. His six-pack was sagging a bit, too. Becoming more of a twelve-pack.

"I've had a busy morning, George. What was so important it couldn't wait? It's not as if our clients are going anywhere." A smile spread across my face at my own joke.

George frowned. He clearly didn't approve of my sense of humor. "Mr. Guthrie passed away last night, and his family is coming in—" George glanced at his watch "—less than an hour to plan his funeral. I need to know what caskets are available for them to choose from. The casket manufacturer we usually order from is on strike, and our supply is getting low. Check out the samples we have downstairs and give the company a call to see what they have in stock."

Should I salute George before I followed his orders? I stuck my tongue out at his back as I followed him down the hall.

I walked into the secretary's office and sat in the desk chair. George followed behind me. I opened the bottom drawer of the desk and stowed my purse. "All right, all right, George. I'll see what other suppliers we can use if we need to. Hopefully the strike hasn't affected them, too." I swore George turned green at my statement.

He wrung his hands. "I hadn't thought of that. What if this is a nationwide casket maker strike? What will I do?"

"You could always hammer together some pine boxes."

George looked up at me. Horror streaked across his face. He was not known for his handyman skills. Replacing a light bulb was a major accomplishment for him. "Very funny, Sam. I've got to get ready for the Guthrie family. Check and see what we can order." He turned and walked out of the office, mumbling to himself.

I saluted his retreating back. "Yes, sir."

* * *

I arched my back and glanced at the clock hanging on the wall. Geez, was it almost five? Thank heavens I'd called Gladys earlier and asked her if she could go next door and feed Porkchop. She'd let him out in the backyard to do his business and for some exercise, too. She was more than happy to take care of him. She often told me she thought of him as her grandpuppy.

I got up and went over to the wing chair in the corner of the room and reached down for my sweater. My eyes were tired and bleary from staring at order forms and receipts all day. Luckily, I was able to order the casket the Guthries wanted for their dearly departed, an oak casket with leaping trout carved into the sides. Mr. Guthrie had been an avid fisherman, and the family thought he'd feel right at home surrounded by his favorite fish for his final resting place.

"Here, let me help you."

I jerked around towards the office door. I hadn't heard George enter the room. He took my sweater from my hands and held it up for me. I slipped my arms into the sleeves and started to move away from him, but his hands gripped my shoulders.

He leaned in and whispered into my ear, "Our marriage was great, wasn't it, Sam?"

I blinked and pulled out of his grasp. I hadn't let him lay a hand on me since the day he proudly announced he was going to be the father of twin boys. What was he talking about? "What are you saying? You ended our 'perfect' marriage six years ago when you decided to do a late-night horizontal tango with Anna."

George had the decency to blush. "A guy can make a mistake, can't he? Are you going to hold it against me forever?"

Heat crawled up my neck, and not from the warmth of my sweater. My temper skyrocketed at his nerve. "Mistake! You tell that to your two sons. Are those boys a mistake?"

I grabbed my purse from the desk drawer and stomped towards the office door. Once there, I turned and said, "I'm done here, George. Call a temp agency."

His mouth fell open. "What am I going to do about the Guthrie funeral and all those casket makers that are on strike?"

A smirk spread across my face. "George, call a temp agency—and as Rhett told Scarlett, 'Frankly, my dear. I don't give a damn.'" I hitched my purse farther up my arm, gave him a two-finger salute goodbye, and then marched out of the Do Drop.

* * *

"I'm telling you, Porkchop, the man really scorches my grits. The nerve of him to make a pass at me. We are so lucky to be rid of him."

My dog wagged his tail as I filled his bone-shaped doggie bowl with kibble. He looked up at me. A deep growl rumbled up from his throat. I took it to mean he completely agreed with me. He and George never did get along. If George got near me, a fierce growl would crawl up Porkchop's throat. My dog was a lot smarter than me. He wised up to the cheater sooner than I did.

I looked at the clock. It wasn't even six, still plenty of time left for Candie and me to do some brainstorming as to who killed Tommy Ray. I reached for my phone and hit her speed dial number.

Candie answered on the first ring. "Hi, cuz. Talk to me. I'm lonely. Mark has a campaign event at the Community Center tonight.

He wanted me to come with him, but I really think the focus needs to stay on him. I'd be a distraction."

"How about if you come over here and keep Porkchop and me company? We need to fix your situation ASAP."

"I'll be there in ten minutes." Candie hung up.

I let Porkchop out the backdoor to do his business so he wouldn't interrupt us when she got here. Business attended to, Porkchop snuggled on the sofa next to me.

The sound of Candie's Precious, her baby blue Mustang, pulling into my driveway caused him to run for the door. I pushed myself off the sofa and went to let her in.

When I opened the door, Candie reached over and hugged me then bent and scratched Porkchop behind his ears. His rear end waggled in contentment. "Evening, cuz." Even with all the stress she was under, Candie still looked fabulous. Rings adorned her fingers. She wore a gauzy rhinestone-studded blouse paired with a swirly skirt. I glanced down at her feet and smiled. "You feel in a butt-kicking mood, don't you?"

Candie lifted her skirt so I could get the full effect of her footwear, cowboy boots with rhinestones that ran up the sides. "You bet. I'm going to stomp all over someone's alibi tonight."

I laughed. "Okay, let's get down to business." I led the way into my dining room. I shoved aside my purse and the day's junk mail littering the tabletop to make room for Candie and me to begin figuring out who killed Tommy Ray.

I reached behind me to the buffet that sat against the wall, a lovely cherry piece that once belonged to my grandmother. When my mother lived here, she kept her silver and linens stored in it. She took those treasures with her when she and Dad retired to sunny Florida. It sat mostly empty now, except for a few placemats and candy dishes I brought with me after my divorce. I opened a drawer and pulled out a pad of paper and pen.

I poised the pen over the paper. "Okay let's write down what Stella Splotz told Gladys at the Senior Center. I think that's the best place to start."

Candie nodded. She tapped the side of her head with a ruby-red manicured fingernail. "Hmm. Like she said, my place resembled Grand Central Station Sunday morning. First, there was Bret Hargrove. Then witchy Babs sauntered over. A couple Stella thought was me and a mystery man stopped by. Stella also mentioned a girl she saw at the campaign rallies was there."

"Yes. I was thinking about what she said, and from her description—you know, short-cropped dark hair, plain clothes—I believe that was Valerie. What do you think she'd want from Tommy Ray?"

Candie shrugged. The rhinestones on her blouse twinkled in the light of the chandelier hanging over the old maple table. "Who knows? What would any of them want from Tommy Ray? I mean, he didn't have any money. At least none I know of. It's the reason I offered him the job of sprucing up my house."

I tapped the pad of paper with my pencil and smiled. "You always were good to all of your exes. Okay, let's go over this list. The person to visit Tommy Ray—the one I think is the most puzzling—was the man and woman she swears was you."

Candie's back stiffened. "We know she's wrong. I was nowhere near my home when Tommy Ray was murdered."

I placed my hand on her arm. "I know, Candie. And we'll prove it."

My phone rang. I glanced at the caller ID and frowned. "Who is it?"

"Susan Mayfield. Why would she be calling me? Momma Mia's is open, and she should be slammed with customers about now."

CHAPTER FIFTEEN

———

I flipped my phone open and put it to my ear. "Hi, Susan. What's up? Is something wrong at the restaurant? I thought you'd be hopping right about now. What? Let me put you on speaker. Candie is here. This way I won't have to repeat everything you say."

I hit the button so Candie could hear Susan's side of the conversation.

Candie leaned towards me. "Hey, y'all. How's things at Momma Mia's tonight?" In spite of Candie living up north for over fifteen years, she still hung on to her Southern accent.

"Hi, Candie. Things are busy tonight. But the reason I called is I have some scoop on Bret Hargrove. I thought it was interesting. Roberta Holden and I ducked into my office so we could escape all the noise and confusion on the restaurant floor. Her husband, Clyde, heard a juicy piece of gossip today at his barber shop, too." Roberta once told us at Loopy Ladies our ears would sizzle right off if we knew what those men said while sitting in his barber chair.

"Go ahead, Susan. Candie and I are sitting on the edge of our seats waiting for your news."

"Okay. As I said, Bret Hargrove was in for dinner tonight with his wife. He said they were celebrating a wedding anniversary."

Candie frowned. "I hope he bought her something really nice for putting up with such a jerk."

Susan's laughter rang over the phone. "I have to agree. But if he did, I hope he used a different credit card than the one he tried to pass off on my waitress when it came time for him to pay their dinner bill."

I turned to Candie and raised my eyebrows. "What are you talking about, Susan?"

"His card was rejected. He tried to shrug it off, but when he handed his waitress another card, that got denied, too. He said it must be a mistake and he'd get in touch with the credit card companies in the morning. I only hope he doesn't stiff us. He ordered the most expensive wine we carry to go with their meal."

I nodded in agreement. "Geez, what a jerk."

Candie grabbed my phone. "Susan, you said Roberta has some info, too?" I gave Candie an evil side-eye and reached for my phone back, but she clutched it in a death grip.

"Hi, Candie. You and Mark should have been here tonight, but you would have needed a reservation, the place is so busy. Brian outdid himself with his lasagna. The tiramisu was to die for. I mean it was worth every calorie it shot to my hips."

I stared at the phone. "Roberta, was this the biggie info you wanted us to hear?" I rubbed Porkchop's back to calm my irritation with Roberta.

Laughter came through the phone. "Oh my, no. Clyde said the gossip at his barber shop this morning was how Bret Hargrove's campaign is bankrupting him. He hasn't been paying his suppliers at his store, The Sound Machine. To top it all off, one of his employees tried to cash his paycheck, and it bounced higher than a rubber ball. What do you think about that?"

"I'd say it is very interesting." I heard a knock on a door and then a voice speaking to Susan.

"I have to go, ladies. A mini crisis needs attention in the restaurant. I thought you'd want this news as soon as possible," Susan said.

I nodded, not that Susan and Roberta could see me. "Thanks so much Susan and Roberta. Candie and I appreciate you keeping your ears open."

Candie leaned over to speak into the phone. "Y'all are a peach. Thank you so much. I sure hope I'll be having my wedding reception at Momma Mia's and not in the county jail."

"Now, chin up, Candie. You'll be the prettiest bride we've ever catered a reception for," Susan said.

Candie blushed. "From your lips to God's ears."

"He won't let you down, and neither will the Loopy Ladies. I've got to go, but I'll let you know if I hear anything else. Bye."

"I will, too," Roberta chimed in.

"Bye," Candie and I said in unison.

"And thanks again." Candie handed my phone back to me, and I flipped it shut.

We sat in silence in my dining room for a few minutes. Porkchop stood on his hind legs, begging me for a few scratchies.

I turned to Candie. "So, what do you make of their info?"

Candie shook her head. "I'd say Bret Hargrove is hiding a whole bunch of secrets we should dig our noses into."

I absentmindedly continued to scratch Porkie between his ears. "I agree, but how do you propose we go about digging up these secrets?"

"A trip to The Sound Machine, tomorrow."

I shook a finger at Candie. "Are you crazy? What reason would we have for going there? Right now, Bret is your arch enemy. He's the guy spreading all those lies about Mark. The one who wants to take him out as mayor."

Candie waved a hand in front of her face to dismiss all my objections. "I know. I know. But I've never dealt with him directly. And he's the one who has the most to gain with Mark tainted by my so-called relationship with Tommy Ray. What if he came to my place to see if Tommy Ray possessed any more pictures of me in a—how should I say it—a compromising position? Maybe he was willing to pay Tommy Ray for those pictures."

I bounced on my seat, excited by what Candie was saying. "Yes, yes, and what if Tommy Ray said they were too personal, and he wouldn't give them up for any amount of money. But from what Roberta said, Bret didn't have any money to spare. What if Bret got so mad, he came back after Mrs. Splotz saw him leave the first time. Bret lost his temper in a rage and killed Tommy Ray?" I squinched up my forehead. "Would becoming mayor be so important to Bret? What would he gain from it? I mean Wings Falls isn't a big town, and he certainly wouldn't get rich on the mayor's salary."

Candie shook her head. Silver hoop earrings slapped against her neck. "I agree if you are an honest mayor. But this is a growing area, and downstate investors are looking to bring their money north."

A light clicked on in my brain. "You're right. I've heard of people wanting to develop some prime areas in Wings Falls. A dishonest mayor could make a lot of money by granting permits to shady people. Money is a big reason to kill someone."

Candie nodded. "Yes, much to the detriment of the Wings Falls community."

"Okay, so tomorrow morning you pick me up and we make a trip to Bret's store," I said.

* * *

"Are you ready to face Bret?" I sat in the passenger seat of Candie's Precious. We'd parked two blocks away from Main Street where The Sound Machine was located. Everyone in town knew her baby blue Mustang, and we didn't want it to be spotted outside of his business. Butterflies danced a tango in my stomach. "Are we going to wing it, or is there more to your plan than wearing these silk scarves and sunglasses to disguise who we are?"

Candie reached for the car's door handle. "We'll make some excuse about the DJ for my wedding canceling at the last minute."

I tucked my curly hair under my scarf. "And we're wearing this disguise because?"

She heaved a sigh. "I don't want word getting back to Mark that we went into his rival's store." Candie stepped out of the car.

I slid out my side of the car and joined her on the sidewalk. A gust of wind whipped around me. I pulled the scarf tighter around my head. "Candie, as soon as you open your mouth, he'll know who you are. You can't hide your Southern accent."

"That's why you're going to do all the talking." She slid on her oversized sunglasses.

We stood in front of the window of a butcher shop. I spied diagrammed posters of pig and beef cuts hanging on the far wall of the shop. My reflection in the window stared back at me. I slipped on the sunglasses and shook my head. "Do you really think this will fool anyone? Who do you think we are, anyway? Cagney and Lacey?" I asked, referring to an 80s TV show that featured two female policewomen.

"Oh, I love that. Do you want to be Cagney or Lacey?" Candie turned and sashayed down the sidewalk. Confidence oozed from every pore in her body.

I wished my shaking legs would absorb some of her bravado. I felt as confident as the hunk of meat hanging from a hook behind the butcher's counter.

CHAPTER SIXTEEN

"Hey, Candie, wait up." I shoved my Michael Kors purse up my arm and scurried down the sidewalk to catch her.

When I reached her, she jutted out her chin and said, "Call me Lacey."

"Oh brother, I've created a monster," I mumbled to myself.

Rain began to fall from the gray skies overhead. The local weather lady had predicted a light rain for today. I hoped she was right, because more often than not, she was wrong. This could be the beginning of a downpour, and I hadn't brought my umbrella with me. I didn't relish a soaking and looking like a drowned rat.

Three minutes later, we entered The Sound Machine. A buzzer sounded as we opened the door. I resisted the urge to cover my ears as hip hop music blared from a speaker attached to the wall behind a glass display counter. The store was divided into different sections for a person's home entertainment needs. One wall featured speakers of every size imaginable. Televisions for both inside and outside use hung from another. There was even a section for marine audio systems. That made sense, since Wings Falls was located only minutes from Lake George, a major lake in upstate New York. I pulled my scarf a little tighter around my head. I'd never been in Bret Hargrove's store before and wasn't acquainted with his sales staff. Wings Falls was a small town, and I didn't want to risk anyone recognizing me who might wander into the store while Candie and I tried to dig up dirt on Bret. I cringed at the thought of Hank's reaction if word about our sleuthing traveled back to him.

"Hey, man, can I help you?" A young fellow with tousled blond curls and bloodshot eyes sauntered out of a back room. A snowboard tattoo curved around the side of his neck. The crotch of his loose-fitting jeans hung down low while his knobby knees poked through fashionably placed rips in the legs. My fingers itched to lean over the counter and pull his pants up. A hint of cigarette smoke clung to him. I wondered if he was catching a few puffs before we walked in.

Candie approached the counter. She grabbed hold of the young man's hand, batted her eyes, and in her sultry Southern accent said, "Sweetie, I'm in desperate need of help."

I blinked. Wasn't I supposed to do the talking? She certainly wasn't hiding her Southern accent.

Beads of sweat popped out on the young man's forehead—Bruce, by the name tag pinned to his "Make Love Not War" T-shirt. His protruding Adam's apple bobbed up and down. Even in disguise, Candie made an impression on men, young and old.

"How can I help you, ma'am?" Bruce fiddled with the neck of his T-shirt.

Candie leaned in closer to him. I feared if Bruce breathed any harder, he'd faint. "You can call me Lacey, and this is my maid of honor, Myrtle." She flicked her free hand towards me.

Myrtle? I mouthed to Candie.

She smiled and shrugged.

"You see, Bruce, I'm in a real bind. I'm getting married in a couple of weeks. And my rascal of a DJ has up and quit on me. Left me in a lurch, and I don't know what to do. My dear friend here—" she nodded towards me "—said The Sound Machine could supply me with a DJ who would make my wedding the event of the year."

Bruce cleared his throat. "Yes, ma'am. We can supply you with anything you want. Here's a brochure on what we offer." He grabbed a brochure from a shelf behind the counter. He unfolded it and pointed to the various packages The Sound Machine offered. "We can even bring a karaoke machine. It's a big hit at parties and weddings nowadays."

Candie clapped her hands together. "Oh, Myrtle, wouldn't karaoke be so much fun?"

I rolled my eyes at her, not that she could see them behind my sunglasses. "Oh, yeah, it would be so much fun." Not in a million years could I see Hank on stage singing along to one of my favorite Elvis songs. "All Shook Up" wasn't going to happen, at least not from my staid detective.

While Candie scanned the brochure, I noticed a stack of flyers promoting Bret Hargrove for mayor sitting on the counter. I snatched one from the pile and waved it at Bruce. "Do you know this candidate for mayor?"

He tore his eyes away from Candie and turned to me. He brushed a lock of curls out of his eyes. "Yeah, the guy owns this place. Kind of."

I raised an eyebrow. "What do you mean 'kind of'?'"

Bruce looked around the room as if he expected someone to overhear what he was about to say. "Well, he's let a lot of the staff here go because he can't afford to make payroll."

Candie waved the DJ brochure at Bruce. "You mean he can't pay his help?" She jabbed a finger at the brochure. "How do I know this DJ will show up for my wedding?"

I nudged Candie. So, Roberta's and Susan's info about Bret's checks bouncing and his bad credit must be correct.

Bruce nodded at the brochure. "Hey, man, I know this guy. He'll do you right. He won't stiff you like Old Man Hargrove."

I stifled a laugh and wondered what Bret would think of his employee calling him Old Man. "So has this Mr. Hargrove 'stiffed' his employees?"

Bruce crumpled one of the Bret's campaign flyers in his fist. "Yeah, my good buddy, Phil. His paycheck bounced higher than a basketball, and he had a car payment due, too. I heard the boss on the phone the other day yelling at someone that they would get their money soon. To give him a little more time. That his election for mayor was in the bag."

Candie's lips formed an *O*. "'In the bag?' What do you think he meant?"

Bruce shrugged. "Heck if I know. He is always on the phone trying to make a deal. Some shady characters have started to hang around here lately. I'm getting out real soon, too."

"You have another job?" I asked.

"Yeah, a buddy of mine hooked me up with a job at Snow Magic, the ski resort. It's open in the summer, too. You know, for mountain biking and kids' summer camps. I love to snowboard and will be able to get in all the rides I want for free in the winter. You ladies mountain bike? I could see about snagging you some free passes."

Candie went into a coughing fit. I pounded her on the back. I knew the very thought of being anywhere in a ski lodge except as a lodge bunny, with her hands wrapped around a mug of hot chocolate, was out of Candie's realm of thinking.

I shook my head. "Thanks for the offer, Bruce, but I think Lacey and I will pass."

Candie grabbed my arm. "Thanks for all the info, Bruce. I'll get back to you. Come on, Myrtle, we better be going."

"Anytime, ladies." Bruce waved as we exited The Sound Machine.

The rain fell heavier now. Large puddles settled on the sidewalk. "Bruce confirmed what Roberta and Susan said last night about Bret's financial situation." A shiver shot through me as I slid my purse up my shoulder. "I think our trusty weatherperson was wrong again. We're in for more of a monsoon than a light rain. Come on. Let's hurry back to your car."

Candie flung the end of her scarf around her neck. "Yes, gossip central at Clyde's barber shop has the facts about Bret correct. Maybe Hank should get his hair cut there. From the information he picks up from those gossipy old men, he could probably solve Tommy Ray's murder."

I didn't think Hank would add Clyde's barber shop to his list of reliable information sources. "Who do you think Bruce meant when he said some 'shady' men were hanging out at The Sound Machine?"

Candie laughed. "Who knows. To a kid his age, shady could mean a guy with slicked-back hair, smoking a cigar." She stopped under a store's awning.

I turned to see what brought her to a standstill. "What? What's the matter?"

"Let's get to the library. I want to research something."

"What's wrong with your phone and Google?" I asked. And using it at my warm dry house while sipping on mugs of tea.

"No, I think this would be easier to find at the library where Jane can help us. I need her to look up the minutes of a town council meeting from this past spring. April, I think." Candie started off again, but this time in the direction of the library, which was at the end of Glen Street, a block over from Bret's store.

I jogged to catch up with her, trying not to slip on the rain-slick sidewalk. I didn't want to land on my rear end. I was already in the drowned rat mode.

* * *

"Hi, Jane," I called out when Candie and I entered the library.

Jane Burrows, the head librarian of the Wings Falls' Library and fellow Loopy Lady, stood behind the library's main checkout counter. She pointed a patron in the direction of the book they were looking for then nodded in response to my greeting. When Porkchop and I come back in another life, I want Jane's job. The library was my home away from home. If I wasn't doing research for an upcoming article, you'd probably find me curled up in a chair, reading a cozy mystery in the many reading nooks situated among the stacks. Jane had booked me for a reading and author signing for my new book when it was released.

Candie pulled off her scarf and leaned against the counter. "Jane, where would I find the minutes of the Planning Committee meeting from this past April?"

Jane tugged at the hem of her sweater, her usual attire for the day, summer and winter—sweater sets and khaki slacks. "You can find them on the computer. They're public record. Type in 'Wings Falls town meeting minutes' and the month you want. Do you need help with that?"

Candie nodded. "Honey, it would be ever so appreciated. I'm all thumbs when it comes to the techno stuff."

I covered my mouth with my hand to hide the smile that spread across my face. My cousin was smart as a whip and could navigate any computer with ease, but if she could wrangle someone else to do the work for her, she'd gladly let them.

Jane led the way into the research room, a small room tucked into a corner of the library. Two rows of tables ran down the center of the room. Computers sat on the top of the tables—five on each side of the table.

Jane pulled out a chair and seated herself at one. "Now, what is it you want to know?"

"The minutes of last April's Planning Committee meeting." Candie pulled a chair closer to Jane so she could read what she brought up on the computer's screen.

Jane turned on the computer. Her fingers flew across the keyboard. I sighed. If my fingers could type as fast as Jane's, maybe I could write more articles and be able to buy more designer purses.

I leaned over Jane's shoulder. The minutes flashed onto the screen. I scanned the page then pointed to the screen. "There. What is this Riglio Investment Corporation Bret Hargrove mentioned?"

Candie shook her head. "Never heard of them before. Jane, can you look them up?"

"Sure." Jane's fingers once again flew across the keyboard. The results of her typing appeared on the screen.

My mouth dropped open.

Candie's ruby-red fingernail tapped on the screen. "Well, bless his heart."

CHAPTER SEVENTEEN

I leaned closer to the computer. "Who is Tony Riglio?"

Candie's eyes widened. "According to this news article, he's from New York City and he's involved in a lot of shady business—gambling, racketeering, loan sharking. You name it, he's got his fingers in the pie."

I loosened the scarf draped around my head for my disguise at The Sound Machine. In spite of the air conditioning, the close quarters of the computer room was becoming warm. "Yes, but he hasn't done any time for his 'businesses.'"

Jane glanced up from the computer and shook her head. "He knows how to stay barely on the right side of the law and not get caught."

I pointed to the computer screen. "See, he also has his fingers in the construction pie. The article said some of the buildings he was involved with were cited for building code violations. When the inspectors caught him, he dismissed it as errors in judgment on the part of his job site foreman."

Candie frowned and shook her head. "The weasel, blaming the shoddy work on someone else and not his instructions."

I agreed. "But no one was ever charged with a crime. Do you think he paid someone off to look the other way?"

Jane's fingers flew across the keyboard again. "Nothing comes up about Mr. Riglio or anyone else connected with his company being arrested. I'll bet a few dollars passed someone's hands."

Candie stood and stomped her foot. "And Bret wants to bring him here to Wings Falls because he has 'experience' in doing major redevelopment. My Dixie will cuddle up with your Porkchop before we let him ruin our town. I wonder how much Mr. 'Sneaky' Bret Hargrove would make on the side?"

I laughed at the thought of Dixie and Porkchop cuddling together—not going to happen. "It is something to ponder. I'd bet my first royalty check from my sales of *Porkchop, the Wonder Dog* there's something in it for Bret."

Jane looked up from the computer. "Do you think Mr. Hargrove would be desperate enough to kill Tommy Ray for more information against Mark?"

Candie furrowed her forehead. "Interesting question, Jane." She looked at me. "Sam, if he wasn't at The Sound Machine this morning, I bet he's at his campaign headquarters."

I grabbed my purse from the back of a chair where I placed it when we entered the computer room and slid it up my arm. "Yes, probably giving his minions orders to get the vote out. I'd say our next stop is a visit to his headquarters."

A smile spread across Candie's face. "My thoughts exactly."

"Thank you, Jane, for all of your help. You certainly were able to dig up this info on Bret a lot faster than Candie or I could. We better let you get back to your library duties."

"Anything to help a fellow Loopy Lady," Jane answered.

* * *

I held the library door open for Candie.

As we walked down the library steps, I asked, "Maybe Bret killed Tommy Ray in a fit of anger because he wouldn't give him any more naughty pictures of you and Tommy Ray. What do you think?"

Candie sighed. "He could have. Tommy Ray and I were young and in love. We did some very foolish things back then. I blush even thinking about them now. He promised to burn all those pictures we took. Obviously, he didn't."

I hooked my arm through hers. "Cuz, don't give it another thought. You're a different person now. Older and much wiser. After all, you're marrying a wonderful man in a few days, which I think is a very wise decision on your part."

Candie looked at me with sorrow clouding her violet eyes. "I hope you're right."

Bret's campaign headquarters occupied an empty storefront on a side street in Wings Falls. Although it was only a few blocks from the library, Candie was tired of avoiding rain puddles from the earlier rainstorm, so we walked back to her car and drove the short distance to Bret's headquarters. Frankly, I thought we would have gotten there quicker walking than we did driving *and* trying to find a parking spot. My Southern cousin ignored those little details.

Unlike Mark's campaign headquarters, which was organized and housed in a building in the center of town, Bret's sat in an abandoned laundromat. Candie and I pushed open the door and gazed around the room. Laptops sat on warped laundry folding tables. Papers spilled from the tops of dented and rusting washers and dryers. Campaign posters with Bret's smiling face lay scattered in a corner of the room. Water-stained tiles hung down from the ceiling. The smell of bleach and detergent still clung to the room.

"Lookie who the storm blew in."

I turned to see Bret Hargrove leaning over a young campaign worker. His hand rested on her shoulder. His fingers toyed with the curls cascading down her back. I wondered if his wife knew how chummy he was with his workers. I shook my head. It was her problem, not ours.

Candie sniffed the air and jutted out her chin. "Yes, a breath of fresh air, unlike the stench clinging to this room."

I poked my cousin in the ribs. "Candie, remember what Memaw Parker use to say: 'You can catch more flies with honey than vinegar.'"

"Maybe I should have brought a hunk of cheese for the rat," Candie said in a soft whisper.

I coughed, trying to stifle my laughter.

Bret walked over to us. He flashed his gleaming white toothpaste-ad teeth at us. "Can I get you a drink of water for your nasty cough?"

I slapped my chest. "No, something I ate must have gotten lodged in my throat."

Bret ran a hand through his surfer blond hair. "So, what brings you two to enemy territory? Are you ready to concede the election?" Bret laughed at what I guess he considered a joke.

Candie stiffened at my side. "Why, sweetie, bless your heart for thinking Mark and I would take the easy way out. But I can assure you, we have only begun to fight. I was wondering, though, why you were trespassing on my property on Sunday morning while my cousin and I were doing our Christian duty and praying for wretched souls like yours at church?"

Silence descended over the room. Campaign activity stopped, and all eyes in the room focused on the three of us.

Bret's face turned beet red. His hands hung clenched into fists at his side. I was glad for our audience, since I didn't know what Bret would have done if we were alone with him.

He gritted those pearly white teeth of his together. "What are you talking about? I am not involved with your lover's murder, and I told the police as much. I have nothing to gain from his death. In fact, he did me and all of Wings Falls a favor by flashing the picture of him and you around at The Round Up on Saturday night, Little Miss Riding Hood."

Candie sucked in her breath. "First of all, he was not my lover. He was my ex-fiancé. Secondly, the picture is thirty years old. And last but not least, Tommy Ray told me he saw you coming out of the Shady Rest Motel last week with a woman. A woman who definitely was not your wife. I would say you have a lot to lose if Tommy Ray had spilled the beans on your extra-curricular activities."

A gasp sounded from behind Bret. The campaign worker whose hair, moments before, Bret was fondling, sat with tears rolling down her cheeks. Her lips trembled. "Tell her that's not true, Bret. You said I was the only woman in your life. You were going to leave your wife when you won the election."

Candie gave the devastated worker a faint smile. "Honey, once a rat, always a rat. At least you found out now before it was too late." She pointed to Bret. "He isn't worth shedding another tear over."

The worker swiped at her tears, nodded, and got up from the table. She walked over to a row of hooks attached to the wall next to the door and grabbed her raincoat. She slid it on and left the building without a backward glance.

If Bret could shoot daggers from his eyes, Candie and I would be mortally wounded right now. I leaned over to Candie and whispered, "I think it's a good time for us to make our exit, too."

Candie slipped her arm through mine, and we turned to go. Candie gave Bret a backhanded wave and a parting shot. "Ta-ta. Have a great day. See you at the polls."

As the door shut behind us, we heard Bret shouting to his campaign workers to get to work.

I tugged the scarf a little tighter around my head to try to ward off some of the rain that had begun to fall again. I wished I had thought to wear my raincoat or at least brought an umbrella.

"So, when did Tommy Ray tell you about seeing Bret with another woman at a motel? It's news to me, and come to think of it, why didn't you tell me?" I puffed out my chest in indignation. When did my cousin stop sharing things with me? At times, I thought we were closer than identical twins. We often shared the same thoughts and could practically read each other's minds.

Candie gazed at me with her innocent violet eyes. "He didn't." She turned and started to walk down the rain-covered sidewalk.

Her statement halted me in my tracks. My jaw dropped open. I blinked then ran to catch up with her. "What do you mean he didn't? But you just said…"

Candie waved her hand at me. "I called his bluff. A rat like him usually has his pants dropped for some bimbo or another."

I stopped in the middle of the sidewalk. A gentleman walking behind me nearly collided into me. I turned, smiled, and gave him an apology. "Candie, you called his bluff?" I started to laugh and couldn't stop. Candie joined me in laughing, and soon tears streamed down our faces. I'm sure people passing us thought we were a little crazy.

Suddenly I had a sobering thought. I placed a hand on my chest and reached out to grab Candie's wrist. "What if Tommy Ray really had let Bret know he'd seen him at a motel with a woman not his wife? If such news got out, it could have sunk Bret's campaign and his chances of making big money from Tony Riglio's kickbacks when he awarded him contracts for expanding Wings Falls."

Candie nodded. "I'd say that was a good reason to want to murder Tommy Ray."

CHAPTER EIGHTEEN

———

With all of my laughing, my scarf had become loose and slid off my head. I bent to retrieve it. The sound of a car gunning its engine flooded my ears.

"Sam, watch out!" Candie shouted as she shoved me up against the front window of a local bar, one of many populating this street. Unlike The Round Up, these bars catered to the hard-core drinkers. They opened their doors before noon and didn't close until after midnight.

An SUV jumped the curb and missed us by inches. Rain from the puddles dotting the sidewalk sprayed down the legs of my slacks. Candie released her hold on my trembling shoulders. She stepped back from me and, with shaking hands, pushed back the scarf falling over her eyes.

I opened my mouth to speak, but no words came out, I drew in a gulp of air and tried again. "What was that—or should I say who was that?"

Candie nodded in the direction of the receding vehicle. Raindrops tumbled off her scarf. Anger flushed her cheeks. "I don't know, but they should be arrested for reckless driving."

I agreed. If not for Candie's quick thinking, I would be patronizing my own funeral parlor right now. The thought sent a shiver up my spine, and it wasn't due to the rain soaking the front of my slacks. "Did you get a look at the driver or the car they were driving?"

"Let me think." Candie's forehead furrowed in thought. "I didn't see the driver, but I noticed it was an SUV."

I shrugged. "Well, that really narrows the field of suspects. Only about ninety-nine percent of the people in the North Country drive an SUV. What about color? Did you see what color it was?"

Candie was silent for a few seconds. "Black, definitely black. Oh wait! There was some kind of sticker on the rear window."

I clapped my hands together. This clue could lead to whoever tried to run me down. "Sticker? Could you read what it said?"

Candie stomped her cowboy boot on the sidewalk. "I didn't have time to pull up a chair and read the sticker. I was too busy trying to keep you from becoming roadkill."

I put a trembling hand on her arm to calm her rising temper. My nerves were still raw from my near brush with death. "Sorry, cuz. If the person is local, I thought it might give us a clue as to who they are."

Candie looked around and pointed at the various drinking establishments lining both sides of the street. "You're right, but from the looks of this neighborhood, it could have been any one of the patrons from these dives. Maybe they imbibed a few too many and couldn't tell the road from the sidewalk."

I nodded in agreement. "I guess we were in the wrong place at the wrong time. When the person sobers up, they probably won't even remember their bumper almost kissed me." I took one last look down the street from where the car came. "Candie, look! Quick, look." I pointed in the direction of Bret Hargrove's campaign headquarters.

Candie's head whipped up. "What, what? Is it the SUV again?" Candie strained her neck to get a good look where I was pointing.

I shook my head. "No, no. Didn't you see who went into Bret's headquarters?"

"No, I didn't. Who was it?"

I frowned. "Valerie."

Candie looked as puzzled as me. "Now why would she go there? I'd think she'd be spending all her time at Mark's headquarters. After all, the primary is next Tuesday."

I agreed with Candie. "Yes, and from what Flossie said last Saturday night at The Round Up, she has a major crush on Mark. So why would she have anything to do with Bret?"

Candie's mouth dropped open. I put my hand up to shut it. "Watch it, or you'll swallow some raindrops. Didn't you know about Valerie's feelings for Mark?"

Candie's eyes widened as she shook her head. "No, I didn't have a clue. She's always been polite to me. Mark hasn't said a thing to me about Valerie's infatuation with him." She frowned. "There better not be anything going on between the two of them behind my back." She opened her purse and pulled out her phone. "I'm going to give Mark a call right now and get to the bottom of this."

I took her hand in mine. I wanted to stop her from making a serious blunder by calling Mark in the state of mind she was right now. Like Memaw Parker used to say, "Words spoken in haste today, you'll regret tomorrow."

"Maybe she knows someone who volunteers for Bret and wants to find out what he's up to next."

Candie huffed out a breath. "Yeah, and I have a bridge in Brooklyn to sell you, too. If a friend of hers was working for his campaign, she could easily call him or her on the phone. And I'd like to know why she was at my house the other morning. What reason would she have for meeting with Tommy Ray?"

I shrugged. "Good question. You really hadn't heard the rumor that she was mooning over Mark?"

Candie shook her head. "No, she never acted lovesick at Mark's headquarters. At least not while I was there." Her eyes widened. "What if it was because I was there?"

"What do you mean?"

Candie pointed towards Bret's building. "What if when I was there, it was all an act? You know, act nicey-nicey when I was there and then all gooey-eyed over Mark when I wasn't. I do have a job and can't be at the headquarters all the time. She *is* one of his most devoted volunteers."

It was a possibility. "Most campaign workers are volunteers, right? So how does she support herself if she's spending so much time as a volunteer? How does she get time off from her job at Sylvia's Bridal Salon? We know Miss Sylvia is a doll, but she does have a business to run and would need dependable employees."

Candie's head snapped up. "I believe I read on her volunteer application she only works at Miss Sylvia's part time, but she also works for her dad. I think she does his books or some such thing."

"Maybe that's why she can get off work so easily, since she works for family and her other job is only part time."

If Candie's eyes were lasers, they'd be boring holes into the front wall of Bret's building. "Yes, and her dad is in the construction business."

A light flicked on in my brain. "Oh, I see. What if she really wants Bret to win? Then maybe her dad could get some of those contracts for expanding Wings Falls that Bret is so big on promoting.

She could have gone to your house to get some dirt on you from Tommy Ray to sabotage Mark's campaign."

Candie's scarf slipped off her head. Raindrops settled on her auburn curls. "I wonder if growing up around the construction business, she knows how to use a nail gun? I say we have a talk with Valerie."

Candie started down the sidewalk. I tugged on the sleeve of her blouse to stop her. "We can't march into Bret's campaign headquarters and start throwing questions at Valerie. We'll have to wait until we can get her alone at Mark's headquarters. It shouldn't be too hard since she's always there. We can ask her about our suspicions in Mark's office."

Candie nodded in agreement. "You're right. It will give us time to formulate a plan. And I also want to tell her to keep her hands off Mark."

I laughed. "You go, girl. But right now, let's get out of the rain. I need to get home, feed Porkchop, and let him out. It will take some coercing with a doggie treat or two. He hates going out in the rain. I can't say I blame him. I'd hate it, too, if my belly skimmed the puddles of rainwater."

Candie chuckled. We started to walk in the direction of her Precious. I couldn't wait to crank up the heater in her car to full blast. My soaked slacks sent a chill through me. After attending to Porkchop's needs, I planned to pull on my fleece-lined sweatpants. I knew it was summer, but without the sun to warm me, I was chilled to the bone. I even owned a fleece-lined top I was thinking of donning. I'd slip on my fleece-lined slippers, too. Fleece was the operative word here. Finally, I would nuke a mug of hot chocolate in the microwave. Porkchop and I would settle on the sofa and watch some mindless TV show and forget about murder and campaigns. Or so I thought.

* * *

Candie had pulled as far up my driveway as she could. The rain was coming down in a steady downpour. I leaned over and gave her a hug then let myself out of her car. I'd have to make a mad dash for my front door. After taking care of Porkchop, I'd put some water in the microwave for my hot chocolate dreams.

I waved at Candie as she pulled away from the curb. "Drive carefully," I shouted after her.

She tooted her horn and returned my wave.

I tromped up my front steps. I opened my front door and was surprised when Porkchop didn't greet me. Concern raced through my body. I dropped my purse on the floor of my entryway. I didn't bother to shed my rain-soaked shoes. Rain puddles followed me as I walked into my living room. "Porkchop, where are you? Mommy is home."

My house was a small rancher, so there weren't many places he could hide. I heard a faint whining coming from behind the bathroom door in the hallway leading to the bedrooms. I raced down the hall and flung open the bathroom door. A trembling Porkchop jumped up to greet me.

"Porkchop, how did you get shut in here?" I cradled his long body in my arms. My eyes scanned the room and came to rest on the mirror over the sink. There was my answer.

CHAPTER NINETEEN

Porkchop jumped at my legs. I sank to my knees on the hard tile floor and gathered him onto my lap. "It's okay, baby, Mommy is here to protect you." I glanced up at the message. *Hands off what is mine!* was scrawled in vivid pink lipstick across the mirror hanging over the sink.

I fumbled in my pocket for my phone. I flipped it open and punched in Hank's number.

He answered on the second ring. "Sam, what's up? I'm a little busy right now."

His abrupt tone of voice jolted me. Tears clogged my throat, but I was able to choke out, "I'm sorry, Hank. I didn't mean to bother you." Then I flipped my phone shut.

I gathered Porkchop's warm body next to me and snuggled into his short red hair. Tears streamed down my face. "Porkie, I don't know what has gotten into him lately. Maybe I read too much into our relationship, and this is his way of calling it quits." My phone rang. I looked at the caller ID—Hank. I ran my fingers over his name. Tears splashed onto the phone. "That's okay. I won't bother you again," I whispered into the warm air of the bathroom.

After about five minutes of wallowing in my loss of what I thought was a growing romance, I stiffened my spine and stood with Porkchop cradled in my arms. I took one last look at the message on the mirror then placed Porkchop on the floor. I opened the doors beneath the sink housing my cleaning supplies. I was about to spray and wipe away the message when the sound of someone pounding on my front door interrupted me.

I looked down at Porkchop. "Who could that be? They certainly are impatient." I walked into my mudroom and peeked out the door's peephole. A frowning Hank stood with his arm raised, about to assault my front door again. He must have broken all the city's speed limits to arrive here so quickly. I flung the door open before he could damage either it or his fist.

"Can I come in?" he asked. I noticed his sport coat was buttoned incorrectly. He looked like he had dashed out of the station in a hurry.

I motioned for him to enter. Porkchop, the traitor, went into his happy dance when he saw Hank.

He reached down and scratched between Porkchop's ears. "How you doing, good buddy?"

My feelings started to betray me. I craved some of the attention Hank was showering on my dog. Hank looked up at me. I still wore my rain-soaked slacks from my morning trip to The Sound Machine with Candie. My hair was a disheveled mess, and I knew my nose and eyes must be red and swollen from crying.

A frown creased Hank's forehead. "Sam, what's the matter? Why did you call?"

I pointed to the bathroom. "It's better if I show you."

"This isn't about a clogged toilet, is it?" Hank asked.

I shook my head and led the way to the bathroom. "Clogged toilets I can handle."

Once we were in the bathroom—a tight fit with Hank, Porkchop, and me crowded into the room—I pointed at the mirror.

Hank's jaw clenched. "What the heck…" This he followed with a few words that would have raised Memaw Parker's eyebrows.

He turned to me. "When did this happen?"

"I discovered the message when I got home after Candie dropped me off. Porkchop didn't greet me when I came in the door. I became really concerned. You know how he's always at the door when I come home."

Hank nodded.

"So, I went in search of him and found him shut in this bathroom." Tears started to well up in my eyes again as I thought of my poor Porkie trapped in this small room and for who knows how long. "Then I saw the message on the mirror."

Hank's hands curled into fists as he read the message. "What time did you go out this morning?"

"Candie picked me up about nine. What does that have to do with this?" I nodded towards the mirror.

Hank folded his arms across his chest and heaved a sigh. "It's obvious someone broke into your house while you were gone and left this message. I'm only trying to pinpoint when it happened."

The meaning of his statement suddenly hit me like a Mack Truck. I was so concerned about Porkchop, I hadn't thought this whole incident through. Someone had broken into my house while I was gone. "But I used my key to unlock my front door."

"Wait here and don't touch anything." Hank left the room with Porkchop trailing after him.

Alone, I started to reflect on what Hank said. Who broke into my house while I was gone, and why? Did this have anything to do with Tommy Ray's murder? Did Bret Hargrove think we were getting too close to proving he killed Tommy Ray in order to cover up his shady business dealings?

I returned to my living room and sat on the sofa. Hank was checking all the windows and doors in my house.

Porkchop jumped up on the sofa and snuggled down beside me. "Did you find anything?" I asked when Hank walked back into the living room.

He ran a hand through his hair, ruffling its thick brown waves. "No, all your windows and doors are secure. I didn't see any signs of forced entry. I'm going to call the station and have them send someone out to check for fingerprints and anything out of the ordinary I might have missed. But at first glance I didn't notice anything disturbed." He pulled out his phone and punched in the number for the Wings Falls Police Station. He asked whoever answered to send an officer to my house.

Thoughts of what-ifs began to float through my brain. What if I came home sooner and walked in on the person who broke into my house? What if they'd harmed my Porkchop? Tears rolled down my cheeks.

Hank slid closer to me on the sofa. He gently picked Porkchop up and placed my dog on the other side of him then drew me into his arms. Porkchop didn't let out a peep. I snuggled into Hank, smiled, and swiped at my tears.

He tilted up my face and rubbed a finger over my tears. "What's brought on the smile?"

"I was thinking about how Porkchop growled at George the other day at the Do Drop, and you moved him away from me and snuggled closer without a bark from him."

A smile spread across his handsome face. "Smart dog."

A knock sounded on my door.

Hank pulled away and stood. "It must be the officer I requested."

I stifled a groan as Hank walked over to the front door. I hadn't realized how much I missed having Hank close to me.

The officer followed Hank back into the living room. "Sam, this is Officer Reed. He's going to check for fingerprints and any signs of forced entry."

Officer Reed carried a small black plastic box about eight inches square. I assumed it was the fingerprint kit.

I nodded. "Yes, I remember you from Sunday morning at Candie's."

Officer Reed tipped his hat in recognition.

I watched as Hank showed him the way to my bathroom.

When Hank came back into the room, he sat back on the sofa and turned towards me. He hitched one knee onto the sofa. "Sam, Reed snapped a picture of the message on your mirror. Do you have any idea who might be warning you away from something and what that something might be?"

I shook my head. I wasn't about to tell him Candie and I were at The Sound Machine this morning. It would only anger him, and we were having a civil conversation right now. I didn't want to ruin it. "No, I don't."

Hank persisted. "Have you done any more investigating on your own into Tommy Ray's murder?"

He wasn't going to let it go.

I twisted my fingers together. "Well, Candie and I did go to The Sound Machine this morning."

Hank frowned. "And what was your reason for going to The Sound Machine? It couldn't possibly have anything to do with Bret Hargrove being a suspect in Tommy Ray's murder, could it?"

I swallowed hard. He was not going to like my answer. "Well, we did ask the nice kid who waited on us about their prices for a DJ for Mark and Candie's wedding."

Hank heaved out a deep sigh. I could tell he was fast losing patience with me. "Sam."

"Okay, okay, we might have gotten around to asking a young fellow named Bruce a few questions. He gave us some interesting information."

Hank arched an eyebrow. "Like what? Would you care to share it with me?"

"He said the paychecks at The Sound Machine have bounced and he overheard a phone conversation Bret had. Bret told the person on the other end that he'd get his money soon because he had the primary 'in the bag.'"

Hank stroked his chin. A five o'clock shadow was sprouting on his square jaw. "'In the bag', huh? Very interesting."

I nodded. "Yeah, Lacey and I thought it was, too."

Hank chuckled. "Lacey, as in Cagney and Lacey?"

I laughed, too. "Yeah, it was Candie's idea, but I was Myrtle."

Hank laughed out loud. Porkchop jumped off the sofa and started to bark at Hank's laughter. He didn't want to miss out on whatever fun Hank was having.

I swatted at Hank's arm. "It isn't that funny."

He swiped at the tears of laughter rolling down his cheeks.

Officer Reed walked back into the living room. "Can I speak to you, Detective Johnson?"

Hank rose from the sofa and joined Officer Reed in the hallway. Hank and Reed spoke in a hushed voice.

Then Reed, fingerprint kit in hand, walked to the front door. "See you back at the station, Detective." Officer Reed nodded at me as he walked past.

Hank rejoined me on the sofa. "Sam, besides you, who else has a key to your house?"

I wrinkled my forehead in concentration. "Only Candie and me."

"Do you know of anyone who might wear the bright-pink shade of lipstick the message was written in?"

I did. And I didn't like where his questioning was leading.

CHAPTER TWENTY

———

"Do you know who wears this shade, Sam?" Hank asked again.

"Candie," I finally told him. Then I quickly added, "But why on earth would she write this on my mirror?"

"To deflect guilt? Throw us off her trail?"

I jutted my chin out defiantly. "Candie was with me the entire time. She could not have written this."

Hank slipped a small notebook from the inside pocket of his sport coat. His hand grazed over the top of his Superman tie. Unlike all the times before, his penchant for cartoon ties didn't bring a smile to my face. I only wished he possessed superpowers like Clark Kent and could prove Candie innocent in a flash. I sat close enough to see him jot down Candie's name and *pink lipstick*.

My spine stiffened, I plucked my damp pants away from my legs and sat straighter on the sofa. "You know as well as I do Candie didn't kill Tommy Ray. She was with me all morning and couldn't have locked Porkchop into the bathroom. More importantly, she loves my dog as if he were her own, so you can just scratch that information out of your notebook." I jabbed at the offending page for emphasis.

Hank huffed out a deep breath. "I care for Candie, too. Heck, I'm supposed to be the best man in her and Mark's wedding, but I have to follow the law, and right now things don't look too good for her." He reached over and tucked a stray curl behind my ear.

I turned my face into his hand and nuzzled into it. His thumb swiped at the tears that trickled down my face. "I know you don't like my sticking my nose into this investigation, but I can't stand by and watch my cousin, who is more like a sister to me, be railroaded to jail. Not when I know she is innocent."

Hank caressed my cheek. "I understand. I might not like it, but I understand. You are a very caring and loyal person. Candie is lucky you are her cousin." He shifted on the sofa and tucked his notebook back into his sport coat. His gaze rested on me. As if realizing for the first time, he touched my damp slacks. "What happened? Did you slip and fall in the rain?"

"No, a car jumped the curb while Candie and I were walking back to her Precious this morning."

A scowl fell over Hank's face. "What do you mean a car jumped the curb? Were you hurt? Why didn't you tell me sooner?"

I blinked at the rapid-fire questions he shot at me. "Well, for one thing, we were trying to figure out who broke into my house. And secondly, you were busy scolding me for going to The Sound Machine this morning."

Hank sighed and rubbed a hand across his eyes. His shoulders drooped. I almost felt sorry for him—almost. I was too worried about Candie to have any more emotions to spare.

"Sam, I wasn't scolding you."

I raised an eyebrow at his statement.

"All right, all right, maybe a little. But don't you realize how serious this all is? I don't want you to get hurt, and I'm terrified with all of your snooping that something will happen to you."

I picked up his calloused hand and held it in mine. I ran my fingers across the back. "I'm truly sorry for all the worry I'm causing you. But you have to know by now that when a friend of mine—and especially a family member, like Candie—is in trouble, I can't sit idly by and do nothing. I have to do everything in my power to help. Someone is setting her up."

Hank stood and pulled his wallet out of the back pocket of his jeans then sat back on the sofa next to me. He flipped open his wallet and pulled out a tattered picture. What was he going to show me? I didn't think this was the time for family photos. He ran a finger gently over the surface of the picture then handed it to me.

My eyes roamed over the photo. It was faded but a shot of a beautiful woman who was very pregnant. Her head was thrown back in laughter. Long black hair fell over her shoulders.

I looked up at Hank with a puzzled look on my face. "She is very beautiful. Who is she?"

Hank gazed at the photo then at me. "My wife."

My jaw dropped open. Questions started to tumble out of my mouth. "You're married and you never told me? Why have you been seeing me? Where is she? She's pregnant in this photo. Where is your child?" I jumped off the sofa and stood rigid in front of him. My hands clenched into fists at my side. How dare he cheat on his wife. Boy, I could really pick them. First George, and now Hank. Are there any true blue, good men out there?

Hank patted the sofa cushion. "Calm down, Sam. Let me explain."

"It had better be a good one," I grumbled out.

Hank ran a finger over the photo. "Her name was Amanda." My brows rose in question. "Was?"

He nodded. "Yeah, was. You remind me of her in a lot of ways. Like you, she was stubborn. Fiercely loyal. And full of life. I was a rookie in the NYPD, and she was a rookie reporter for one of the big papers in the city. We'd only been married a year, and she was expecting our first child, a boy. She was due to go on maternity leave in two weeks, but she had one last big story she wanted to cover. It was about the gangs taking over a certain neighborhood."

A chill shot through my body as I anticipated what he was about to say. "That must have been a dangerous assignment."

Hank shrugged. "Tell me about it. Mandy insisted on covering this one last story before she went out on leave. When she left that morning, she promised me that she'd be safe since she wouldn't be going into that area alone. Allen, her photographer, would be accompanying her. Next thing I knew, a message came over my car radio that a gang fight had broken out in the neighborhood she was reporting on. Shots had been fired. I got to the scene in time to hold her in my arms as she and my baby breathed their last breaths."

Tears rolled down my face. "I didn't know. Your aunt Gladys never said a word."

"It wasn't her story to tell. She figured I'd mention it to you when I was ready." Hank pushed off the sofa and stood before me. A crooked smile spread across his face. "So that's why I get so concerned when I think you are putting yourself in danger. I've kinda figured out that you are fiercely loyal to your family and friends. I'll just have to stock up on antacids."

"Antacids?" I asked.

He grinned. "For all the worry and heartburn your snooping will cause me. But you're worth it."

My heart did a skip of joy. He really did care. I stood and pointed to mismatched buttons and buttonholes on his jacket. "You must have been in a hurry to get here."

He looked down and smiled. "You could say that." He rebuttoned his sport coat.

He hooked a finger under my chin and tilted my face towards him. Leaning down, he placed a gentle kiss on my lips. I reached up, encircled his neck with my arms, and pulled him closer, deepening the kiss.

In a hoarse voice, he said, "If I'm going to make sure Candie can walk down the aisle with Mark, I'd better get back to the station."

Reluctantly, I withdrew my arms from his neck and stepped back. "Okay, as the big shot detectives say on TV, 'bust this case wide open.'"

Hank laughed. "I'll give it my best." He scratched Porkchop between the ears. With one hand on the doorknob, he wrapped his other arm around me and pulled me close for another kiss. "Be careful," he whispered against my lips. Then he opened the door and walked down the steps to his car.

I glanced down at Porkchop. "We'll try, won't we, Porkie?" A shiver ran through me. "I'd better get out of these pants before I catch pneumonia. Then we'll call Candie." Porkchop trotted beside me as I walked back to my bedroom.

CHAPTER TWENTY-ONE

———

I drove my egg yolk–yellow Bug while Candie sat in the passenger's seat cuddling Porkchop. I called her as soon as Hank left my place to go back to the police station. He needed to figure out why someone would shut my pup in my bathroom and leave a threatening note scrawled onto the bathroom mirror in what looked like Passion Pink lipstick. This, added to trying to solve Tommy Ray's murder, would make for a late night for him.

"How is my Porkie Workie? Why would someone do such a nasty thing to a sweet doggie-woggie like you?" Candie crooned to Porkchop while she stroked his ears. From the sighs of contentment coming from my dog, he was eating up all the attention his aunt Candie showered on him. "Dixie sends her love. She became very upset when I told her what happened to you."

I rolled my eyes upward. Dixie is Candie's calico cat. Bret Hargrove would look like a choirboy before love flowed between our two pets. At the best of times, Dixie and Porkchop barely tolerated each other. When my ex, George, announced he wanted a divorce after doing the late-night bump fuzzies with the secretary of the funeral parlor we co-owned, the Do Drop Inn, Porkchop and I bunked in with Candie and Dixie for a few months. As soon as I got my feet back on the ground, and not soon enough, my parents retired to Florida, and I moved back into my childhood home before any more fur could fly.

We were on our way to Mark's campaign headquarters to help the volunteers with some last minute "get out the vote" phone calls. I wasn't about to leave Porkchop home by himself in case the person who invaded my home returned. I had called a locksmith to change the locks on my doors, but he said he was booked for today and couldn't get there until tomorrow morning at the earliest.

Candie turned in her seat and looked at me. "What's with people leaving you threatening notes, anyway? Remember last year when the receptionist at the vet's left you one taped to the visor of your car? She was afraid you were asking too many questions about the murder of the pet shelter owner and would discover that she, in fact, was the killer."

I shrugged my shoulders. "I don't know. Maybe the person thinks that by threatening me, he—or possibly she—will scare me off of asking questions about Tommy Ray's murder." I glanced towards my cousin, who sat hugging Porkchop close to her. I wished I could absorb some of his comforting vibes right now, too. "Do you think Tommy Ray's murderer broke into my house?" In spite of the eighty-degree heat outside the Bug, my hands started to shake and my teeth began to chatter. Not a good combo when trying to drive.

Candie squealed. Porkchop let out a yelp. "Ohhhh. I hadn't thought of that. Sorry Porkie, I didn't mean to hug you so tightly. Do you think it was a woman since the message was written in pink lipstick? Thank heavens I was with you all morning, or that toad Sergeant Peters would love to pin this one on me, too."

I had to agree with Candie. I could see Peters trying to do anything he could to get back at me, just because I wanted to play in a clean sandbox back in kindergarten. Who wanted to make castles in pee-soaked sand? He knew how close Candie and I were and how much it would hurt me if anything happened to her. "I guess because the message was written in lipstick, it could indicate that Tommy Ray's killer was a woman, but a man could just as easily have bought a tube of Passion Pink at Walgreens to throw off the police. Everyone knows that shade is your signature lip color."

Out of the corner of my eye, I could see Candie flip down the car visor and slide open the mirror attached to it. She pursed her lips and turned her head from side to side. "Oh, that it is."

I laughed. "Candie, you are an original."

My cousin laughed in return. "Sweetie, there is only one Candie Parker, and it's me."

"That's for sure." I turned the Bug into the parking lot of Mark's campaign headquarters. Mark had rented a space for his campaign in what was once a sporting goods store. The store had outgrown the space and moved to a mall that sat outside Wings Falls, near the interstate. The space worked out fine for Mark, though. It was spacious, with large picture windows along the front of the building. An office area was located in the back of the store. There was even a storeroom Mark equipped with a refrigerator for the volunteers' cold drinks, lunches, or whatever snacks they brought with them while working to reelect Mark mayor.

"Come on, Porkchop. Time for us to get to work and make sure Mark beats Bret Hargrove next Tuesday." I clipped on Porkchop's leash. He hopped across to the driver's seat and into my arms.

"That's right, Porkie. Your soon-to-be-uncle has to get reelected. He's the best mayor Wings Falls ever had." Candie opened the car door and stepped out.

My cousin was a tad bit prejudiced about Mark since she was about to marry him in little over a week, but I agreed with her. Mark had done a lot to make Wings Falls one of the most desirable towns to live in Upstate New York.

I pushed open the door to the headquarters, and the sounds of volunteers on telephones asking people to vote for Mark bombarded my ears. Unlike the disarray of Bret Hargrove's headquarters, Mark's was neat and orderly. Long tables ran down the middle and sides of the room. Folding chairs were pushed up against them. Volunteers sat on either side of the tables speaking into their phones. Posters featuring Mark's face and printed with the slogan *Reelect Mark Hogan for Mayor* hung from the walls. You could almost touch the energy flowing through the room.

"Hi, Candie and Sam. Who is this sweet pup?"

I turned to see Dan Brewer, Flossie Garner's date from last Saturday night at The Round Up. He stood behind me, a phone clutched in his hand. He bent and scratched Porkchop between the ears. Porkchop tilted his head up and licked Dan's bearded chin.

I laughed. "Sorry about that, Dan. But he's only showing his appreciation for you hitting his sweet spot. Scratch him between his ears, and you're his friend for life."

Dan returned my laughter. "I'm glad to have a new friend in town. A person can never have too many friends." He slid his phone into the back pocket of his jeans. "I think I'll grab a bite to eat out of the fridge."

"It's so nice of you to help out with Mark's campaign. I didn't think you were going to be in town this long." Candie shifted her purse up her arm. It sported rhinestones like most of her wardrobe.

Dan fidgeted with the sleeve of his T-shirt. "Oh, umm, I thought I'd spend a little more time visiting with Flossie. It's been a while since we've connected."

"That's nice. How did you two meet? I don't think she told us on Saturday night when we were all at The Round Up. Your accent has a tinge of Southern in it," Candie continued.

I shot my cousin a quizzical glance. What was with her grilling Dan? He was here to help out on Mark's campaign. On this crunch week before the primary, we could use all the help we could muster. It had been a hard-fought campaign, what with Mark having to deal with all of Bret Hargrove's lies.

"Umm, I went to college in Atlanta. I must have picked up a little accent from hanging out with my buddies. If you'll excuse me, I need to grab my sandwich out of the fridge. I want to get back to the phones." Dan hurried past us to the back room.

I shook my head in bewilderment. "Now what was that all about? We can't go alienating our volunteers right before the election."

"Come on. Let's stow our purses in Mark's office and I'll tell you. I think Mark might have some dog treats with Porkchop's name on them."

I followed Candie to the back of the room where Mark's campaign office sat. Candie opened the door and walked over to a closet in the corner of the room. An oak desk held court in the middle of the room. Padded faux-leather chairs sat in front of it. Campaign posters and flyers were stacked on the desk. Candie placed her purse on the top shelf of the closet. I handed her my red-handled, C-printed Coach purse then sat in one of the chairs in front of the desk.

Candie opened the top drawer of the desk and took out a handful of small doggie treats. "Here you go, Porkchop."

Porkchop trotted over to her and ate them out of her hand.

I raised an eyebrow. "Mark had doggie treats in his desk?"

"What can I say? Mark is always prepared for all kinds of visitors, whether two-legged or four-legged." Candie pulled a tissue out of a box sitting on the desk and wiped off Porkchop's doggie slobber.

"Okay, now tell me what were all the questions for Dan about? He's helping out here, manning the phones. We can't afford to lose any volunteers right before the election."

Candie sat beside me. The sunlight radiating through the window behind her highlighted her auburn hair. "Flossie said he was in town for the weekend. Why is he still here? And why would he want to spend his time at Mark's campaign headquarters? Maybe you didn't notice his Southern accent, but I did. A true Southerner will pick up on things like that. Besides me, how many people with a Southern accent do you know here in Wings Falls? If a person gets agitated, their accent becomes more pronounced. The more I questioned Dan, the more his accent came out."

I frowned, not knowing what Candie was getting at. "So, he has a Southern accent. That's not a crime, even up north here with us Yankees."

Candie shook her head. "No, it isn't. But don't you remember? My nosey neighbor, Mrs. Splotz, said one of the voices she heard arguing on my balcony had a Southern accent."

My eyes widened and my mouth formed an "O" as I realized what Candie meant.

CHAPTER TWENTY-TWO

Porkchop lay at my feet, snoring softly. "You're right, he does have a slight accent. And Mrs. Splotz did mention that one of the people who visited with Tommy Ray on Sunday morning had a Southern accent?"

Candie tapped her fingers on the arm of her chair. "That's what I just told you. One of his visitors spoke with a Southern accent. If that person was agitated enough with Tommy Ray, his accent might have become more noticeable. But why would Dan Brewer have anything to do with Tommy Ray? At The Round Up last Saturday night, Flossie said he was a friend visiting from out of town."

"Mrs. Splotz also said there was a woman with him on the balcony. She thought it was you because of the hair coloring." A jolt of excitement shot through me. Maybe we'd nailed another person with a possible motive for killing Tommy Ray. *Oops, wrong choice of words.*

"I think we'd better ask Flossie a few questions about this so-called friend of hers, who I think should be added to the suspect list along with Bret Hargrove. I believe she's due in soon to help man the phones. It's all hands on deck this week since the primary is next Tuesday." Candie rose from her chair.

I placed a hand on her arm to detain her for a moment. I had more questions tumbling about in my brain. "Flossie acted like Dan was a little more than a friend on Saturday night—or at least would like to be. If so, why isn't she here with him right now? And speaking of him being here… Why is he? I mean, he doesn't know Mark. He's a stranger in Wings Falls. What does he care about our local politics?"

Candie nodded and sat back down. My questions caused her to frown. "You're right. We all think Mark is the greatest living mayor, but Dan Brewer isn't from here, so why would he care? Oh.

Oh." Candie bounced in her seat. "He was out with Flossie on Saturday night, and we're guessing that Sunday morning he was with another woman at my house arguing with Tommy Ray. I wonder if Flossie knows he was two-timing her in less than twenty-four hours. The cad. I think I'll go right out there and give him a piece of my mind. Flossie has been a valuable worker for Mark's campaign. She doesn't need someone like Dan breaking her heart." Candie started to rise from her chair again.

"Candie, now don't go getting your buns in a knot over Flossie. You know she has designs on your job as Mark's secretary once the two of you are married."

Candie shook her head. "I don't know where she would have gotten that idea. I've never told Mark I want to quit being his secretary. I happen to love my job. As much as I love him, I certainly don't want to be completely dependent on him."

I smiled. That was my Southern cousin for you. Sexy as all get out, the embodiment of all things feminine, but as fierce and independent as her cat Dixie.

"Okay, so what's our plan?" I asked.

Candie and I put our heads together. End result—to flat out ask Flossie about her relationship with Dan Brewer.

It didn't take long for the opportunity to arise to shoot questions at Flossie as the object of our cross-examination. As we were about to leave the office, she walked into the campaign headquarters.

The morning had turned windy, and a gust accompanied Flossie in the door. "Phew, it certainly is windy out there. It practically knocked me off my feet." Flossie laughed as she untwirled the scarf draped around her neck and stuffed it into her purse. She ran a hand through her heavily frosted brown hair that skimmed her shoulders. She glanced around the room. Her eyes fell on Dan Brewer. "Hi, Dan. I didn't know you were here. I called your phone, but you didn't pick up. We could have driven here together if I'd known you were coming, too."

Dan's face turned almost as red as his hair. "Ahh, sorry. It was a last-minute decision. I know how committed you are to Mark's campaign, so I figured I'd take a chance that you'd be here."

"Do I detect a little trouble in paradise there?" Candie whispered out of the side of her mouth.

"If it wasn't so warm outside, I'd say there was going to be a dip in the temperature—and not one forecasted by the weather person," I whispered back.

"Hi, Flossie," I said. It was time to set our plan in motion and find out exactly what Flossie knew about Dan Brewer. Did he murder Tommy Ray, and for what reason?

Flossie turned towards Candie and me. "Oh, hi. I didn't notice you two standing there."

"Yeah, too busy trying to find out why Danny-boy there wasn't at her beck and call," Candie said for my ears only.

I put a hand over my mouth to stifle a giggle. "I think you're right."

When Flossie started to move away, I stopped her by asking, "Flossie, can we talk for a few minutes?" I pointed to the office's doorway to indicate that we wanted the conversation to take place away from prying ears.

"Umm, sure." Flossie walked towards the door, saying hello to fellow volunteers who waved on her way past them.

I closed the door to the office behind her and took the seat I'd vacated moments before. With my hand, I motioned for Flossie to sit in the other. Candie leaned against the desk.

"What's this all about? Has something happened with Mark's campaign? That Bret Hargrove isn't spreading any more lies, is he? I'd love to wring his scrawny neck. That man wouldn't know the truth if it smacked him in the face." Flossie was on a tirade, and it didn't look like she was about to wind down anytime soon.

Candy leaned over and patted Flossie's hand. "Flossie, no, it isn't anything like that. Everything is going smoothly with the campaign, thanks to your hard work along with the other volunteers'. Believe me, Mark and I really appreciate all you have done."

I cleared my throat. Heat crawled up my neck. This was so awkward, digging into someone's personal life. "I don't know how to delicately ask you the questions we need some answers to."

Flossie sat up straighter in her chair and cocked an eyebrow. "What kind of questions? What is it you want to know? You're starting to worry me. Get on with it."

Candie brushed her hands down the front of her filmy skirt. "Okay. How long have you known Dan Brewer? Do you know him well? Where did you meet him? Why do you think he'd want to volunteer at Mark's headquarters?"

Flossie swallowed hard and twisted her hands in her lap. "My, those are some rather personal questions. Before I answer them, I want to know your reason for asking those questions."

I placed my hand on top of hers to still their fidgety motions. "Candie's neighbor, Mrs. Splotz, said she heard a person with a Southern accent arguing with Tommy Ray on her balcony the morning he was killed. Don't you think it's a bit strange that Dan wants to hang out here? Also, outside of Candie, how many people do you know in Wings Falls that have a Southern accent?"

The color drained from Flossie's face. She started to sway in her seat. I stood and placed an arm around her to keep her from falling out of the chair. "Candie, quick, get Flossie a drink of water. I bought some bottled water the other day. It's in the fridge in the back room."

Candie raced out of the office but was back in seconds with a cold bottle of water. I handed it to Flossie. She grasped it in shaking hands. Beads of sweat gathered on her forehead.

She took a sip of the water, and then with trembling lips, she asked, "Do you think I'm seeing a murderer?"

CHAPTER TWENTY-THREE

———

To quote one of my cousin's Southern phrases—I felt lower than a snake's belly. Flossie may have found the love of her life, and here we were, telling her he could be a murderer.

"That's what we don't know. Candie and I have a few questions about why Dan Brewer is really here. We thought you might have the answers."

Candie waggled her jeweled fingers. "That's right, sweetie. We only want to make sure you're not dating some kind of scoundrel."

Tears rolled down Flossie's cheeks. "It wouldn't be the first time I've dated a loser."

Candie and I looked at her with a frown on our faces and questions in our eyes.

Flossie drew in a large, shuddering breath. "On a scale of one to ten when it comes to picking duds for a boyfriend, my luck would be an eleven. I knew it would be too good to be true to have a guy as great-looking and nice as Dan interested in plain old Flossie Garner."

"Flossie, now stop right there. You're a very attractive woman, and any fellow should consider himself lucky if he dated you." I fingered my curly brown hair that had a mind of its own. If only my hair would fall to my shoulders like hers did. A fellow could get lost in her sapphire-blue eyes rimmed with eyelashes to die for.

Flossie shot me a weak smile.

"Can you tell us how you happened to meet him? He said you two met online. Is that correct?" Candie asked.

Flossie swiped at the tears running down her cheeks with the back of her hand. "Well, kind of. I knew his sister from college. I hadn't heard from her in years. You know how it is—life happens and you lose touch. About a month ago, she emailed me and said her big brother was going to be in Wings Falls on some kind of business, and would I mind showing him a good time while he was here?"

Hmmm, Dan had given us the impression that they had met before but had lost touch.

Candie leaned forward from her perch on the desk. "You never met him before Saturday night at The Round Up?"

"Not exactly. He arrived in town on Wednesday. We went to dinner at The Smiling Pig. You know, the new barbeque place on Main Street that Marybeth Higgins' brother has opened up?"

I smiled. Our quiet Loopy Lady, Marybeth, was starting to come out of her shell as the hostess at her brother's new restaurant on her days off from the hospital. "Yes, I've heard great things about it. I haven't had the chance to go yet, but Hank and I hope to real soon." To steer us back onto the Dan Brewer track, I asked, "How did he act? Did he ask you any unusual questions? Did you go out any other days besides Wednesday and Saturday?" I felt bad about throwing all these questions at her, but finding Tommy Ray's killer was more important right now than her feelings.

Flossie wrinkled her brow in thought. "Now that you mention it, he knew about Candie and Mark and their upcoming wedding. I didn't think anything of it at the time. This is a small town, and not much is secret. I guess I was too flattered that he wanted to see me to take notice of anything unusual."

"Did he say why he was in Wings Falls?" I asked.

"He said something about investigating a deadbeat father. It sounded like he's some sort of private investigator. He was pretty closed-mouth about his job." Flossie tipped the water bottle to her lips and took a long swallow.

Candie turned her violet eyes on me. "Private investigator. Now that's interesting, and he knew about me and Mark. Could he have known about us before he arrived in Wings Falls? Were we the real reason he came here?"

I shook my head. These were very interesting questions. What was Dan Brewer's real reason for coming to Wings Falls? "How did you say you know his sister? What is her name?"

"Like I said before, I knew her from college. We were pretty close then, but like most college friendships, we drifted apart after graduation. Her name is Darlene Hopkins. Her mom was married a bunch of times. Dan is her stepbrother. I think he grew up in Ohio, but I'm not sure. Darlene said her mom moved around a lot with all of her marriages."

Candie scrunched up her brow and tapped the side of her head with her finger. "Darlene! That's the same name as Tommy Ray's girlfriend."

"It is?" I asked.

Candie nodded. "Yes. They couldn't be the same person, though, could they?"

I had one last question for Flossie. "Did you notice his Southern accent when you were out together?"

Flossie frowned and stared at the ceiling in concentration. "Not really. All I noticed was his deep, sexy voice. Why? Did you detect something I didn't?"

Candie stood and walked around the desk. "Well, I can't be sure, but he got riled up when Sam and I questioned him earlier, and I thought he spoke with a bit of a Southern drawl."

"No, I can't say I heard that, but he did say he went to school in Atlanta. You know how it is when you hang with people who speak in a certain way. You tend to mimic their pattern of speech."

I pointed to Candie and laughed. "There's always the exception to the rule." Candie's accent was as strong as the day she moved to Wings Falls.

Candie put her hands on her hips and jutted out her chin. "It isn't my fault that you Yankees don't know how to speak properly."

"He may have gotten some of his accent from living with his sister. I told you their mother was married a bunch of times."

Candie and I nodded.

"If I remember right, Darlene's father was a Southerner. In fact, I think she grew up in Tennessee, but after college she remained in Georgia. She didn't mention moving back to Tennessee."

Candie leaned so far forward she almost slid off the desktop. She jerked upright to catch her balance. "Tennessee? I wonder if she lived anywhere near where I grew up in Hainted Holler?"

"There's one way to find out." Flossie pulled a phone out of her coat pocket and punched in some numbers. "Oh, hi Darlene. Flossie here. Umm, yes, Dan and I have had a really good time getting to know each other. I have a question for you. I'm sitting here talking about the south with a couple of friends of mine. One of them is from Tennessee. I mentioned that I thought you grew up there, too. Did you live anywhere near Hainted Holler? What's that? What the…?" Flossie stared at her phone then looked up at Candie and me. A blank look came over her face.

"What did she say? Did she tell you where she lived?" I asked, puzzled as to why she was staring at the phone.

Flossie shook her head. Her frosted brown hair skimmed the collar of her coat. "No, she hung up before answering me."

"Why would she do that?" I asked. "It was a simple enough question."

"It may have been a simple question to you, but maybe not to her if she has something to hide," Candie said.

"So, she lived in Tennessee. I wonder if she still does. How could we find out?" I asked.

Candie turned to Flossie. "What is the phone number you dialed?"

Flossie scrolled through the contact list on her phone."615-555-5555."

Candie jumped out of her chair. "Tennessee! That's an area code in Tennessee."

"She has a Tennessee area code. Big deal. So do thousands of other people," I said.

Candie looked at me as if I were the village idiot. "Don't you see? Tommy Ray had the same area code. Maybe there's a connection between Tommy Ray, this Darlene, and Dan Brewer."

My eyes widened at what Candie had said. "You're right, there must be some kind of connection. There are too many coincidences here for there not to be."

CHAPTER TWENTY-FOUR

Candie walked towards the office door. With her back rigid and her chin jutted out, I knew her Southern temper was on the rise. "I'm going to march out there and ask Dan Brewer if he knew Tommy Ray. He has some serious explaining to do."

Flossie and I trailed after her.

Dan sat at one of the long tables talking on his phone. He didn't notice us entering the room. The heads of other volunteers swiveled towards us as Candie approached him. When Candie got to his seat, she stood behind him with her hands on her shapely hips, tapping her foot in agitation.

She poked him on the shoulder to get his attention. "Dan, I want to talk to you."

He jumped the proverbial mile out of his seat. "Geez, Candie, why don't you scare me to death." He sucked in a deep breath and placed a hand over his heart.

"I want to ask you a question. Can you end your conversation with whomever you are talking to?" Candie nodded to the phone clutched in his hand.

"Umm, sure." He told the person on the other end of the phone that he had to go then placed the phone in his jacket pocket.

"Why are you really here?" Candie asked, pinning him with her violet eyes.

Dan looked towards Flossie. "I told you before, I wanted to meet Flossie. She sounded like a really nice girl, someone I thought would be my type."

Now, that was a change of tune. Earlier, he'd said they had "lost touch," giving Candie and me the impression he'd known Flossie before coming to Wings Falls.

Flossie leaned towards Dan. "Don't lie to me. We only emailed each other a couple of times, and you thought I would be your 'type' from those few emails? How naive do you think I am?" Tears started to flow down her cheeks again.

The room had become eerily quiet. All the other volunteers sat listening to our conversation. Getting-out-the-vote calls were suddenly on hold.

Dan had the good grace to blush. "I thought you sounded intriguing, and I wanted to get to know you better."

I think all three of us did an eye roll at the same time. "Flossie said your sister is Darlene Hopkins."

Dan nodded. Sweat started to bead on his forehead. "Yes, she is. So what?"

I continued with my questions. "Does she live in Tennessee?"

"Look, none of this is any of your business, and I don't see why I have to sit here and be interrogated by the three of you." Dan stood and started to walk towards the front door.

"One last question, Dan. Did you know Tommy Ray Clements?" Candie shouted after him.

Dan's step faltered. With his hand on the doorknob, he turned to look at us. All the color had drained out of his face. "Not that it's any of your business, but that fellow is a first-class scum of the earth." With that parting remark, he opened the door and stepped out into the rising heat of the morning.

Candie, Flossie, and I stood with our mouths open. Candie was the first to recover from what Dan had said as he left the headquarters. "Well, if that don't beat the band. Flossie, he told you he was some kind of investigator and that he's up here looking for a deadbeat dad?"

"That's what he told me," Flossie said, swiping at the tears on her cheeks.

I jerked to attention. "Wait, wait, wait a minute. His parting shot was at Tommy Ray. Could Tommy Ray be that deadbeat dad he was looking for?"

Candie's mouth dropped open. "Darlene—she is Tommy Ray's current—or was his current girlfriend."

I shook with excitement. Maybe we had found Tommy Ray's killer and Candie could walk down the church aisle free of any suspicions. "Could Tommy Ray have a child with this Darlene or, at the very least, gotten her pregnant? Did you know anything about that, Candie?"

Candie shook her head vigorously, sending her auburn curls into a frenzy. "No. He didn't mention anything about this Darlene being pregnant or having a child. If he did, I would have sent him packing back to Tennessee to take care of them. I don't cotton to deadbeat fathers."

A thought struck me. "Flossie, what does your friend Darlene look like?"

"As I said, it's been years since I've seen her. We've kept in touch via email, but I don't do Facebook, so I haven't seen any pictures of her. She said she has a boyfriend in construction but that he was out of town doing a job."

Excitement started to build in me. "I wonder if it was out of town, as in Wings Falls? I know you said you haven't seen her in years, but can you recall what she looked like when you last saw her?"

Flossie scrunched up her forehead in thought. "Like I said, it's been a long time. But that last time I saw her, she was on the plump side, with short black hair cut in a pixie style."

My heart sank. There went my theory. I thought maybe Mrs. Splotz had mistaken Darlene for Candie. Candie, while having a full figure, wasn't plump by any means, and her hair was long and auburn. She wore it in a loose bun at the nape of her neck with tendrils caressing her cheeks. Nope, it was a far stretch to think Darlene resembled Candie. I related my musing to Candie and Flossie, and they agreed with me.

The front door opened, and the wind blew Valerie into the building. She came to a halt in front of the three of us. Her eyes widened when she saw Candie.

"What's the matter? Do I have something on my face?" Candie asked.

"Um, no," Valerie stuttered. "But I thought I just saw you outside getting into a car with Dan Brewer."

"What are you talking about? You can see I'm here in the flesh," Candie said.

Valerie's eyes narrowed. "I could have sworn that it was you getting into a red Ford Escape with Dan. It did seem strange since you are engaged to Mark and all. I mean, why would you be going off with another man when you are supposed to be getting married in a little over a week? I'd better get busy and start making phones calls so that my mayor can get reelected." Valerie walked over to the chair that Dan had vacated moments before, saying hi to other volunteers on her way. She sat and pulled out her phone then picked up a list of registered voters that lay on the table and started to punch the buttons on her phone.

Candie clenched her slim hands into a fist. "What does she mean by 'my mayor'? And the nerve of her insinuating that I'd go off with another man. Let me at her so I can tell her who the mayor belongs to."

Flossie turned towards me. "I told you that Valerie has a crush on Mark."

I nodded. "Yes, you did, and I mentioned it to Candie."

Candie was starting to breathe heavily as she stared at Valerie. I needed to get her out of the room before she exploded. "Candie, come with me to the office. You can calm down in there."

"I'll start manning a phone," Flossie said and left Candie and me.

Candie and I walked towards Mark's office. "You'd better get me out of here before I have a duck fit."

Oh, no. A duck fit was the Southern version of a major step above a hissy fit.

I pointed to one of the chairs we had sat in when we were in the office before. "Now sit, and I'll go get a bottle of water from the back room." I left the room for the water but was back in seconds.

"Where does Valerie get off calling Mark 'my mayor'?" Candie sat, still stewing over Valerie's remark.

I handed Candie the bottle of water I'd retrieved from the fridge. "I don't know. She is a devoted volunteer, and Flossie did say she had a crush on Mark."

Candie slumped farther down in her chair. "A crush is one thing, but she acts as if she's the one engaged to him, not me."

Maybe there was something to this "crush" Valerie supposedly had on Mark that Flossie had mentioned. Gone was the shy, church-mouse Valerie I had witnessed at the beginning of Mark's campaign. The woman I'd seen a few minutes ago had a sharp tongue—ready to do battle. But why was she at Bret's headquarters?

There was a knock on the door. Flossie stuck her head in. "Sam, Candie, I have something I think you may want to see." She walked in holding her phone in her hand. She held it out for Candie and me to see what was on it.

CHAPTER TWENTY-FIVE

———

When Flossie showed us what was on her phone, I don't know whose mouth hung open lower—Candie's or mine.

"Why that hussy! I'm going to tear her hair out and right now. Let me at her. We'll see whose mayor Mark is!" Candie was way beyond a duck fit now. She was in flying duck fit territory. A hissy fit would be a blip on the radar compared to a flying duck fit.

"Flossie, where did you get this picture?" I stared down at the image on her phone. Valerie stood curled up next to Mark, an arm around his neck, planting a kiss on his lips. How she'd managed to take the picture is anyone's guess. She had to be part contortionist not to have pulled her shoulder out of joint to snap this picture.

"Valerie got up from the table and went into the back room to fetch a bottle of water. I accidentally knocked her phone off the table. When I picked the phone up off the floor, this image came onto the screen." Flossie nodded at the phone.

Candie's face was flushed red as a beet with anger. Her lips trembled with rage as she spoke. "Flossie, I should have looked into your claim that Valerie has a crush on Mark. That crush had better not go both ways."

"Now, Candie, there has to be a simple explanation to that kiss. You know Mark is head over heels in love with you. Heck, I think he fell in love with you the first time you walked into the mayor's office five years ago. He fought hard to break down that one-date maximum rule you had imposed on men after you broke up with fiancé number eleven," I said. There was no way I would ever believe that Mark was cheating on Candie, not after all he went through to win her heart—and win it, he did.

A smile spread over Candie's lips. "I guess I did give him a wee bit of a hard time when we were first dating."

"A hard time? Climbing Mount Everest would be like scaling a sand dune compared to getting a second date with you."

The early days of their courtship were a lesson in perseverance and patience as I watched Mark woo Candie. Wings Falls' florist shops did a booming business in the early days of their courtship. Not that he still didn't send her flowers for no other reason than it may be a Tuesday or National Buttermilk Pancake Day. Mark is a true romantic. Hank not so much, but that was okay with me. I knew he cared, if for no other reason than he feared for my safety when I've gotten tangled up in the last two murders to occur in our quiet little upstate New York town.

Candie pointed at Flossie with ruby-painted fingernails. "Okay, let's get to the bottom of this picture and now. I've got enough complicating my life with Tommy Ray's murder, Mark's election, and our upcoming wedding. I don't need Valerie adding to it. If she wants a fight over *my* man, I'll give it to her." With her shoulders thrown back, Candie marched towards the office door.

I put a hand on Candie's arm to detain her. "Candie, wouldn't you like to have this conversation with Valerie in the privacy of this office? You know—keep it between the four of us?"

Candie shrugged off my hand. "Honey, that woman doesn't know who she is messing with. You fool with what's mine, and you have a battle on your hands. She fired the first shot, but she won't get the last one in. That's mine, along with Mark. Remember Memaw Parker's saying?"

We linked arms and chimed in together, "You don't mess with us Parkers."

Candie and I, with our arms still hooked together, marched out into the room full of campaign workers chatting away on their phones, hopefully encouraging people to vote for Mark next Tuesday. Flossie brought up the rear.

Silence descended upon the room as we made our way to Valerie's chair. Phones were suspended midway to worker's mouths, fingers poised over phone buttons. As if finally noticing the quiet that enveloped the room, Valerie looked up from her phone and spotted Candie, Flossie, and me standing behind her. She turned back to her phone and said, "I have to go, Mark. I'll call back later." She swiveled in her chair to face us. "Is something the matter?"

More than Valerie's attitude had changed. Gone was her polyester wardrobe from Saturday night. Today she wore a pair of snug jeans and a bust-hugging tank top. I blinked at the transformation. I hadn't noticed it when she first entered the headquarters, but now that I stood next to her, she looked quite stunning. She had even made up her eyes with a shimmery bronze eye shadow that complimented her skin and dark hair coloring. Was this all to attract Mark? And why change her appearance so late in the campaign? She'd been working for Mark for months now, and she'd never worn make-up or changed her wardrobe from her baggie polyester pants and tops to the form-fitting clothes she was now wearing. Was she getting desperate, since Candie and Mark's wedding was fast approaching? Was she afraid her chance of hooking up with Mark was quickly slipping away?

"You could say there is a slight problem." Candie held out her hand to Flossie. "Your phone please, Flossie."

A smirk crossed Flossie's lips as she gave her phone over to Candie. She seemed to be enjoying this confrontation between Candie and Valerie a little too much, I thought. What was in this for Flossie? She didn't have any designs on Mark as far as I knew. She did want Candie's job as Mark's secretary. But that was only a part-time position. How could she live on the salary the city paid her? I imagine she would have to find additional employment elsewhere to make ends meet. The job fitted Candie fine because she had her income from the romance novels she wrote to supplement her needs.

Valerie's bronzed eyelids widened. She started to stutter. "W-w-where did you get that?" She quickly regained her composure and grabbed at the phone. "That picture is private property. Did you hack into my phone?" She glared at Candie then turned her "if looks could kill" vision on Flossie and me.

Candie's quick reflexes pulled the phone out of Valerie's reach. She turned the photo in question to her and tapped the screen. "That's not the question of the hour, hussy. I want to know why you have your lips locked on to *my* Mark in this selfie you obviously took of the two of you in his office over there." Candie pointed to the headquarters office.

Valerie waved a hand in front of her face as if to dismiss Candie's question. "Don't be silly. I was only showing Mark my gratitude for a favor he did for my dad's construction business. Mark was able to cut through some red tape my father was having with the bureaucrats in Albany. You know how they are—paperwork, paperwork, paperwork. You call down there, and they pass you from one agency to another."

I had to agree. Even with my ex, George's, and my funeral business, there were times that we had to deal with the government when burying a body. People sometimes had strange requests as to where they wanted to bury their loved ones. It wasn't like they could dump their ashes into Lake George, no matter how many summers they vacationed on the lake when they were alive. There were strict regulations we had to follow.

"Why were you speaking to him on the phone a few minutes ago?" Candie's fingers still white knuckled Flossie's phone. She wasn't going to dismiss the photo so easily.

"I wanted to give him an update on how grateful my father is for all that Mark did. That's all." Valerie shot sad eyes at us.

Did I believe her? I wasn't sure, but her explanation was plausible. I did understand how difficult it could be dealing with government agencies, no matter how big or small.

The red suffusing Candie's face moments before was slowly starting to recede. She handed Flossie back her phone. "Next time you want to express your gratitude to Mark, send him a Hallmark card."

Valerie hung her head and nodded. She looked properly chastised.

With Candie's mission accomplished, she and I turned to walk back to the office. All eyes followed us as we made our way past the workers. Flossie moved to a seat farther down the row from Valerie. I could only imagine how cold the air would be between the two of them now that Flossie had ratted Valerie out.

Before we reached the office door, Candie turned back to the room. "And Valerie…"

Valerie gazed up from her phone at Candie.

"Delete that picture from your phone. *My* phone is the only place where his photo resides."

Valerie ran her fingers through her short hair and nodded in return.

"Okay, folks, the show's over. Time to get to the phones."

The campaign workers snapped back to punching numbers into their phones at Candie's statement.

Candie sank into a chair and heaved a sigh when we closed the office door behind us. I knew that while my cousin was a strong woman, she hated confrontation. But she would do what she had to in order to defend her own. And Mark was hers. Weariness weighed down her shoulders.

I leaned down and gathered her into a hug. "It's over now, sweetie. You said your piece, and Valerie understands that it's hands off where Mark is concerned."

Candie looked up at me. Tears rimmed her violet eyes. "Do you really think so?"

CHAPTER TWENTY-SIX

———

At the sound of Candie's sniffles, Porkchop raised his head. He had been snoozing on the floor in a corner of Mark's office and had slept through all the commotion in the call center of the headquarters. He stretched his long body and walked over to Candie. My precious dog stood on his hind legs and placed his head on Candie's lap. He lovingly gave her hand doggie kisses.

Candie reached down and patted the top of his round, reddish-brown head. "You are such a sweetie, Porkie. I love you, too." Porkchop nestled his head into her hand. Candie raised her eyes and gave me a tremulous smile. "He's like my Dixie. They know when we humans are hurting and want to comfort us. I think we are way better because of their unquestioning love. All our pets want are a full tummy and a warm place to sleep. In return, they give us unconditional love. Maybe I should give up on humans and stick with Dixie? She certainly won't betray me, ever."

I sat bolt upright in my chair. Porkchop looked from me to Candie. He could sense that I was becoming agitated. "Candie, what are you talking about? Who would betray you?"

"Mark" was her one-word answer. Tears streamed down her face as she drew in hiccupping sobs.

"What! What are you talking about? Mark loves you." I hoped the workers in the other room hadn't heard my screech.

I jumped out of my chair and knelt beside Candie. Porkchop was on one side of her and I on the other. I gathered her into my arms. My cousin's body shook with her sobs. Porkchop let out a soft whine that I was sure was his way of trying to comfort her.

"Didn't you hear Valerie talking to Mark on the phone when we first approached her? She seemed pretty cozy in their conversation," Candie gasped out between sobs.

"Yes, I heard her mention Mark's name, but she said it had to do with Mark helping her father with some red tape concerning his construction company."

Candie nodded. "Okay, but why couldn't she talk to him about it here at the campaign headquarters? Why did she have to call him on the phone? And why does she have his personal phone number?"

I had to agree with Candie, these were all very valid questions. Ones I would want an answer to, also.

Candie sat and idly stroked Porkchop's sleek fur. "Maybe Mark thinks I'm too much of a liability to his career and his campaign for mayor."

I leaned back on my heels and shook a finger at her. "Candie, hush your mouth. If I were Memaw Parker right now, I'd be threatening to wash it out with soap. Mark thinks no such thing."

A tremulous smile spread across Candie's lips.

I leaned up and brushed a tear off her cheek. "Do you think that after all Mark went through for the last five years to win your heart that he's going to give up on you?"

Candie's auburn curls bounced about her face as she shook her head. "I'm praying he doesn't. My life was just about perfect until this past Sunday morning. Mark was going to win the primary, despite all of nasty Bret Hargrove's dirty tricks, and I was going to marry the love of my life." Candie heaved a large sigh. Despair etched her face.

It was time for some tough love. I placed my fingers under Candie's chin and raised it so she was looking me in the eye. "Now listen here, missy. I'll have no more talk like that. There is no more 'was' about it. Mark *will* win the primary. He's the greatest mayor Wings Falls has had in ages, and the people of this town know it. You *will* walk down the aisle at Saint Anthony's in a week and a half and marry the love of your life—Mark. I didn't get poked and prodded at all those dress fittings at Sylvia's Bridal Salon on my bridesmaid dress for nothing. Finally, look at poor Porkchop there. You promised him he could be your ring bearer. Look at those eyes." I tilted Porkchop's head up so Candie could get the full effect of his Hershey-brown eyes. "Are you willing to disappoint my sweet pup? He's been practicing almost every night walking up and down my hallway with the ring pillow strapped around his body. It's all I could come up with to replicate the church's aisle."

Candie laughed and hugged Porkchop closer to her. "No, you're right. I'm wallowing in my own misery. I need to snap out of it and figure out who really did murder Tommy Ray."

I nodded. "You're right. I know Hank is doing all he can to solve this murder, but a little help from the Sleuth Cousins wouldn't hurt."

"But he's not going to like you interfering. You know how upset he was when we poked our noses in the last two murders we were involved in," Candie said.

I waved a hand in front of my face to dismiss what Candie had said. "Who said I'd be interfering. He can conduct his own investigation, and we'll do a little of our own. Now hand me my purse so I can get out the piece of paper we wrote down our list of suspects on. And in case Hank forgot, we did solve those two murders for him."

Candie smiled then placed Porkchop on the floor at our feet. "You did help discover who killed the animal shelter owner, and if it wasn't for your fine detective work, Hilda Pratt's murder in the spring at the hook-in may not have been solved."

I wiggled my fingers at Candie. "My purse, please."

Candie scrunched up her freckled nose and stuck her tongue out. "Bossy."

"Just give it to me. We have work to do. Now what did Mrs. Splotz say about Sunday morning and the voices she heard coming from your balcony?"

Candie tapped a finger against the side of her head. "Okay, let's review what we have. According to Mrs. Splotz, it was a party on my balcony, so many people were coming and going."

"We have a pretty good idea who some of them are. We only have to figure out which one pulled the trigger on the nail gun and killed him." I shivered at that thought.

Candie pointed to the piece of paper I held in my hand. "Put Bret Hargrove on the top of that list. He has the most to lose. From what his employee, Bruce, at The Sound Machine said, it sounds like Bret is in deep financial doo-doo. He needs to win the mayoral race in November so he can award building contracts to that Tony Riglio from New York City. He would be pretty desperate, I'd think. Those guys from New York City play for keeps. If Bret got mixed up with them, he'd be the small potatoes I imagine the big city boys wouldn't hesitate twice about mashing."

I picked a pen off the desk and underlined Bret's name. "You're right. Bret's in way over his head and, I imagine, would do anything to win this primary. Mrs. Splotz mentioned a fancy-dressed woman in high heels. I'm going to guess that's Babs. What lengths do you think she'd go to win her 'Markie' back?"

Candie shrugged. "Beats me. You know the old saying about a woman scorned being madder than a wet hen."

I laughed. "Well, that is a broad translation of that biblical saying."

Candie stuck her tongue out at me. "Smartie pants."

I laughed. "I'll add her to the suspect list. Who knows. She may be more desperate to win Mark back than we know. After all, why would she come to Wings Falls? Our quiet little town certainly won't live up to her social standards."

Candie nodded. "Don't forget Dan Brewer and the mystery woman. He obviously came to town to find Tommy Ray. That whole thing about wanting to meet Flossie is a big lie. He used her as an excuse to come to Wings Falls and not look suspicious."

"I agree. And if he lied about why he really was in town, would he kill Tommy Ray? He certainly was mad enough when we questioned him about why he was here. Who could that mystery woman be, the one who looks like you? The one Valerie saw getting in the Ford Escape with Dan a few minutes ago."

I rubbed my forehead. All this trying to find a murderer was starting to give me a headache. "There was one more person who visited Tommy Ray on Sunday morning—the person who went to Mark's campaign rallies. That could be anyone in Wings Falls. How will we narrow down that person's identity?"

"Hello, ladies."

Porkchop barked and wagged his tail. Candie and I looked up from the piece of paper we'd written our suspects on. Mark and Hank stood framed in the office's doorway.

"What are you up to?" Hank asked with a devilish look in his eye.

I smiled and swept the piece of paper back into my purse. "Oh, you know, campaign business."

"Uh-huh," he said, stepping into the room with Mark, who only had eyes for Candie.

We both stood and walked over to the loves of our lives. I slipped my arms around Hank as he entered the room. Happiness filled me, knowing we had resolved our differences, kind of, about my helping to prove Candie innocent of Tommy Ray's murder. He pulled me close and placed a kiss on the top of my head. He then bent and scratched the top of Porkchop's head.

"Anyone up for some barbeque at The Smiling Pig?" Mark asked.

"Yes!" Candie and I both said at once.

"Then it's a date. Let's get going." Mark pointed to the door.

I blinked and looked at my watch. The phone room was empty, and it was dark outside the headquarters. Where had the day gone? It was after five. "I need to take Porkchop home first and feed him his dinner."

"Okay, we'll follow you home. You get your pup settled. Then we'll have a nice, relaxing dinner and forget about all the turmoil from this past weekend," Mark said as he handed Candie her purse.

I only wish that was how the night had ended.

CHAPTER TWENTY-SEVEN

The heat of the day had chilled as we entered The Smiling Pig, necessitating a light jacket. The scent of barbequed meat enveloped us. Saliva flowed in my mouth as my stomach thought it had gone to heaven, anticipating what I was going to send its way.

"Hi, guys. Here for some of Clint's tasty barbeque?"

I turned to see Marybeth Higgins hugging an armload of plastic-coated menus to her petite body. Her long brown hair was pulled back into a ponytail. A smile spread across her face, and her eyes sparkled with excitement.

I returned her smile. "Hi, Marybeth. The whole town is raving about your brother's barbeque. We thought we'd see what all the excitement was all about. Right?" I asked Hank, Candie, and Mark. The three of them nodded in unison.

"I don't know. I've got some pretty high standards when it comes to barbeque."

"How's that?" Marybeth frowned at Candie's statement. She laid the menus on the hostess stand and placed her hands on her narrow hips. "I know you Southerners think you've got the barbeque market cornered, but Clint's will give any of your Southern recipes a run for its money."

Candie fidgeted with the strap of her purse. I couldn't believe my bold cousin was actually a little nervous. "Oh, never mind. I should know when to keep my thoughts to myself."

Like that would ever happen!

"No, no. I want to know who our competition is. It's best to know what we are up against." Marybeth wasn't about to back down from what I believed she thought was a challenge to her brother's cuisine.

Candie glanced up at Mark. "Umm, someone from my past." She looked back at Marybeth. "Well, it's no secret that I've been engaged a few times."

I laughed. "Yeah, that's like saying the Grand Canyon is a rut."

Candie poked me in the ribs. Luckily, my purse for the evening, my raspberry pink Kate Spade, blocked her jab, and it had no effect on me.

"Anyway, if Miss Smartie Mouth here will let me finish, one of my fiancés owned a barbeque joint in Tennessee, and folks came from all over the state to dine on his sandwiches, chicken, and ribs." Her violet eyes sought Mark's face. "I'm sorry, sugar, for mentioning him. You know you're the one who owns my heart."

Mark pulled Candie into a hug and kissed her forehead. "Don't give it another thought. I'm the one you're marrying in less than two weeks. Your past is what made you the wonderful gal you are today. I'm the luckiest fellow on earth."

Candie giggled and snuggled closer to Mark. "Don't y'all see what a gem I have here?"

I rolled my eyes. "Okay, you two lovebirds. I'm starving. You can carry on with your canoodling after I've eaten."

Hank grabbed my hand and whispered into my ear, "Canoodling? I like the sound of that. Care to do any later on?"

Heat shot through my body from the touch of his breath on my neck. I smiled up into his crystal-blue eyes. "I think that could be arranged."

"Anyplace special you'd like to sit?"

Marybeth's question yanked me back from my thoughts of Hank and me snuggling later on my sofa. "What? Oh, yeah, How about near that yummy fire crackling in the fireplace?"

"You're in luck. A couple finished at that table a few minutes before you came in. With the weather we're having, it's been a popular place to dine this evening. That's weather in the North Country—we sweat during the day and need sweaters at night."

We all laughed as Marybeth led the way to the vacant table.

As we trailed behind Marybeth, patrons called out, "Hi Mark."

"How's the campaign going?"

"You've got my vote next Tuesday."

Mark responded to each well-wisher with a "Thank you" and a handshake. He didn't take one vote for granted.

"Here you go." Marybeth placed the menus on the rustic pine table. "Take your time, and I'll let your waitress know you're here."

We all thanked her and shed our light jackets over the back of the hickory chairs. Hank helped me out of mine, and Mark helped Candie with hers. Our Memaw Parker must be smiling down from heaven right now at the good manners our fellows were showing us. I hung my purse on top of my jacket. We picked up our menus to peruse the restaurant's offerings.

"Oh, my. I don't know if I can make up my mind between the brisket, the pulled pork, or the chicken," I lamented. "My taste buds are calling out for a taste of all of it."

Candie tapped on her menu. "Lookie here. Why don't you try their sampler platter? Then you won't have to decide. You can take a taste of everything."

"That sounds like the perfect solution to satisfying my barbeque cravings." I rubbed my hands together in anticipation of my meal.

"I think I'll second you on that order," Hank said, closing his menu and laying it on the table.

Mark laughed and placed his menu in front of himself. "I'll third that."

"Well. I'm not going to be the odd man, or should I say woman, out. I'll fourth that order," Candie placed her menu on top of Mark's.

We all laughed. At least we were going to make this an easy order for our waitress. Speaking of which, she approached our table. Her name was Shiloh, according to the tag pinned to her denim shirt. The wait staff had no formal uniform, from what I saw circulating the room. Shiloh wore a light-blue denim shirt that she'd paired with jeans and red Crocs. I had thought that my hair was curly, but her curl factor far surpassed mine. A blue headband pulled the curls away from her face.

She pulled an order pad out of the pocket of the short black apron tied around her tiny waist. I'd kill for a waist that small, one I hadn't possessed in years and, after tonight's meal, would never see again in my lifetime. "Had enough time with the menu?"

I tapped my menu. "You make deciding what to eat really hard. I want to try everything. So, we're all going with the sampler platter."

Shiloh jotted our order down on the pad. "Good decision. I don't think you'll be disappointed. What do you want to drink with your meal?"

Hank spoke up. "Do you have Trails Head beer on tap?"

Shiloh nodded. "Yes, we do. Anyone else want one?"

We all added a Trails Head to our order. Shiloh flipped her order pad closed and said she'd be back in a few minutes with our beers.

When she left our table, I leaned back in my chair and took in the restaurant's décor. The room was filled with pine-topped tables surrounded by hickory chairs, a style popular in the Adirondacks. The walls were covered with rough-cut barn wood siding that was stained a soft gray. A bar hugged the wall opposite our table. You could see beyond it to the kitchen, where meat smokers and open barbeque pits worked their magic. The aromas floating out of the kitchen were divine.

Neon signs of *Hot Meat*, pigs, and chickens decorated the walls. I had to laugh at the neon sign proclaiming *No Meat, No Life*. Happy customers enjoying their meals filled every table.

"From the looks of the crowd, we're lucky to have gotten a table," Mark said.

Candie hooked her arm through Mark's. "You're right, sugar. This place sure is busy—and for a Tuesday night. I can't imagine what a weekend night would be like."

"I've heard there is a waiting line out the door on Saturday nights," Hank said.

"You're probably right." I glanced around the room. My eyes widened as they came to rest on the person standing at the front door waiting to be seated. Oh, no. So much for the hope this was going to be a peaceful meal.

CHAPTER TWENTY-EIGHT

———

I nudged Hank's arm and nodded towards the door. Mark and Candie sat with their backs to the door, so they didn't notice the new party that had entered The Smiling Pig.

"What? What's up?" Candie swiveled in her chair to see the object of my attention. "Ugh. I think I have indigestion. And I was really looking forward to some of Clint's delicious barbeque."

"Sweetheart, what are you talking about?" Mark turned to see the cause of Candie's sudden upset stomach. He slid his arm across her shoulders. "Don't give them another thought. We're here to relax with our good friends and enjoy our meal."

"Mark's right, Candie. We'll pretend they aren't even here." My brow furrowed. "He's married, right? Is that mousy-looking woman clinging onto his arm his wife? Why is Babs with them?"

Mark nodded. "That's Ashley. His long-suffering wife. Beats me why Babs is with him. There've been rumors about his having affairs, but he's never paraded them around town before. But from my unfortunate past experience with Babs, I wouldn't put anything past her," he said, referring to his brief marriage to Babs when he was a young, struggling lawyer.

Babs stood next to Bret with her arm entwined with his. She looked a little too chummy if you asked me.

We were distracted from the scene at the front door by Shiloh delivering the beers we had ordered to our table. She informed us that our platters would be up in a few minutes. I took a sip of my Trails Head and closed my eyes. The mellow brew slid down my throat and eased away all of the tension that had taken hold of my body since Sunday when Candie discovered Tommy Ray's body.

Hank leaned towards me. "Do you want to be left alone with your beer?"

Candie and Mark laughed.

I flipped open my eyes and blushed. "Was it that obvious I was enjoying it?"

Candie reached across the table and squeezed my hand. "Sweetie, if I didn't know better, I'd say you were thinking of what you and Hank would be doing after we leave here."

My cheeks got hotter. "Candie! Although, that would have been nice. But no, this beer—" I held the bottle up in front of me "—erased some of the tension I've been feeling since Sunday morning."

"Right about now, I'd need a whole case of beer to ease my woes, but I don't fancy the headache I'd have afterwards plus the inches it would put on my waistline. My wedding dress would be tighter than an Olympic swimmer's spandex."

We all laughed at Candie's colorful description of her dress.

"Sweetheart, you'll be the most beautiful bride who ever walked down the aisle at Saint Anthony's." Mark kissed Candie's smooth cheek.

"I'll toast to that." I raised my beer bottle to my lips.

"I hope you're not doing any premature celebrating, folks. Mayor, your little lady here might be spending your honeymoon in the county jail." Bret slapped Mark on the back, causing beer to spill down the front of Mark's gray and black–striped shirt.

Babs, still latched on to Bret's arm, wore jeans so tight I wondered how she could possibly sit in them. She'd topped them with a red blouse that let a person know her triple Ds were front and center. She laughed at Bret's remark and playfully swatted his arm. "Oh, Bret, you are so funny. Isn't he, Ashley?" She moved closer to Mark. "Markie, I'm sorry you didn't take advantage of all of my assets and how valuable I could be to your campaign. Luckily, Bret did, and he's hired me as a consultant for his campaign. Isn't that right, Mr. Future Mayor?" She flashed him a megawatt smile.

Unlike Babs, Ashley looked worn out and drab—drab skin, drab hair, and drab clothes.

"I think we should follow the hostess to our table," Ashley said in a voice barely above a whisper.

Marybeth stood nearby, nervously fingering a stack of menus.

Mark rose from his seat and was mere inches from Bret. "That's good advice, Mrs. Hargrove. You should pay attention to her, Bret. Good evening, Babs."

Babs reached over and traced her inch-long ruby-red fingernails down Mark's face. Candie shot up out of her chair and pushed Babs's hand away. "Look, you hussy, keep your hands to yourself."

All eyes in the restaurant were now trained on us. Diners had their phones poised midair, recording the events at our table.

I rolled my eyes towards the ceiling. *Great! What happened to what I hoped would be a peaceful night out eating barbeque? This is turning into a circus.*

I whispered to Hank, "Please, do something before some blood is spilled." If not by Mark decking Bret, then by either Candie or me punching Babs in her cosmetically sculpted nose.

Hank stood. "Mr. Hargrove, I think it would be in everyone's best interest to continue on to your table."

Bret sucked in a deep breath. "If you say so, Officer."

"I say so." Hank motioned towards Marybeth.

"Please follow me," she said in a shaky voice.

My heart went out to her. She was extremely shy, and I could tell by her shaking hands that this incident rattled her.

Before departing our table, Babs leaned over and kissed Mark's cheek. "That's to remember me by, Markie."

Candie balled up her fist and pulled back her arm. I reached over the table and grabbed her arm before she could lay a good one on Babs. Not that I could blame her, but with all the phones in the restaurant recording what was going on at our table, I didn't think it was a picture either Candie or Mark wanted in the morning paper or spread across Facebook.

"Your girlfriend has quite the temper, Mark. Are you sure she didn't kill Tommy Ray?" Bret called over his shoulder as he and his party followed Marybeth.

Candie sank back into her chair. "I'm so mad I could chew nails and spit out a barbed wire fence. I can only imagine the type of consulting she's doing."

Despite the tense situation we had endured, thanks to Babs and Bret, I had to laugh. My Southern cousin had a way of expressing herself.

"Hi, folks. I hope I have your vote next Tuesday. I'm the man to bring change to Wings Falls."

I watched as Bret campaigned on his way to his table. He passed out flyers he dug from the back pocket of his jeans and shook hands with the people trying to enjoy their meals. A few diners took his brochures, but most people ignored him and continued eating their meal.

"You folks ready to enjoy the best barbeque in town?"

"Shiloh, I didn't hear you. We were a little distracted by one of the customers." I sat back in my seat so she could place my order in front of me.

Shiloh shook her head. "That man's a menace to Wings Falls." She finished placing the other platters of barbeque on the table.

I frowned at her statement. "What do you mean by that?"

"He's not the first politician I've heard promise a town the moon and then take the taxpayer's money to line their own pocket. The same thing happened where I lived before moving here, and it led to all kinds of corruption and people losing their savings. The people of Wings Falls better not be taken in by Mr. Hargrove's fancy talk. But that's enough of my opinion. Enjoy your meal, folks." Shiloh waved and walked over to the table next to us, who wanted another round of beer.

I watched her retreating then turned to my table. I shook my head. "Bret really wants to be Wings Falls' next mayor. Do you think he could have killed Tommy Ray to get information that would guarantee him winning the election?"

"We're not ruling him out as a suspect. He certainly has the most to gain by implicating Candie in Tommy Ray's murder," Hank said, slicing off a piece of chicken from the plump breast on his plate.

Candie dabbed at her lips to remove any sauce that may have landed there. "His throwing the suspicion of murder on me certainly could give him an advantage at the polls. Who would want their mayor married to a murderer?"

Mark patted Candie's arm. "Now, sweetie, I know you didn't have anything to do with Tommy Ray's death, and Hank here is going to prove it. He'll arrest the killer."

Tears formed on Candie's eyelashes. "I hope it won't be too late. The election is only a few days away."

"I'll arrest the murderer. Don't worry, Candie. Remember, I rented that monkey suit—I mean tux—for your wedding. I'm not going to let it go to waste." Hank smiled and bit into his chicken.

"You might want to ask some questions of Dan Brewer and why he's in Wings Falls," I said.

Hank picked up the pulled pork sandwich lying next to the chicken on his plate. "Why's that?"

I swallowed a bite of my chicken. "Remember Mrs. Splotz?"

He nodded. "What does she have to do with all of this?"

"She mentioned that one of the people visiting Tommy Ray had a Southern accent. Well, Dan was at Mark's campaign headquarters today, and Candie asked him a few questions about why he was in Wings Falls. He got a little agitated and let a Southern accent escape." I related to him our conversation with Flossie, too.

Hank put down the sandwich he had raised to his lips. "Dan Brewer, hmmm? Interesting."

CHAPTER TWENTY-NINE

———

Mark wiped his mouth with a barbeque sauce–stained paper napkin and patted his stomach. "Well, the rumors are true."

I took one last bite of my pulled pork sandwich then swallowed. If I wasn't out in public, I'd be licking my fingers to savor every last drop of the sauce smothering my sandwich. "What rumors? You're not referring to Tommy Ray's murder, are you?"

Mark shook his head. "No. I'm talking about how delicious Clint's barbeque is. Ever since he opened The Smiling Pig this spring, I've heard that it is the best around. People weren't exaggerating when they made that comment." Mark pointed to his empty plate. "This is, by far, the best I've ever tasted."

Candie dabbed at the corners of her mouth with her napkin. "I certainly don't mean to be disloyal to my Southern kin, but I have to agree with you, Mark. I'm so full I'm about to pop."

The theme from *Star Wars* resonated from Mark's shirt pocket. He put down his beer and retrieved his phone. A frown creased his forehead.

Candie placed her hand on Mark's arm. "Sugar, what's the matter?"

"It's Oliver, the elderly man who lives in the apartment next to mine. What could he be calling me about?" Mark said.

Hank set his beer bottle next to his plate. "There's one way to find out. Answer it."

Mark laughed. "Brilliant suggestion." He swiped his finger across the surface of his phone.

"What? You've got to be kidding. Tell Peters I'll be right there. He'd better not get crazy and knock my door down." Mark disconnected and looked up at us.

The three of us shot quizzical glances at Mark.

Hank was the first one to ask about Mark's phone call. "What was that all about? Why is Peters at your apartment?"

"I haven't got a clue. Oliver only said that he was banging on my door, asking me to open up. He has two other officers with him." Mark turned to Candie. "I'm sorry to cut this night short, but I've got to get home and see what Sergeant Peters is up to. Hank, can you drop Candie at her house?"

Candie sat up straight in her chair. "Sweetie, you're not going to face Peters by yourself. I can feel it in my bones, and I know this has to do with Tommy Ray's murder. I'm coming with you. I'd trust a snake slithering in the grass more than that man. I'm the reason he's pounding on your door."

"But Candie…"

"There's no buts about it, Mark. I'm coming." Candie reached behind her and gathered her purse and jacket off the back of her chair.

A smile split my lips. Mark had better give up the argument right now. When my cousin made up her mind, there was no way of stopping her. "I couldn't have phrased it better myself. You'd be insulting the whole snake population by comparing him to one of them."

"Mark, you and Candie head on out. I'll take care of the bill." Hank motioned for Shiloh, who was clearing the table next to us, to come over.

"You sure?" Mark asked as he placed his phone back into his pocket.

"Yeah, get going before Peters busts your door down. I'll be along in a few minutes to see what he's up to." Hank reached into the back pocket of his snug jeans for his wallet.

"Thanks, man. We'll settle up later." Mark placed his napkin on the table then stood. He helped Candie out of her chair.

I stood and reached over to hug Candie goodbye. "Everything will be all right," I whispered into her ear.

Tears started to form on her eyelashes. "I hope you're right, but I have a nasty feeling that this is all my fault."

I gave her a squeeze. "Hush. As Memaw Parker would say, 'Don't go borrowing trouble.'"

A smile trembled on her lips. "I'll try not to, Memaw."

After Mark and Candie left, Shiloh appeared with our bill. Hank paid for our meals, and I grabbed my jacket. I glanced towards Bret Hargrove's table and saw him leering at me as I headed towards the door. Did he really just lift his beer in my direction?

As we settled into Hank's Jeep, I turned in my seat towards him. "What do you think Peters is up to at Mark's apartment?"

Hank shrugged his shoulders then placed the car key into the ignition. It roared to life, and we pulled out of The Smiling Pig's parking lot. "Your guess is as good as mine. Nothing was mentioned at the station for the police to go to Mark's place. But I don't put anything past him. He's bucking for a promotion, so who knows what he'd do."

My blood was boiling. I pounded the armrest that sat between us. "Promotion? That idiot! I'm surprised he made sergeant." Would he try to make rank off the good reputation of my cousin and the mayor? How low would he sink? Candie was right… Comparing him to a snake did a major injustice to the reptile family.

* * *

Fifteen minutes later, Hank pulled his Jeep into the parking lot of Mark's apartment complex. For years, Mark had led a simple bachelor life. Content to live in a two-bedroom apartment, that is until he met and fell in love with Candie. Now they were going to share her purple-painted Victorian home. The home that Candie had been having her late ex-fiancé, Tommy Ray, rehab. She felt that it needed to be "just right" for the two of them to begin their married life together—giving the house's gingerbread trim a fresh coat of white paint, replacing the house's front steps, and of course, that fatal last job of fixing the railing on the balcony that led off the master bedroom. Mark had told her not to bother, but Candie wouldn't hear of it. Things had to be perfect for the lovebirds.

Mark's apartment consisted of two bedrooms, so he'd insisted that Tommy Ray bunk in with him. He'd said it was the least he could do if Candie was footing the bill for the renovation costs. Tommy Ray had given her a break on his bill because the room was provided for him.

Two cruisers sat outside Mark's apartment. The light bars on top of the cars sent eerie red flashes up the sides of the apartment building. Their color reflected off the tenants' windows. The red glow shot a chill through me. A vision of Tommy Ray's blood, spilled out on the floor of Candie's balcony, floated before my eyes.

Hank pushed open the driver's-side door of his Jeep. "Stay here while I find out what Peters is up to."

I watched as Hank walked towards Mark, Peters, and two other officers. Tenants from the apartment complex huddled in the small parking lot in front of Mark's apartment door. They clutched their coats and robes to their bodies to ward off the chill evening air. With their heads together and hands gesturing towards the police cars, I was sure they were talking about the excitement that was unfolding before them. A knock on my passenger-side window startled me out of my reverie. Candie stood next to Hank's car with tears streaming down her face.

I opened my door and stepped out of the car into the chilly night air. I gathered her into my arms.

Between hiccupping sobs, Candie said, "Sam, what do you think Sergeant Peters is up to? I know this has to do with Tommy Ray's murder. This is all my doing."

"Candie, hush that kind of talk. Should we go over and see what is happening?"

"Mark told me to stay here and that he'd take care of Peters."

I stood back from her and swiped my hand across her smooth cheeks. "Since when do you take orders from anyone, even if that person is your fiancé?"

A chuckle escaped her lips. "I guess you're right. I love Mark with all my heart, but that ring on my finger doesn't change the fact that I am my own woman. I'm going to march over there right now and find out what Sergeant Peters is up to." Candie nodded and jutted out her chin. She turned towards Mark, Hank, and the other men gathered next to the building.

I reached out and grabbed her arm. "Whoa, one minute."

Candie swiveled around towards me. "What? A minute ago, you said I'm an independent woman. And as such, I'm going to ask some questions about why Peters is here."

"Yes, I did, but you're not going to do it without me."

Candie and I laughed. We linked our arms together and set off to see what had my childhood nemesis pounding on Mark's front door this late at night.

CHAPTER THIRTY

———

The sound of my shoes clicking on the sidewalk leading up to Mark's apartment pierced the night air. I gazed around at some of the senior tenants gathered in curiosity at the police activity. Gossip central was in full force. Heads filled with pink curlers or sporting bedhead huddled together.

As Candie and I approached Peters and the two officers standing with him, I recognized them as the Officers Reed and March. They had come to Candie's house on Sunday to assist with Tommy Ray's murder investigation. Both officers politely nodded and said, "Ma'am," as we took our places next to Hank and Mark.

Sergeant Peter's turned and scowled at the officers. I swear I saw an eyeroll from Officer March when Peters' back was to them. I did a mental happy dance, knowing that these young recruits were, as Yogi Bear used to say in the old cartoons, "smarter than the average bear."

Sergeant Peters stood in front of Mark with his chest puffed out. His thumbs were hooked into the top of his holster belt. I wondered if he realized his stance only made him look like he was about to topple over as his spindly legs tried to support his large upper body. "Would you rather I get a search warrant, Mr. Mayor?"

Hank stepped forward. A frown creased his forehead. "Why wasn't I informed about this search?"

A grin slashed Sergeant Peters' pudgy face. "I overheard you at the station mention you were going out to dinner tonight. I didn't want to interrupt your meal."

I couldn't hold my tongue any longer. "Sandy, I mean Joe, then you assumed that Mark was going to be dining with us also? What would you do if Mark wasn't here? Bash his door in?"

Peters fidgeted from one foot to the other. Obviously he hadn't thought his grand scheme through.

"It's okay, Sam," Mark said, trying to relieve the growing tension between Peters and me. Maybe I should have stayed in Hank's Jeep. I certainly wasn't making the situation any better.

"Sergeant, I'm assuming this has to do with Tommy Ray's murder," Candie, who to my surprise had remained silent until now, spoke up.

Peters turned his beady eyes on Candie. "We understand that the victim lived here with the mayor."

Candie nodded. "That's correct. Part of his payment for fixing up my house was a free room."

"Why did he want to take this job? You were engaged to him at one time. Wouldn't that have been a little awkward?" Peters asked.

Candie placed her hands on her hips. Oh, boy, I could see her temper rising. "As I told you on Sunday at my home and again at the police station, Tommy Ray and I may have been engaged once, but we parted on good terms and are friends. I've remained friends with all of my exes."

Peters' face turned up in a sneer. "Yeah, I bet," he mumbled under his breath.

Mark stepped forward. "Exactly what do you want to do in my apartment?"

"With your permission, we would like to search his bedroom."

I couldn't stay silent another minute. "For what?"

Peters looked down his bulbous nose at me. "Anything that we could link to his murderer."

Mark shook his head in disgust. "Why didn't you say so in the first place? Come on. Let's go inside."

Mark lived on the first floor of the two-story apartment complex. He led the way to his front door. Sergeant Peters, with Officers Reed and March, walked right behind him. Hank, Candie, and I brought up the rear.

Once at the door, Peters turned to the small crowd gathered in the chilly night air. "Show's over, folks. You can go back to your Ovaltine and cookies while I carry out official police business here."

If there was a contest for the biggest jerk of the year, Sandy—I mean Joe Peters—would win first place, hands down. Nobody would even come close to him.

Mark inserted his key in the door's lock. After opening the door, he stood back and let us all precede him into his apartment. I'd never been in his apartment before. As I looked around his small living room, I'd classify the décor as "early bachelor." Brown was the dominant color scheme—a brown and tan–plaid sofa, brown recliner, brown stained end tables with a matching coffee table in front of the sofa. This all sat on a brown shag carpet. A fifty-four-inch television hung off the wall facing the sofa. Nothing else decorated the other three walls. Moving into Candie's fancy Victorian home with its purple and white–painted gingerbread trim and overstuffed velvet furniture would be a whole new experience for him. Beyond the living room, I could see into a small but efficient kitchen with all the necessary appliances needed for preparing meals—a microwave, stove, and refrigerator. In Mark's case, take out or frozen dinners probably would have comprised his menu options. Unfortunately, I didn't think once he and Candie were married that his dining options would improve much. Memaw Parker often lamented that her one big failure in life was that Candie and I didn't follow in her culinary footsteps. Every summer Memaw won first place for her blueberry pie at Hainted Holler's summer festival.

Sergeant Peters stood in the middle of the living room with his hands on his hips. "Where's the murder victim's bedroom?"

"He had a name. Tommy Ray," Candie said.

Oh, brother. My cousin was really ticked off at Peters. "Calm down. You're not helping things. Hank will handle Peters," I whispered out the side of my mouth.

Mark pointed down a hallway that led off the living room. "Down the hall. The last room on the right. After the incident on Sunday, I closed his door and haven't opened it since. I was waiting for his next of kin to claim his belongings."

I turned to Candie. "Do you know who that would be?"

She shrugged. "I know he had a brother, but I think he passed a few years back. But other than that, I don't know what kin he still has. Until he came north to work on my house, it's been years since we've been in contact, other than our yearly Christmas cards."

I smiled. She may have been engaged eleven times before finding the true love in her life, Mark, and still friends with all her exes, but I couldn't say that other than on a business level at our funeral parlor, The Do Drop Inn, I was friendly with my ex, George. Yearly Christmas cards, not going to happen.

Hank and Mark followed Peters and the officers down the hallway. Candie and I remained in the living room.

Peters turned to Hank. "No need to bother yourself with this search, Detective Johnson."

"No bother at all, Joe. No bother at all. A little oversight won't go to waste."

Peters' jaw tightened. He wasn't thrilled to have his authority questioned, especially in front of the new officers.

After about ten minutes of sitting on the sofa in the living room listening to drawers and doors opening and slamming shut, I turned to Candie. "I can't take it anymore. I have to see what they're doing."

Candie had spent the time twisting her fingers and picking at the red nail polish on her usually perfectly manicured fingers, a sure sign she was nervous. "Me, too. Let's see what they're up to."

The two of us stood and quietly crept down the hallway. I peeked into Tommy Ray's bedroom. My eyes flew open at the sight before me. The room was a total disaster. The contents of the dresser drawers were dumped onto the floor. The clothes in the closet were thrown across the top of the bed. Lined up on the bottom of the bed were pictures of Candie and Tommy Ray from when they were engaged—some racy, others sweet and romantic.

Candie's gasp drew the officers' attention to us.

Peters stood in the middle of the room holding a small, tattered book. "So, Ms. Parker, when were you going to break your engagement to the mayor, or were you going to carry on your affair with your ex-fiancé after you married him? Was Tommy Ray Clements going to spill the beans about what you two were up to? Is that why you killed him?"

CHAPTER THIRTY-ONE

———

Candie's eyes widened in shock. "What are you talking about? I never cheated on Mark. Not once. Tommy Ray was my handyman. Hired to do some repairs on my house before Mark moved in."

Sergeant Peters tapped a dog-eared page of the small book with a pudgy finger. "It looks like your handyman kept a diary of his 'so-called' work at your house. It says here, in what I presume is your lover's own handwriting, that the two of you were enjoying yourselves in, what do they call it, the 'biblical sense' while he was fixing up your house. Was that part of his payment?"

I wanted to smack the sneer that crossed his lips right off his face, but I didn't think that would help Candie's situation.

Candie grabbed for Tommy Ray's diary, but Peters held it up out of her reach.

Mark stepped forward. "That's enough, Sergeant. What are you insinuating?"

"I'm not insinuating anything, Mayor. It says right here in black and white that your girlfriend was fooling around with the victim before he was murdered." He practically danced in his shiny black shoes with glee.

Tears streamed down Candie's cheeks. She looked up to Mark with a pleading look in her eyes. "Mark, I never did such a thing. I never would cheat on you. I love you."

Mark pulled Candie to him and kissed the top of her head. "I know you wouldn't, sweetheart."

I shook my head in disgust at what Joe Peters was doing. I feared he was taking his dislike for me out on my cousin and not looking at this investigation with an unbiased eye. "Joe, this is all Tommy Ray's side of the story. He and Candie have remained friends, despite having been engaged before. He was having troubles with his current girlfriend. In fact, I talked to a fellow named Dan

Brewer today who is in Wings Falls tracking down Tommy Ray. He said that Tommy Ray was a deadbeat dad. What if this Dan Brewer or the unknown mother killed Tommy Ray for running out on her?"

Peters shook the diary at us. "So why did he write in this diary of his that he was bopping Candie in that big ol' bed of hers?"

My mouth dropped open. I shook my head. "Maybe in his dreams he was, but Sandy—I mean Joe—I know my cousin. She would never do anything like that behind Mark's back." I couldn't contain my anger any longer. I didn't mean to call him by his hated childhood nickname, but my tongue got the better of me.

"Sergeant, we've found something that might be of interest." Officer Reed held up a bundle of what looked like old letters. A purple ribbon tied them together.

The blood drained from Candie's face. She started to sway on her feet. Mark pulled her to him for support.

Peters reached his hand out for the letters. "Let me see what you've got there, Reed."

The officer did as he was instructed and handed the bundle over to Peters. Joe extracted one of the letters from the stack and pulled violet-colored paper out of the envelope. He proceeded to silently read it.

"Oh, no. Why would he have those with him? They're over thirty years old." Candie's voice was barely above a whisper.

"What are they?" I asked.

"Love letters I wrote to Tommy Ray. When we were first engaged, he was in the Army Reserves. When he went away for his training, I'd write to him every day. I missed him so."

"I remember that. You were in love. Sergeant, any young couple in love would do that," I said to Peters.

Hank had remained silent during all of this, but I could feel his body becoming more rigid by the moment. "Joe, I know you're trying to pin Tommy Ray's murder on Candie, but you're all wrong here. If you pursue this any further, I'll testify that you're harassing her so you can get a conviction. Is the promotion you want so badly worth arresting an innocent woman?"

Peters had the decency to blush. "Detective, you're too close to the woman involved in this murder. You can't look at this case with an unbiased eye."

Hank ground his teeth. Now I knew he was really ticked off. "Peters, if I thought my own mother had killed Tommy Ray, I would have arrested her. I know by what little evidence we've collected in this case that Ms. Parker here is innocent."

"But these letters here and his diary…" Peters waved at Hank.

Hank brushed away the letters. "I don't care about some delusional scribbles of an unbalanced murder victim. I care about the facts, and the facts say that Ms. Parker is not the murderer."

I couldn't have been prouder of Hank at that moment. My heart burst with love for him and the way he spoke up for my cousin. I grabbed his hand and gave it a gentle squeeze to let him know how I felt.

Mark pointed at the letters and diary clutched in Peters' beefy fist. "If his diary and some thirty-year-old love letters are all you have found, I think your search here is finished. I'd appreciate it if you and your officers left my fiancée, my friends, and me in peace."

"But…" Peters stuttered out.

"I let you into my home in good faith and without a search warrant. Now I would like you to go. I wouldn't want Detective Johnson here to have to arrest you for trespassing." Mark nodded at Hank.

I couldn't help it. I laughed out loud. The look of rage on Peters' face was priceless. I did feel sorry for Officers Reed and March, though. Having to follow orders from such a buffoon must not be easy.

"I'm going to take this diary and the letters," Joe said, holding them up for all to see.

Mark crossed his arms. His face was flushed with anger. "Take what you want. I have nothing to hide, but please leave."

Joe Peters turned to Reed and March. "Come on, men. We're finished here. I think we've gathered enough incriminating evidence."

As Officers March and Reed left Tommy Ray's bedroom and passed by Hank, they acknowledged him with a respectful tip of their hats and a "Detective Johnson."

"Hurry up," Peters growled at them. "I want to get this evidence back to the station."

Once they had left Mark's apartment, we all settled in the living room, Candie and Mark on the sofa and Hank and me on chairs facing it. We sat in silence trying to digest what had happened to our evening. One that had started out with us dining on fabulous barbeque at The Smiling Pig.

Candie sat curled up next to Mark, silently crying. "I never knew Tommy Ray was writing that diary. It's all a lie. I thought he was involved with a woman named Darlene. At least that's what he had told me. I was only interested in the renovations he was doing to my house. I wanted it to be perfect for you, Mark, for when you moved in after we were married. Now, I don't know if that will ever happen."

Mark tilted Candie's chin up and swiped at her tears. "Now scrub that thought from your brain, sweetheart. We're getting married a week from Saturday. I don't want to hear another word about that."

"Porchop has been practicing day and night to get his ring-bearer strut perfect. You can't disappoint him," I said, thinking about my sweet doxie with the ring pillow strapped to his back, waddling down my hallway. He was going to be the hit at Candie's wedding.

A weak smile curved Candie's lips. "No, I guess I can't. If I'm not behind bars, he'll be able to strut on down the aisle before me."

We all laughed. This was my cousin rising to the occasion. Her Parker pride wouldn't allow her to be down for long.

Hank leaned forward in his chair, his fingers intertwined on his knees. "Candie, I'm not saying this will be an easy murder investigation to wrap up, but I know you're innocent, and I will do everything to prove that."

"But what about the diary and letters Sergeant Peters took with him?" I asked.

Hank leaned forward in his chair. "Those letters are what, over thirty years old? They have nothing to do with his murder on Sunday. The diary is his word against Candie's. Candie says what he wrote never happened, and there is no way to prove that it did. Candie has a spotless reputation here in Wings Falls, and that would go a long way with any judge if this ever went to court, which I don't think it will."

I picked at the arm of my chair. "This is Joe Peters trying to make a name for himself and get that promotion he wants so badly. He doesn't care who he has to walk over to get it. He's been a jerk all of his life."

Hank reached over for my hand. "I can't say I always approve of his tactics, but he is a good cop."

I held up a hand to stifle a yawn.

"Come on, Sleeping Beauty. Let me get you home before you fall asleep in that chair." Hank stood and held out his hand to me.

Mark pushed off the sofa. "Yes, you two get going. I'll look after Candie. We'll be fine."

Candie nodded. "I need some cuddling time with Mark. Thank you both for being here for me."

I bent down and hugged her, whispering in her ear, "I love you. All will be fine. Remember what Memaw Parker would say."

Together we repeated our grandmother's mantra. *"We're Parkers, and we can do anything."*

I chuckled. "That's right, and don't forget it."

We said our goodbyes and left.

*   *   *

It was a short ride from Mark's apartment to my house, only about ten minutes. Hank and I were both quiet on the trip. In fact, I started to doze off. The night's activities had exhausted me. I was jolted awake by Hank slamming on the brakes of his Jeep and emitting a curse, a word he had never said in front of me.

CHAPTER THIRTY-TWO

"What the…?" I rubbed my hands across my eyes to swipe away my sleepiness.

Hank shoved the Jeep into park and opened his door, saying, "Stay right here."

Yeah, like I was going to sit here while he investigated what had him so upset. I opened my door and went around to his side of the vehicle where he stood shaking his head. I glanced at what had caught his attention. My hands flew to my mouth. "Hank, what's happened to my lawn? And look at my mailbox. It's demolished." My dachshund-shaped mailbox lay in a smashed heap on my lawn. I walked over to it and picked up the remaining pieces. I turned to Hank. "This was a housewarming gift from my parents when they signed the house over to me." Tire tracks had chewed up my lawn. Someone had had a fine time doing circles on it. I brushed away the tears forming on my eyelids. Anger started to well up in my body. "Why would someone do this?"

Hank placed his arm around me and pulled me into the warmth of his body. He tucked me under his chin. "I don't know, but we'll find out. I'd like to blame it on a rowdy teenage prank, but with what has been going on, I'm afraid it is more serious than that."

I nodded. "No teenagers live on this street. Most of the people are my parents' age or older, like Gladys next door."

Hank turned toward Gladys's house. "A light is still on in her living room. I wonder if she saw or heard anything."

I tugged at Hank's hand. "Let's go find out. I won't be able to sleep anyway. Tonight's events have me too keyed up."

We turned and walked down my drive towards Gladys's house. I clung to Hank's hand, afraid that my shaking legs wouldn't manage the short distance.

As we climbed the wooden steps of Gladys's porch, I could hear a baseball game blaring on the television through her window.

Both Gladys and her live-in boyfriend, Frank, were hard of hearing, as the volume was turned up full blast. Someone must have scored a hit, because they were both cheering.

Hank knocked on the front door but got no response.

"You're going to have to knock harder for them to hear you." I didn't think this boded well for them hearing anything that pertained to my yard next door.

Hank shook his head and pounded on the door louder. The door rattled in its frame.

"Hold your horses. I'm coming. You don't have to knock the door down. Frank, turn the television down. We've got company," Gladys shouted.

I smiled in spite of what had happened to my front lawn. Gladys was one of a kind. A real original. The mold was certainly broken when she was born.

The door opened. Gladys stood dressed in a green and orange–plaid cotton robe tied at her waist. Her purple curls were wrapped in a red silk scarf. Fuzzy pink bunny slippers encased her feet. Their noses poked out from underneath her robe. "Hank and Sam? What are you doing here this late at night? What's happened?"

"Evening, Aunt Gladys. I was wondering if I could ask you a couple of questions?"

"Why of course, Hank. Don't stand out there letting the mosquitoes eat you alive. Come in out of the dark. Frank and I were only watching a baseball game on television. Frank gets so caught up in them. I watch to keep him company."

I smiled. Only minutes before she was shouting as loud as Frank when a hit was made.

Frank shuffled into the entryway. "Who are you talking to, honey buns? Oh, hi Hank and Sam. What's got you two out this time of night?"

I had to bite the inside of my cheek to keep from laughing. Frank stood before us wearing a navy-blue robe with Superman's "S" emblazoned across his chest. His stick-thin hairy legs poking out below the robe ended, with his feet encased in Minion slippers. Their googly eyes bounced around when his feet moved.

Hank was the first to speak. "Hi, Frank. I was dropping Sam off at home. When we pulled into her driveway, we noticed damage to her front lawn. I was wondering if you two saw anything unusual this evening or heard any ruckus coming from next door?"

"Let me see what damage was done." Gladys flipped on her porch light as we stepped outside. Her wrinkled hand flew to her mouth. "Oh, my. How terrible. We were enjoying a baseball game on the television. I'm afraid Frank here is a little hard of hearing, so we had the volume up a wee bit."

It was all I could do not to roll my eyes. Gladys was as hard of hearing, if not more than, as Frank. Every spring when she threw her windows open, most of the neighborhood could hear her police scanner blaring.

Frank shook his head in disbelief. "Do you think it was some crazy teenagers out for a little fun?"

"I can think of a lot better ways to have fun than tearing up a person's lawn. They should be home, playing on their Xboxes or whatever teens do today."

My dander was rising by the minute. Are kids so different than in my teenage days? If I did something like this, I'd first have to face my parents' punishment, but then when summer came, and I went to Hainted Holler to visit Memaw Parker, the look of disappointment on her face would be worse than anything my parents could have doled out to me.

Gladys extended a thin finger toward my yard. "Oh, look! Your poor dachshund mailbox was knocked down, too."

I nodded. "Yes, I think I'm more upset about that than anything else. Mom and Dad gave it to me as a housewarming present when I first moved back in."

Gladys slipped an arm through Frank's. She fingered the collar of his Superman robe. "My Frank here is really handy. I bet he could build you another one like the one that was destroyed. Right, pookie bear?"

"Really, Frank? I would appreciate that," I said.

Frank squeezed Gladys's arm. "No problem. I'll start on it tomorrow and have another whipped up in no time."

Hank motioned to the red brick Cape Cod across from my rancher. "We don't want to take up any more of your time. I want to stop across the street and ask if those folks saw or heard anything."

I didn't know the young couple living there, as they moved in only a few weeks ago. I needed to call on the Pillsbury Dough Boy and whip up a batch of brownies and welcome them to the neighborhood.

Gladys nodded towards the house in question. "Oh, they wouldn't have seen anything. They've gone to visit her parents for a few days. Her dad has some health issue, and they went to help her mom out."

Why wasn't I surprised she knew this? My house sat on a large lot, over an acre, surrounded by large trees and shrubs that secluded it from all the other houses on the street. I doubted that anyone else would have seen the vehicle that carved up my lawn.

I was afraid this was a mystery that wouldn't get solved. "Thank you, Gladys and Frank. We'll let you get back to the baseball game. I hope your team wins. Come on, Hank. I think I'll have to chalk this up to a bunch of teenagers out for a joy ride."

Hank held my hand as we walked back to my house. "Sam, I'm not convinced this is a carload of teens getting their jollies driving all over your lawn."

My head snapped up. "Do you think it could have anything to do with Tommy Ray's murder?

"I'm not ruling anything out," Hank replied.

CHAPTER THIRTY-THREE

———

As we walked back to my house, I mulled over Hank's words. "Why do you think whoever took a joy ride on my lawn is involved with Tommy Ray's murder and not someone turfing up a lawn for kicks?"

Hank wrapped his strong arm around my shoulder. "I'm not saying it couldn't be, but I'm not ruling out someone trying to send you a message, too."

I looked up at him and frowned. "A message?" A chill shot through me again, and it wasn't from the cooling night air.

Hank gently massaged the back of my neck, easing the tension I didn't realize was gathered there. "Yeah, like *keep your pretty nose out of investigating Tommy Ray's murder*."

I had to smile. "Do you remember the first time you said that to me?"

Hank looked down at me. A frown creased his brow. "Said what?"

A chuckle escaped me as I thought back to almost a year and a half ago. "Don't you remember when I got involved with the murder of Calvin Perkins, the pet shelter owner? You told me, and I quote, 'stop poking your pretty little nose into things.'"

Hank laughed, too. "Yeah, I seem to remember saying that, but you didn't listen to me then, and I don't think you are going to listen to me now. Am I right?"

I cleared my throat, reluctant to answer his question. "Weeelll…"

"I thought so. I'll just hope your pretty little nose doesn't get hurt when you're poking it where it doesn't belong."

I slipped my arm through Hank's and hugged it to my side as he guided me up my driveway. "I promise I'll always be careful."

We had arrived at my front door, and I could hear Porkchop barking on the other side. Hank turned me to face him. He bent and kissed the tip of my nose. "I guess that's the best I can ask for. I kind of like that nose and the rest of you that goes with it."

My body leaned into him and his warm embrace. "Do you want to come in and do some of that canoodling we were talking about earlier at The Smiling Pig?"

Hank rested his chin on my head. "There's nothing better that I would love to do, but I better get to the station and write up your lawn incident. I'm going to have a patrol car keep an eye on your house until we solve Tommy Ray's murder, so don't be concerned if you spot a black and white riding by periodically."

I snuggled closer to him, wanting to melt right into his solid body. His concern for my safety warmed my heart. "Do you think that's really necessary? After all, I have Porkchop to fend off any possible intruder. He'd protect me right down to his last rawhide bone."

Hank smiled. "I've no doubt that my buddy would protect you, but a little added security wouldn't hurt."

Porkchop's barks became louder and, if I wasn't mistaken, more menacing. I believe he'd heard Hank and was showing him how brave he was. "Speaking of Porkchop, I think he's letting me know that he's craving one of his bones right now."

Hank pulled back from me and stared into my eyes. A smile lifted the corners of his lips. "You're probably right. Give him some extra scratches for me."

I handed my keys to Hank, and he unlocked my front door. Porkchop jumped at his legs, begging for some of those scratches Hank mentioned a moment before. "Take good care of your mistress." Hank bent and gave Porkchop the attention he craved.

Hank once again pulled me to him and gave me a long and passionate kiss. One that would have to carry me through the night. Breathing heavily, he tucked a curl that had fallen forward back behind my ear. "I'd better get to the station to fill out that report, or I'll never leave here. I'll send an officer over in the morning when it is light out to do a thorough report on what happened."

I shook my head. "Is that really necessary? Aren't we making too much out of a broken mailbox and some tire tracks on my front lawn?"

Hank placed a finger on my lips to hush me. "Humor me on this, please." He leaned over and placed a light kiss on the tip of my nose then turned and walked back to his Jeep.

I stood watching from my front door as his taillights faded into the night. "Okay, Porkchop. I guess it's only you and me tonight. How about one of those rawhide bones you love so much? We can snuggle together on the sofa and see if there are any late-night movies on the television."

His slim tail wagged as he strutted beside me into the kitchen.

* * *

"Lordie. What happened to your front yard? It's all tore up." Candie stood in the middle of my living room. We had an appointment this morning with her florist to finalize the flowers for her wedding. Porkchop stared up at her, hoping for some scratchies from his aunt Candie. Not one to disappoint him, she bent and scratched between his ears. His back leg thumped the carpet.

"Yeah, it's a mess. All right. The worst part is whoever did it ran over my mailbox, too." I still mourned the loss of my dachshund-shaped mailbox.

Candie placed her hands on her hips and jutted out her chin. "Why, that dog. The person who did it I mean, not your mailbox. Did anyone see who did it?"

I shook my head. "Hank and I went over to Gladys's, but she and Frank didn't hear anything. I think a train, along with a marching band, could have tramped over my lawn and they wouldn't have heard it. They were engrossed in a baseball game and had it up to full volume. But Frank said he'd make me another mailbox to match the one that was destroyed."

"How sweet of him. What about the people across the street? Did Hank question them?" Candie pointed in the direction of the brick house.

"Gladys said they're away for a few days visiting her parents. Her dad is having some health issues."

Candie nodded. "Yep. Gladys would know the news on your street. Too bad she missed the biggest thing happening last night."

I had to agree with her. Gladys's news radar was certainly on the fritz last night.

I grabbed my pink and green–flowered Vera Bradley purse off my sofa. I needed the bright pattern to cheer me up. I glanced at my wristwatch. "We'd better get going. Your appointment with the florist is in twenty minutes." I bent and patted Porkchop. "Be a good boy while I'm away." He wagged his tail then trotted over to his bed. He climbed in, circled the cushion three times, lay down, and shut his eyes. Before Candie and I reached the door, soft snores came from his bed. I smiled. He was settled for the morning until I got home.

As we walked to Candie's Precious, a patrol car cruised past my house. Hank was true to his word about having the police keep an eye on things.

Candie turned to me and raised an eyebrow.

I shrugged. "Hank is concerned that there is more to trashing my lawn than some teenager out for a joy ride."

"Smart guy," Candie said as we climbed into her car.

I buckled my seat belt. "You don't think he's being a little overly cautious?"

Candie slipped her key into the ignition, and her baby blue Mustang roared to life. "No, I don't."

I sank into my seat and pondered this on the ten-minute ride to Blooms, Candie's florist. It wasn't in the best part of town—not that Wings Falls had any really bad areas, but it had seen better days. There were a number of boarded-up buildings, and paint flaked off the sides of most of them. We pulled into Bloom's parking lot, and I glanced over to the Star Dust Motel that sat next door.

The motel was known as a "meeting place" for couples. The neon sign announcing the motel's name sputtered on and off. The *s* and the *t* in Dust were burned out. Paper cups and newspapers were blown against the walls of the motel. Pink paint peeled off the side of the building. A late-model car with a flat tire was parked in front of one of the motel's units. I was surprised to see three newer cars in the parking lot. Must have been people from out of the area who weren't aware of the motel's reputation.

A door to one of the rooms swung open. A man and a woman, both wearing dark sunglasses, emerged from the room. The man wore a baseball cap pulled low over his forehead. The woman had a red silk scarf tied loosely around her head. But that tight red dress, I'd recognize it anywhere.

CHAPTER THIRTY-FOUR

I gasped and nodded towards the motel. "Candie. Quick! Look who that is coming out of the Star Dust."

Candie turned in her seat to see where I was pointing. A stiff wind blew up and tugged the woman's scarf from her head. If the red dress wasn't a dead giveaway, the wind tugging off her scarf revealed Babs's face.

Candie grabbed for her purse. She reached inside and pulled out her phone.

I pointed to the phone. "What are you going to do with that?"

"I'm going to take a picture, ninny. I'd bet my favorite pair of rhinestone-studded cowboy boots that's Bret with her." Candie opened the car door, leaned on the roof of her car, and posed her phone in their direction. "Say cheese," she shouted at the couple.

Startled, the man darted to a car with a Bret Hargrove for Mayor sticker attached to its bumper. Candie and I walked over to Babs, who stood with her mouth hanging open. Babs shook her finger at the retreating car tearing out of the parking lot of the motel. "Why that rat, leaving me all by myself to deal with you two."

"Giving him some campaign advice?"

Candie thumbed through her phone for the picture she snapped.

Babs turned on her. "Not that it's any of your business, but yes, I was counseling him."

"Yeah, I bet," I mumbled under my breath.

Candie shook her phone at her. "I'm sure Rob Anderson at the *Tribune* would love this picture of you and Bret that I took." Candie turned her phone in Babs's direction to show her the image of her and Bret indulging in a passionate kiss.

Babs grabbed for the phone, but Candie was too quick for her and yanked it out of her reach.

"You wouldn't," Babs screeched and stomped her stiletto so hard, I was surprised the heel didn't break.

Candie took a step towards Babs. "Want to make a bet? How about you tell me what you were doing at my house on Sunday, the morning Tommy Ray was murdered. And why are you here with Bret if you're still pining for Mark?"

Babs fiddled with the ends of her scarf. She jutted out her chin. She heaved a deep breath. "You wouldn't understand."

Candie folded her arms across her chest and tapped the toe of her cowboy boot. "Try me."

My cousin wasn't about to let Babs slither away without answering her questions. I almost felt sorry for Babs. *Almost.*

"I'm in a desperate straight for money. My last lover, may he rot in jail, stole my credit cards and ran them up. He also emptied my bank account. I heard through a friend about Mark running for reelection and figured that if I could get back with him, things would work out for me."

Candie folded her arms across her chest. "And how did you think you could manage that when he is engaged to me?"

Babs rubbed her trembling hands down the sides of her dress. "Mark and I had a pretty good thing going years ago when we were married. I thought I could remind him of all the good times we had together."

Candie jabbed at the air with her finger. "Yeah, until you cheated on him with his law partner. Or did you forget that?"

Babs had the good grace to blush. "A gal can make a mistake, and Mark is a very forgiving person."

"Not that forgiving," Candie ground out through gritted teeth.

I stepped between them, afraid this conversation might get really nasty. "Ladies, we're getting off track here. Babs, why were you at Candie's house on Sunday morning? How did you even know where she lives?"

Babs flung the ends of her scarf over her shoulders and tilted up her chin. "After you all left The Round Up on Saturday night, I walked up to the bar where Tommy Ray sat. He was still crying into his beer and mooning at his picture of you, Candie, dressed as Little Red Riding Hood."

Candie rolled her eyes and groaned.

"So, what does that have to do with you going over to Candie's house?" I tapped my shoe on the cracked pavement. My patience was running thin.

"I thought if Tommy Ray had any more racy pictures, I could show them to Mark and convince him I would make a better wife for him than you. I told Tommy Ray that Candie would then be free for him."

Candie clenched her fists at her side. "Why, you snake."

I put a hand on her arm to keep her from inflicting any damage on Babs. "There you go again, insulting snakes," I whispered. I felt her relax a little. Candie had made enough newspaper headlines this week. She didn't need another for assaulting Mark's ex-wife.

"So, did he have what you wanted?" Candie asked.

Babs nodded. "He said he had other pictures he could share with me. He gave me Candie's address and said to meet him there Sunday morning and he would give them to me."

I waggled my fingers at her, anxious to get to the end of her tale. "Soooo, did he have them when you got there?"

Babs shook her head. "No. He changed his mind. He said if Candie came back to him, he wanted it to be because she loved him and not because she was blackmailed into it."

Candie sucked in a breath. "Oh, my dear Tommy Ray. He was such a sweetheart. Well, most of the time." Then she frowned. "So, is that why you killed him?"

Babs's eyes widened. "No, he was alive when I left him. In fact, why don't you ask that Dan fellow who was at The Round Up on Saturday night? I saw him pull up in your drive as I left. I even waved to him."

"How about your new boyfriend? Do you think he killed Tommy Ray?" Getting to the end of her story was like pulling teeth. I had to yank every detail out of her.

A puzzled look crossed Bab's face. "My new boyfriend? Who do you mean?"

Candie laughed and pointed her phone at Babs to remind her of the picture she had just taken of the loving couple. "How soon we forget. You know, the one you've been giving 'advice' to on his campaign, Bret Hargrove."

Babs's shaking fingers plucked at the sleeves of her dress. "I passed him as I turned onto your street. I can only assume he was coming from your house. Tommy Ray was definitely alive when both Bret and I left him. As I said, ask that Dan fellow. He had a woman in the car who looked an awful lot like you."

"Okay, I guess that puts you and Bret in the clear for killing Tommy Ray. But my suggestion to you is, leave Mark alone. Honey, he's mine and all mine. I don't take kindly to someone poaching my territory. Understand me?" Candie said with a firm nod.

Babs's eyes widened. I could tell she understood exactly what Candie was telling her. "I believe I'll start packing my bags and go back home as soon as the police tell me I can. Umm, best wishes on your wedding, Candie. Mark's a good man. He'll make you happy. I'm sorry I didn't realize that years ago when he was mine."

I tugged on Candie's arm. "Come on, Candie. We're late for your florist appointment."

* * *

Candie and I had finished our meeting with the florist to finalize the flowers for her wedding. Her choice of white roses and violet-tinted carnations would be stunning. We were walking across Bloom's parking lot to her car. "So, I guess from what Babs said earlier, it scratches her and Brett Hargrove off of our suspect list for Tommy Ray's murder."

Candie faced me and nodded. "I'm afraid so. We're back to square one. From what Mrs. Splotz told Gladys at the Senior Center, it leaves someone who looks like me, Dan, and a person who follows Mark's campaign rallies."

We climbed into her car. Candie slid her phone with the incriminating picture back into her purse.

"Yeah, sort of like looking for the old needle in a haystack," I said. "Are you going to do anything with the picture of Bret and Babs?"

Candie picked her phone back out of her purse and swiped it with her finger. She stared at the picture then shook her head. "No, I can't bring that pain on his wife, Ashley. I'd be no better than Bret if I gave it to Rob Anderson for his newspaper." She deleted it from her phone.

I was busy buckling my seat belt when I heard shouting from the Star Dust parking lot that drew my attention.

"Dan, I told you we should go to the police. You know we're innocent of his murder."

"Are you crazy? The police would arrest us in a heartbeat," Dan answered in an angry tone of voice.

I poked Candie in the ribs. "Look! Look! Over there!"

Candie's head snapped towards the direction of the loud voices.

CHAPTER THIRTY-FIVE

———

Candie swiveled in her seat. Her mouth dropped open. "People say everyone has a double somewhere in the world, but look at that woman Dan Brewer is talking to. She could be my twin sister."

I pulled the door handle up and got out of the car. "I'm going to find out who she is."

Candie scurried out to join me. "Not without me, you're not."

The two of us, once again, marched over to the Star Dust Motel's parking lot. A wind had picked up, blowing discarded papers about our feet.

"Dan! Dan Brewer," I called as we approached his car.

He looked at us like a deer caught in headlights. "Um, yeah. What do you want? I'm in a hurry." He grabbed for his car's door handle.

Candie pointed to her look-alike. "I bet you are. Who's your friend here?"

I scanned Candie's double up and down. If I wasn't up close to her, I could easily mistake her for Candie, although a much younger version. She had the same hair coloring as my cousin and wore it in the same style. In fact, she was the exact height and build as Candie. Maybe Mrs. Splotz mistook Dan's friend for Candie on Sunday morning. After all, she only saw who was on the balcony with Tommy Ray from a distance. And Dan Brewer did slip into a Southern accent when he got agitated at Mark's campaign headquarters. Could they have killed Tommy Ray?

Candie placed a hand on Dan's arm. "Why Dan Brewer, fancy meeting you here. Do you want to introduce us to your friend? It's amazing how much she looks like me. If I recall, my neighbor said a woman, who she believed was me, stood on my balcony Sunday morning. You know, the morning Tommy Ray was killed. She also mentioned that the woman had a gentleman friend with her who spoke with a Southern accent, Dan, like the one you try to hide when speaking to us Yankees. Not that I'm a Yankee. Oh, no, I'd never try to disguise my Southern roots like you're doing."

The woman standing next to him started to cry. "Dan, I can't hide like this anymore. Tell Candie the truth as to why we are here."

Dan pulled away from Candie and placed an arm around the woman's shoulder. "Hush, Darlene. You'll get the police on us. They'll never believe we didn't murder that no good deadbeat you were involved with."

Candie raised her eyebrows in disbelief. "Are you all talking about Tommy Ray? What do you mean he's a deadbeat? He was the sweetest fellow when I knew him."

Dan pointed a finger at the woman next to him then turned to Candie. "Oh yeah, he was a real sweetheart. Look at my sister, Darlene. She's a shadow of herself since she got hooked up with him. Don't you see how she resembles you?"

"I have to admit that she does."

"Yeah, and that's because he never got over her." Dan nodded in Candie's direction.

Candie's mouth dropped open. "What do you mean? It's been over thirty years since we broke up."

Darlene sniffled then blew her nose into a crumpled tissue she pulled out of the pocket of her slacks. "I know, but he never really forgot you. He wanted me to dress like you. Dye my hair the same shade as yours and style it like you do." A smile flittered across her face. "He even had me change my wardrobe to include lots of rhinestones."

Candie glanced down at the rings on her fingers. "Yeah, he did like my sparkles."

I couldn't resist asking, "But why? Why would you do that? You're an attractive woman. Any man would be proud of you."

Dan shook his head. "That's what I kept telling her, but she wouldn't listen to me. But his running out on her when she got pregnant with his baby was the last straw."

Candie and I turned to each other. "Baby?" we both said at the same time.

Darlene hung her head and nodded. Tears streamed down her face. "Yes, I'm expecting his baby. He said he wasn't sure he could handle the responsibility of a baby, so when you invited him to do repairs on your house, he took off. That's when my brother, Dan—" she pointed at Dan Brewer—"said we needed to hunt him down. We trailed him up here to Wings Falls, not that it did us any good."

Candie placed a hand on Darlene's arm. "I'm so sorry. I didn't know. If I had, I would have sent his sorry rear packing. I don't cotton to a man shirking his duties like that. I heard he was dating a woman by the name of Darlene, but I had no idea he'd run out on his responsibilities."

A wind had picked up and blew my hair into my eyes. I tried to tuck the unruly curls behind my ears. "That explains the Candie look-alike appearance. You could pass for her twin."

Darlene heaved a shuddering breath. "I was so blinded by my foolish love for him, I went along with whatever he wanted."

Who was I to judge? It was hard to imagine that a woman would go to such lengths to please a man she was in love with, but there was a time when I probably would have done the same when I was married to George. That is, until I found out he was belly bopping the secretary of our funeral parlor.

I needed to ask the question of the hour. "I'm sorry things have turned out this way for you, but I have one last question. Did you kill Tommy Ray?"

Darlene blinked and took a step back as if I had slapped her. "Why would I do that? I loved him, and I'm expecting his baby."

Dan moved between his sister and me. "We came north to make him take responsibility for his child. Killing him would certainly have been counterproductive. No, he was alive when we left him on Sunday morning—grumbling to himself about how he was going to support Darlene and the baby. I may have wanted to wring his neck for running out on Darlene, but he was definitely alive."

I turned to Candie. "Come on, let's go. I think we're done here."

We walked back to Bloom's parking lot and settled into Candie's Mustang. "So, what do you think? Do you believe them?"

Candie inserted the key into the ignition and turned it. Her Precious roared to life. "As much as I need to find Tommy Ray's killer, my gut feeling tells me they are innocent. I can't imagine her pulling the trigger of the nail gun. Dan maybe, if he was mad enough, but I don't believe they did it."

Whenever Candie's "gut" told her something, she was usually right. "So, I guess we can cross them off our suspect list."

"I suppose so. The list is getting smaller and smaller. If we don't find the murderer soon, only my name will be on it." Candie shifted the car into reverse and backed out of Bloom's parking lot.

"And wouldn't Sandy Peters love that. Do you mind stopping at the Shop And Save on the way home? I've run out of coffee, and I need some to start my day, even if it is only decaf."

I stuck out my tongue at Candie as she laughed at my lament over not being able to drink caffeinated coffee. I blamed my ex, George, because my blood pressure began going up about five years ago, around the time he'd started cheating on me.

* * *

Candie turned Precious into Shop And Save's parking lot. "Boy, the parking lot certainly is packed for a Saturday afternoon. If we hadn't had to meet with the florist, Dixie and I could have slept in, getting more beauty sleep."

Not that I wouldn't have loved to have caught a few more ZZ's this morning after our late night at Mark's apartment dealing with Joe Peters, but my cousin was a natural beauty and didn't need more sleep to enhance her appearance. I pointed out her car's front window at an SUV backing out of a parking space. "Over there. I see a car leaving."

"Come on, Precious. Momma is going to slide you right into that spot."

I smiled. Candie talked to her baby blue '73 Mustang as if it were a real person. I wouldn't be surprised if it answered her. If David Hasselhoff's car KITT could communicate with him, then why not Candie's Precious? But hopefully, not when I was present. It would give me a heart attack if I heard anything other than the purr of Precious's motor.

Candie maneuvered Precious into the vacant slot. I glanced out my side window and groaned.

CHAPTER THIRTY-SIX

———

Candie's head snapped towards me. "Are you all right? What's the matter?"

I nodded at the object of my displeasure. Since George had made that pass at me at our funeral parlor while I filled in for our secretary, I'd tried to avoid him. "I don't want to talk to him."

Candie rolled her eyes. "Since when do you let anyone, especially a man, determine where you can go? Now get your buns out of Precious and march up to the store. I'll be right next to you."

Candie was correct. Our Memaw Parker would not be proud of me hiding in a car so I wouldn't have to encounter George. I jutted out my chin and slid my red Michael Kors handbag farther up my arm. I rounded the car and practically bumped into George, who was trying to keep a hold on his twin boys, Larry and Harry. I pasted a smile on my face. "Hi, guys. Shopping day?"

They gave me a vigorous nod. The mop of blond hair on their heads fell across their eyes. Larry, or was it Harry—after five years I still couldn't tell them apart—pointed at his brother. "Yeah, but Harry gots us in trouble." He glared at his twin.

"He did?" I bent down to Harry's level. I may not have any love left for their father, but the boys were adorable. "What happened, Harry?"

Harry sniffled. "I wants some cookies, but Mommy said I couldn't have any 'cuz they would rot my teeth out of my head."

I glanced up at George. "A cookie. One lousy cookie."

George shrugged his shoulders. "What can I say? Anna is on a healthy food kick with the boys."

It certainly wasn't my place to say anything since I never had any children, but I certainly couldn't see the harm in one cookie. "Where is she? Still shopping?"

"Yeah, I told her I'd take the boys to the car so she could finish the grocery shopping in peace." Harry and Larry started to tug on his hands.

"George, what are you doing?"

Uh-oh. Here came the object of our discussion walking towards us, and she didn't seem pleased that I was with her hubby.

"She doesn't look too happy that you are talking to George," Candie whispered out of the side of her mouth.

I had to agree with my cousin. If looks could kill, the one Anna shot me would put me in my own funeral parlor, but as a customer and not the owner.

"Umm, umm," George stuttered. "I ran into Sam and Candie while going back to our car."

One of the twins, Harry I think, pulled away from George and approached the shopping cart Anna was pushing. "Yeah, Momma. Aunt Sam says that a cookie wouldn't hurt us, like you says."

Whoa. Like the old saying about seeing steam coming out of a person's ears, Anna's were spouting full bore. She gritted her teeth so hard I thought they would snap.

"Harry, I've told you over and over that woman is *not* your aunt, so don't call her that."

Poor Harry. I felt really sorry for the boy as he slunk back to his father's side. I started to walk past George and noticed their SUV. The grill of the car was damaged, and the bumper had a large dent in it. "George, were you in an accident? Are you all right?" Even though he was my ex, I wasn't so heartless as to not care about his well-being.

"I'm fine. Anna got side-swiped by a car when she was out at her weekly mah-jongg meeting last night. You know how bad the roads are this time of year with all the crazy tourists crowding the highways."

I shook my head. "Yes, especially with the tourists coming up to vacation in Lake George." I lived close to a very beautiful area of New York—Lake George—and from Memorial Day to Labor Day, all roads leading into and out of that town are jammed with people in a hurry to begin their vacations. I turned to Anna. "I'm glad you're all right."

She ignored my concern.

Candie tugged at the sleeve of my blouse.

"What?" I asked.

She pointed to the damaged grill of George's car. My eyes widened as I bent and looked closer. Stuck in the grill was a small red metal flag. The kind attached to a mailbox.

I pulled the flag out of the grill then straightened and glared at Anna. "You say you were playing mah-jongg last night. I wonder if your fellow players would back you up. You weren't possibly trashing my front lawn and running over my mailbox? In case you're interested, I filed a police report about it."

The way Anna's face paled and her hand shook as she brushed a strand of hair out of her eyes told me everything I needed to know. I guessed she didn't think she'd get caught or that a police report would be filed on the damages.

Anna's body began to tremble.

George turned to her. "Anna, what is Sam talking about? You said you got side-swiped by a car. Is that what really happened?"

Tears began to slide down her cheeks. "I can't take it anymore. You're always going on about how great Sam can do this and do that. How do you think that makes me feel?"

My mouth dropped open. Since when did George ever sing my praises? If my memory served me correctly—not for a good many years. At least not for the last few years of our marriage. I glanced down at Harry and Larry, who stood staring wide-eyed at their quietly weeping mother. My heart ached for them. They were too young to understand the foolishness of adults.

George had the good grace to blush. "I'm sorry. I didn't mean anything by what I said, but you are always so busy with the boys that you don't have time for me."

I rolled my eyes. How shallow could he be, jealous of his own children? A lightbulb clicked on in my brain. Maybe I could solve one mystery plaguing me. "Anna, did you try to run me over the other day when I was walking with Candie? And did you break into my house and leave a message on the mirror of my bathroom?"

She gave a slight nod.

George jerked back as if a fist had hit him in the chest. "Anna?" he said in a voice barely above a whisper.

"How did you get into my house?" But I think I knew the answer. I held my hand out to George. "Hand it over. I was foolish not to ask for it back when you left me for your sweet tart here."

George dug into his pocket and pulled out his key ring. He fumbled with the keys until he came to the one I was demanding back—the key to my house. I had neglected to ask for it back after our divorce. My life was enough of a mess at that time, what with dissolving my twenty-five-year marriage. I was going to correct that mistake right now.

My fingers curled around the key as he placed it into my hand. He looked at me with the sad puppy-dog eyes that used to work on my heart when we were married, but not anymore. "I'll be sending you the bill for the repair to my lawn." I turned to Candie. "Come on, I've got some shopping to do and don't have any more time to waste on them."

As Candie and I walked towards the store, I could hear one of the boys ask, "Daddy, what is a sweet tart? Is that some kind of candy Aunt Sam was calling Momma?" My heart squeezed in my chest for those two young boys.

"I want to get a six-pack of Trails Head beer in case Hank can get free and stop over this evening." I pulled a slip of paper out of the side pocket of my purse where I had jotted down some items I was running low on. It was a short list—nachos, salsa, pizza and, of course, Hank's favorite beer. At the bottom was listed a rawhide bone. Couldn't forget my other main man.

Candie's phone pinged from her purse. "I wonder who that could be. I know Mark is busy with meetings today."

I laughed and pointed to her purse. "There's only one way to find out—look at your phone."

She joined in my laughter and did as I instructed. She zipped open her purse, a turquoise sequined affair, and reached in for her bejeweled phone. A frown creased her brow.

"What is it? Or should I say *who* is it?"

"It's a text from Valerie. She said she has a question concerning the alterations to my wedding dress. She wants me to come to the back door of the salon, as Sylvia is closing early today. Something about a cousin coming to town to visit her. But Valerie is going to take care of the dress emergency since the wedding is only a week away."

I shook my head. "What question? Everything seemed all right when we were there the other day. The hem only needed a little adjusting." That was all Candie needed—a screw up with her dress along with everything else happening lately. "Drop me off at home. I need to feed Porkchop and let him out. Then I'll join you at Sylvia's."

Tears trembled on the tips of Candie's eyelashes.

I reached over and gave her a hug. "You're having pre-wedding jitters. There is nothing Sylvia can't make right. Now, let's see what Valerie wants." Shopping trip forgotten, I parked the grocery cart I had grabbed in the nearest corral and walked back to Precious. We climbed into Candie's car, and she placed it in reverse. We headed out of the parking lot.

CHAPTER THIRTY-SEVEN

"Hi, sweet pea. Did you miss me while I was out with Aunt Candie?" Porkchop greeted me at the door with his usual barking and tail wagging. I picked him up and cuddled him close to me, nuzzling my face into his neck. "I need to meet Aunt Candie at the bridal salon. She got a text from Valerie about her wedding dress. I want to go over there and see what the problem is. You know, for the moral support we Parkers are famous for." Porkchop looked up at me with those chocolate-brown eyes of his. The ones that I could never say no to. "Okay, how about I give you some kibble? You do your business and come along with me to Sylvia's?" I swear he understood everything I said to him. His tail started to wag a mile a minute as if he approved of my plan.

Fifteen minutes later, a well-fed and exercised Porkchop lay curled on the passenger seat of my Bug as we headed to Sylvia's Bridal Salon. I had texted Candie we were on our way but had not heard back from her. I assumed she was busy being poked and prodded by Valerie.

I pulled up to the front door of Sylvia's and frowned at the darkened interior of the salon. I wondered why the lights weren't on, but since it was late in the day, and I knew she had closed early. Valerie and Candie must be in the back of the store tending to her gown emergency. I shrugged and climbed out of the Bug. Porkchop jumped towards me. "Oh, I don't know about you going into the salon. There are too many beautiful gowns in there that don't need your paw prints as part of their design." Porkchop whined and turned his sad eyes on me. "Okay, but you'll have to stay in the reception area. You can't follow me back to the fitting room, where I presume your aunt is." My darling pup hopped up and down on the car seat at my suggestion. I guess what I said met with his approval. I clipped on his leash and helped him down from the car seat.

Valerie's text told Candie to use the back door, but I was going to see if the front door was open so I could leave Porkchop in the reception area. I was pleasantly surprised when I turned the doorknob. It turned under my hand, and a bell chimed over the door as I pushed it open. "Porkchop, you'll have to stay out here while I see about the problem with Candie's wedding dress." I looped the handle of his leash under the leg of a gilded chair sitting in the corner of the room. I was puzzled that Valerie hadn't called out to us when the bell over the door chimed. I would have thought she would at least be curious as to who entered the salon. I gazed about the room. It was gloomy with all the lights turned off.

"Candie," I called out as I pushed aside the curtain separating the reception room from the fitting area of the salon.

I blinked then blinked again. I had to be dreaming, and it wasn't a good one—more of a nightmare. "Candie," I screamed and rushed towards her. She lay on the Persian rug, unconscious. Blood pooled next to her head mingled and with her auburn curls. Pieces of gold plaster of Paris from the cupid—which looked so charming the other day sitting on the white column—were mixed in with her hair. "Candie, what happened? Did you slip and fall?" I sank to the floor next to her. My trembling fingers clasped her wrist and searched for a pulse.

A groan escaped from her lips as she tried to lift her head. "My wedding dress…" she moaned.

"What the…" I looked down at what she was wearing—her lavender lace wedding dress. Not the lovely lace affair she had tried on the other day, but a dress that was now stained with blood and slit in a number of places. "Where is Valerie? Does she know that you had an accident? I need to call 9-1-1 for an ambulance." I dug in my purse for my phone and then did a palm plant on my forehead. I had left it in the Bug.

I chided myself for being so forgetful. "Valerie," I called out. Surely she must know that Candie was injured. I started to rise, when the curtain separating the fitting room from the storeroom area of the salon slid open. Valerie stood framed in the doorway dressed in a beautiful white satin wedding gown. A lace veil covered her head and flowed to the floor. Her eyes had a glazed look, as if she was seeing me but didn't really know who I was. She clutched a pair of scissors in her hand.

"Oh, an unexpected visitor. As you can see, your cousin has had an accident. Oops. Has her wedding dress had a few alterations? These little scissors that Lucy gave out at Candie's shower have come in very handy." Valerie waved them at me and giggled. A laugh that sent chills up my spine. Then she frowned. "Is that your filthy dog making all that noise? Why did you bring him here to the salon?"

I shook my head. I'd been unaware of Porkchop's fierce barking before Valerie mentioned it. I guess I was too absorbed in Candie and what had happened to her. Now I prayed that someone walking past Sylvia's would stop and investigate all the commotion.

Valerie stepped over to Candie and bent down. She jabbed the point of the scissors into Candie's upper arm. Blood tricked out and ran onto her dress. I stepped forward, but the look in Valerie's eyes halted me. Deranged was the only word that I could think of to describe her at this moment. "I'll be a more beautiful bride than her—the slut. I'd never have embarrassed Mark the way she has with those awful pictures of her and that ex-fiancé she was carrying on with."

I gazed around the room. My mouth dropped open in astonishment. Pictures of Valerie and Mark hung from the wall. Mark and Valerie hugging and kissing, the two of them in various loving poses. When had they been taken? Talk about carrying on. Was Mark having an affair behind Candie's back? Flossie did mention that Valerie had a major crush on Mark. Maybe Mark took advantage of Valerie's devotion to him? I shook my head. *No, not the Mark I knew.*

Then it dawned on me. How desperate was Valerie to have Mark's attention? Would she frame Candie for Tommy Ray's murder so she could have Mark all to herself? Was she so blinded by her obsession for Mark that she would kill Tommy Ray?

I pointed a shaking finger at Valerie. "You killed Tommy Ray, didn't you?"

"That fool. He wouldn't give me any of those nasty pictures of him and this hussy. I even stopped by Bret Hargrove's campaign headquarters to see if he had any to give me. I had to do what was necessary to free Mark from her." A sneer crossed her face as she pointed the scissors at Candie. A drop of blood slid off the tip onto the carpet.

Now I understood why Candie and I saw her going into Bret's headquarters. I think Valerie would have tried to strike a deal with the devil if she could have had Mark for her own. "But why murder him?" I still couldn't wrap my head around her killing Tommy Ray to gain Mark's love.

"Oh, must you be so dense?" Valerie shook her head in frustration.

True, there were times when I might not pick up on things as fast as I should, but murder? I couldn't see how Valerie could justify killing Tommy Ray.

"I've told you, it was the only way to free Mark of Candie so he could marry the woman who truly loves him and could help him in his career—me. The nail gun was handy, and I know how to use it since I've helped my dad in the past on some of his construction jobs."

A crash resounded from the reception room, and Porkchop's barks grew louder. A streak of reddish-brown fur dashed past me then disappeared under Valerie's gown.

"Ouch! Ouch! Get your mangy mutt off of me." Valerie pulled up the wedding dress she was wearing. Porkchop had his teeth sunk into her ankle and wasn't about to let loose. The lace veil, that moments before was so carefully arranged on her head, now hung over her face and wrapped around her arms, making it difficult for her to move.

I leapt forward and pushed her to the ground. Porkchop was hanging on to her ankle as if it were one of his prized rawhide bones. I reached over, unclipped his leash, pulled Valerie's flailing arms together, then tied them with it. She lay on the floor, the once pristine wedding dress now tangled about her body, along with the lace veil ripped and torn where Porkchop's nails had caught it. She sobbed and mumbled, "Mark, I love you. I did this for you," over and over.

I spied Candie's purse resting on the tufted sofa. I scrambled over and dug into it for her bejeweled phone. My shaking fingers grasped the phone on the bottom of her purse. I pulled it out and punched in 9-1-1. On the second ring, the operator answered.

"Please, I have an emergency. Send the police and an ambulance right away to Sylvia's Bridal Salon. And notify Detective Johnson I'm here with Tommy Ray's killer," I screamed into the phone.

CHAPTER THIRTY-EIGHT

―――――

The 9-1-1 operator asked me to stay on the line, but I declined. I needed to tend to Candie until help arrived. Valerie was in good hands, or should I say teeth, with Porkchop. He had let go of her ankle and now lay on her back, growling and baring his teeth every time she made a move.

It was only minutes, although it seemed like hours, until I heard sirens screaming down the street. The front door of the salon burst open. "In here," I shouted.

The first person to rush through the curtain was Mark, followed by Hank. An ashen-faced Mark rushed over to Candie and collapsed on the floor next to her. He leaned over her and gently brushed back her hair. Blood coated his fingers from the gash inflicted by cupid. He placed a tender kiss on the wound. "I'm here, sweetheart. You're going to be all right."

Candie opened her eyes, and a faint smile crossed her lips. "Mark, you're not supposed to see me in my wedding gown before the wedding."

I smiled. Leave it to my cousin to bring some sunshine into a dire situation. My heart filled with my love for her.

Mark patted her hand. "Darling, I'm not looking at your dress. I'm drinking in your beautiful face."

"Really?" Candie's eyes fluttered closed.

Mark swiped at the tears trickling down his cheeks. "Really."

Hank placed a hand on Mark's shoulder. "Mark, let the EMTs do their job. You can ride in the ambulance with her to the hospital."

Mark nodded and rose from the floor. Two young EMTs took his place and began to attend to Candie.

Hank strode over to Valerie, lying on the floor. Porkchop still stood guard over her prone body, his paws on her arm. "Come on, buddy. You've done a great job protecting your mistress and Candie. I'll take over now."

Porkchop growled one last time at Valerie as Hank bent down and helped her to stand. Valerie let out a yelp when she put weight on the ankle Porkchop had chomped on moments before. She stumbled into Hank's body as he untied the leash and deftly slipped handcuffs onto her wrists. He led her over to the sofa and motioned to one of the EMTs. "This woman's ankle needs attention."

An EMT walked over and knelt before Valerie. He lifted the hem of the now tattered and blood-stained gown. "That little guy did a number on this ankle. I'll call in for another ambulance to take her to the emergency room. Until they get here, I'll clean the wound and bandage it to help stop the bleeding."

Valerie held a pleading handcuffed hand out to Mark as he walked beside the gurney carrying Candie out to the waiting ambulance. "My wedding dress. I picked this dress out especially for you, Mark. You would have loved it. That evil dog has ruined it." She pointed a shaking finger at Porkchop then turned to Hank, who stood behind the EMT wrapping her ankle. "You know Mark loves me and not that hussy the EMTs are wheeling out of the room. He was always praising the work I've done for his campaign. He said I was the best campaign worker he's ever had. That proves how much he loves me."

I shook my head. I almost had to feel sorry for her. She was obviously living in a delusional dream. Porkchop lay cradled in my arms. I bent and whispered into his ear. "Don't listen to her. You're the hero of the day. You saved me and your aunt Candie. After I check with Mark about how she is doing, I'm going to stop by the butcher shop and buy you the biggest bone they have."

Hank walked over to me. He stroked Porkchop's head then caressed my arm. Concern mirrored in his eyes. "Are you all right? How did this all go down?"

I shook my head and tried to relive all that had happened since Porkchop and I arrived at Sylvia's. "While Candie and I were at the grocery store, she got a text from Valerie saying that there was a problem with her gown, and since the wedding is next Saturday, it needed to be attended to ASAP. Oh, by the way, we ran into George and his family while we were there. I discovered that it was Anna who trashed my lawn, tried to run me over, and broke into my house. She thought George wanted me back. As if that would ever happen."

Hank's hand stilled on my arm. "Do you want me to bring her in for questioning? Issue her a citation?"

I smiled. "No. Apparently George is going through some midlife crisis. Living with him is punishment enough for Anna."

"Just so he leaves you alone. So, what happened after that?"

I continued my story. "I had Candie drop me off at home. I told her I'd join her at the salon as soon as I let Porkchop out to do his business. But I felt so bad for having left him alone for so long that I brought him with me. When we got here, the place was dark. I hooked Porkchop's leash under the leg of a chair in the reception room, but the good doggie that he is, he realized that Candie and I were in trouble. He broke loose and rescued us."

Porkchop leaned into Hank's hand as Hank scratched his head. Hank bent down and whispered into Porkchop's floppy ear. "Good job, buddy, for rescuing my girl and Candie."

My heart skipped a beat when he referred to me as his girl. My eyes caught the pictures of Mark and Valerie hanging about the room in affectionate poses. "Hank, look at those. What do you make of them?"

I pointed to a particular picture showing Mark and Valerie engaged in a very passionate kiss. "Do they seem altered in any way to you?"

Hank looked closer at the pictures. He took a moment to study them. "They appear to have been photoshopped."

I nodded in agreement and pointed to one in particular. "Look there. The fellow is wearing high-top sneakers. I've never seen Mark wear a pair of those, and the woman has stilettos heels on. Candie would never wear high-heeled shoes with Mark. See, they are both about the same height. She'd tower over him if she wore those shoes. Valerie really was in her own dream world about Mark." The hairs on my arms stood on end. Valerie had given the appearance of a very meek and mild person.

CHAPTER THIRTY-NINE

———

It was late, but we all gathered around Candie's hospital bed. "All" meaning Hank, Mark, and myself. She sat cranked up in the bed in a sitting position. A bandage was wrapped around the upper part of her left arm where Valerie had jabbed her with her scissors from Candie's own bridal shower. Her head was also wrapped in a gauze bandage from the damage done by the gilded cupid landing on her head. A blood pressure cuff was wrapped around her other arm.

Mark sat in an orange plastic chair, pulled up next to the bed. He clutched her hand as if afraid to let go. Concern etched his face. "When I think of how close I came to losing you today—I don't even want to think of it."

"Sweetheart, we Parkers are a tough bunch. Right, Sam?" Candie nodded at me then placed a hand on her forehead and groaned. "Oh boy, I still have a whopping headache."

Hank pulled a notebook out of the back pocket of his jeans. He was in his detective mode. "Do you feel up to telling me exactly what happened when you got to the salon?"

"Do I really have to go over all that nastiness again?" Candie batted her eyelashes at Hank. I wanted to laugh but knew Hank had to get all the details as to what happened to Candie today while it was still fresh in her memory. Candie trying to sweet talk Hank wasn't going to work on him.

Hank poised a pen over the notebook, ready to jot down Candie's statement. "I'm afraid so. I need a solid story in order to hold Valerie on attempted murder charges and the murder of Tommy Ray. She's at the station right now. She says you slipped and knocked the cupid off the pedestal."

My mouth dropped open. "You can't possibly believe her! Look at that wound on Candie's arm. I saw Valerie do that with my own eyes."

Candie's blood pressure monitor started to beep. A nurse poked her head into the room then walked over to the side of Candie's bed and stared at the monitor. Candie's blood pressure was falling back to a normal range. "Are you all right, dear? Is something upsetting you?"

Candie shook her head then winced. Her headache was obviously not subsiding. "No, I'm fine."

The nurse straightened the covers on Candie's bed. "Okay, but if you need anything, please buzz me." She pointed to the buzzer clipped to Candie's bed.

Mark folded Candie's slender hand in his. "Hank, can't this wait until the morning? The doc said if Candie feels okay in the morning, she can be discharged."

Candie patted his hand and looked into Mark's eyes. "It's okay, sweetheart. I might as well get this over with. Like Sam told you, I got a text from Valerie saying there was an issue with my gown. Since our wedding is next Saturday, I knew I needed to get over to Sylvia's as soon as possible. I dropped Sam off at home then drove to the salon. Valerie's text stated I should come in the back door. When I entered Sylvia's, my gown was hanging in the dressing room. Valerie shouted out from the storage room that I should slip it on and she'd see what needed to be altered."

Hank was busy writing down Candie's statement. "Did you notice the photographs she hung around the room?"

Candie squinched up her nose. "No. Were they of any importance?"

I was quick to butt in with an answer. "No, honey. Just a few items from a fantasy she made up."

Mark nodded in agreement. "More like her deranged mind." "Well, when I came out of the dressing room, I was shocked to see Valerie dressed in a wedding gown and donning a full-length veil. The next thing I knew, she was asking me what I thought of the gown and would Mark like it when he marries her. I told her she was crazy to think Mark would drop me and marry her. I guess it made her mad, because she lunged towards me and knocked me into the pedestal holding the gilded cupid. Last thing I remember is it toppling over and hitting me on the head. I don't remember anything until I saw Sam bending over me."

Hank looked up from the notebook and turned to me. "I've got your statement. Is there anything you want to add to what Candie has said?"

"No. I've already mentioned how Valerie stabbed Candie in the arm and that she confessed to killing Tommy Ray. She thought that with Candie out of the way, she'd have a clear field in marrying Mark."

Mark leaned over and gently kissed Candie. "As if that would ever happen. You are the love of my life—now and forever."

Tears trembled on the tips of Candie's eyelashes. "I love you, too, Mark. With all my heart."

I cleared my throat. "I did mention who the hero of the day is, right?"

Candie tore her eyes away from Mark and smiled. "Yes. Porkchop."

Mark sat back in his chair. "I owe that pup a lifetime supply of his favorite rawhide bones."

We all laughed.

The nurse who had checked on Candie earlier poked her head in the room. "Pardon me, folks, but visiting hours are over and Miss Parker needs her rest if she wants to be discharged tomorrow."

Candie put a hand to her mouth to stifle a yawn. "I guess it has been an eventful day, and I do want to be sprung from here tomorrow morning. Sam, will you pick me up?"

"Absolutely. I'll bring Porkchop with me so he can see that his aunt Candie is fine."

Mark started to protest. "I'll scrub my agenda and pick you up."

"Hush your mouth. The primary is this Tuesday, and you need to get out the vote. I'll be fine."

I stood and gathered up my purse. "Really, Mark, I don't mind."

Mark opened his mouth to protest again, but Candie held up her hand. "You can't argue with me. I'm in a fragile state."

I laughed. "Huh. You, fragile? That will be the day. Come on, Hank. Let's leave them alone so they can say a proper good night."

I bent over Candie's bed and kissed her on the forehead. "I love you, cuz."

She wrapped her arms around me as best she could since she was hooked up to hospital machines. "I love you, too."

We left Candie and Mark to say their goodbyes.

"Don't be late tomorrow," Candie shouted out the door.

I laughed as Hank and I walked down the hospital corridor to the elevators at the end of the hallway.

The elevator doors swished open. I punched the button marked for the first floor then leaned back against the metal wall of the elevator. I closed my eyes. A deep sigh escaped my lips. Exhaustion swept through my body. I felt Hank pull me close to him. I nestled up to his warmth.

Tears I'd kept at bay all day started to roll down my cheeks. My body shook with sobs, soaking Hank's shirt.

The elevator shuddered to a stop, and the doors slid open. I pushed away from Hank and scrubbed my tears away with my fists. "I'm sorry," I said, rubbing the front of Hank's shirt.

"Hush. It's only a shirt." He lifted my chin and looked into my, what I knew had to be red-rimmed, eyes and then bent and placed a sweet kiss on my lips.

A torrent of tears threatened to break loose again. I shook my head. "I'd better get home and see to Porkchop. I know you need to go to the station and deal with wrapping up Tommy Ray's murder."

Hank nodded. "Let me walk you to your car first."

When we arrived at my Bug, he turned me around into his arms. He rested his chin on my head. "Sam, what am I going to do with you? I know you are loyal to your friends and have to help them when they are in need. I admire that trait in you, but you get yourself involved in the darndest situations. I'm so afraid of losing you. I don't think my heart could survive if anything happened to you."

"Hank. I know you lost your wife in a tragic accident, but I'm not her. I'll always do my best to stay safe. I promise you."

Hank smiled. "Pinkie promise."

I laughed out loud. I wondered if the couple walking past us to their car thought we had escaped from the hospital's psych ward. "Pinkie promise." I held out my little finger for him to hook on to.

Hank then pulled me into a hug and kissed me deeply.

CHAPTER FORTY

───────

I fluffed Candie's pillow then walked back to her kitchen to get the cup of chamomile tea I had steeping on the counter for her. Mark had won the battle over who was going to bring her home from the hospital this morning, but Candie had insisted he return to work and that I could fuss over her just as well.

"Here you are." I handed her the mug of tea. "Is there anything else I can get you?"

Porkchop lay at the end of the sofa, snuggled at Candie's feet. Dixie glared at him from across the room as she sat curled up on the cushion of a purple velvet wing chair. Candie had insisted I bring Porkchop with me this morning so she could properly thank the pup who had saved her life.

Candie cradled the mug of tea in her hands. "What am I going to do about my wedding dress? It's ruined, and I was so in love with it. The dress fit me perfectly!"

I sat at the end of the sofa next to Porkchop with my legs curled up under me, sipping on my mug of tea. "Already taken care of. Sylvia phoned me this morning and said she put a rush order in for a new dress and it will be here by tomorrow."

Candie breathed a sigh of relief. "Cuz, you are the best. What would I do without you?"

I smiled. "And that's not the best part!"

Candie raised an eyebrow. "What are you talking about?"

"Sylvia said that because of what Valerie did, the dress is a wedding present to you—free of charge."

Candie waggled her fingers at me. "No, she can't do that. Hand me my phone. I'm going to call her right now. It's not her fault Valerie killed Tommy Ray and tried to kill me, too."

"She feels responsible because Valerie was her employee."

"I've tried to put that woman out of my thoughts, but I can't fathom why she acted the way she did. What possessed her to think that a few compliments from Mark meant he was in love with her?"

"I talked to Hank this morning, and it seems her life hasn't been a happy one. She never received any praise or encouragement from her parents. She has an older sister who is their pride and joy. Apparently the sister was smarter, prettier, and more talented than Valerie and was constantly thrown up to her." Having been raised by two loving parents, it was hard for me to imagine what Valerie's childhood must have been like.

Candie tapped her chin with her finger. "So, when Mark was kind to her and complimented her on a job well done, she took it to mean he loved her."

I nodded. "That appears to be the case."

Candie's phone rang. I reached over to the marble-topped coffee table sitting in front of the sofa, picked up her bejeweled phone, and handed it to her.

"Hi, sweetie. Yes. I'm doing fine. Sam is waiting on me hand and foot."

I nudged her leg and got a frown in return.

"You want me to turn on the local news? Okay. I'll see you after work." Candie sent some air kisses Mark's way.

"What did Mark want?" I asked.

"He only said to turn on the local news. There's going to be a segment after the commercial about Bret. Here, hand me the remote." Candie pointed to the oversized end table that matched her coffee table.

She punched the television on, the only thing in the living room that didn't have a Victorian flare to it.

A camera focused in on the local newswoman, a trim thirty-something blonde clutching a mic. She stood on the sidewalk and pointed her slim hand at Bret Hargrove's campaign headquarters. Two state police cars sat in front of the building with their lights flashing. "Charlene Hastings here with breaking news. It's been reported the state police have been conducting a secret investigation into Mr. Hargrove's finances and business dealings. The police allege Mr. Hargrove has been passing bad checks and was even using stolen credit card accounts to fund his campaign. With the primary election only days away, this cannot bode well for the man challenging incumbent mayor, Mark Hogan."

My eyes widened and my mouth dropped open. I scooted to the edge of my seat to get a closer look at the television.

Candie sat up straighter on the sofa but winced at the pain the movement caused. "Why, the dirty dog. And he wanted to be the mayor of our good city."

I pointed at the television screen. "Look." Bret was being led out of the old laundromat with his hands handcuffed behind him, his head bent down to his chest.

The reporter stepped up to him and shoved the microphone into his face. "Do you have any comments to make, Mr. Hargrove?"

He scowled at the camera. "I'm innocent, I'm telling you. Someone is trying to frame me."

The troopers escorted him to their car then placed a hand on Bret's head so he could safely enter the rear seat of the vehicle.

The camera focused on the retreating police car. "This is Charlene Hastings, reporting from the deserted campaign headquarters of Bret Hargrove. Back to you in the studio."

I picked up the remote and clicked off the television. "What do you make of that?"

Candie adjusted the neckline of her blouse. She may have come home from the hospital a few hours ago, but she was dressed as if she were going out on the town—her usual rhinestone-trimmed blouse paired with a flowing skirt. Only thing to suggest she wasn't about to step out were the fuzzy violet slippers on her feet. "Very interesting. I think we all knew something was fishy with that man."

I nodded in agreement. "Yes, but he remains on the ballot for next Tuesday's primary election. There are people who will still vote for him."

Candie shook her head. Her auburn curls bounced about her shoulder. "The people of Wings Falls are smarter than that. They know Mark is a winner and will vote for him."

* * *

"Porkchop, are you ready? This is the most important walk of your life. I know you will do a great job." I bent down and adjusted the violet satin pillow strapped around his middle. Mark's and Candie's wedding rings were tied to the pillow with a matching violet ribbon.

Porkchop looked up at me with his soft, chocolate-brown eyes as if to say, *"Got this one in the bag, Mom."*

I chuckled and scratched between his ears.

I turned to Candie. We were standing in the back of Saint Anthony's church. Father Pete had just walked out onto the altar. White roses and violet-tinted carnations decorated the altar in silver vases. Sprays of the same flowers were tied to the ends of the pews. The first notes of "The Wedding March" by Mendelssohn floated down from the organ loft overhead. Mark and Hank stood in front of the altar next to Father Pete, waiting for us. Mark had a grin spread across his face.

A small group of people—Mark's and Candie's closest friends—were seated in the pews. After all that had happened, Candie wanted to keep the ceremony an intimate affair. All eyes were trained on the back of the church, waiting for the bride to start down the aisle.

"You ready to do this?" I clutched my bouquet of white roses and violet-tinted carnations in my hands.

Candie nodded. The violets entwined in her hair quivered. "I've been waiting all my life for this moment. Let's begin."

I did a last-minute adjustment of the folds of her violet-hued wedding dress. Sylvia was true to her word and had had a new dress delivered to her shop in record time. The carnations in Candie's bouquet matched it perfectly. "Okay, Porkchop, let's get this show on the road." I motioned for him to begin his strut down the aisle.

Ooh's and *ahh*'s followed us down the aisle. I smiled as the Loopy Ladies waved and pointed at Porkchop as he pranced by them. Gladys's violet curls certainly matched the color scheme of the day.

I thought Mark's face would split from the smile on his face. Warmth flooded me as I realized both he and my cousin would spend the rest of their life enfolded in their great love for each other. After Candie stepped up to Mark's side, Porkchop and I stood next to Hank. My heart skipped a beat. If I thought his tight jeans looked sexy on him, the tux he wore outdid them. Too bad I couldn't convince him to wear one more often.

He leaned over and whispered to me, "You look beautiful."

"You don't look too bad yourself for a gumshoe."

He chuckled and reached for my hand, giving it a gentle squeeze as Father Pete began the ceremony.

CHAPTER FORTY-ONE

"I now pronounce you man and wife."

Father Pete blessed Mark and Candie, and then they turned towards the congregation. Porkchop, who had been an angel sitting at my feet during the ceremony, barked, as if giving his blessing to his aunt Candie and new uncle, too. The organist started up again, and the newly married couple started down the aisle, waving to their guests.

Tears of joy and happiness trickled down my face. Hank turned to me and took my arm to follow Mark and Candie.

"Come on, Porkchop. Your work today is done, and you did a fantastic job." I reached down and petted my pup.

Greetings of "Congratulations!" and a few "Finally's" followed the bride and groom as we walked past the well-wishers.

Hank leaned towards me, concern etched on his face when he saw my tears. "Are you all right?"

"I'm just so happy for Mark and Candie."

Hank shook his head. "You're happy, so that's why you're crying? Women."

I swiped at my tears. "I know, crazy. But so much has happened. I wondered if this day would ever come."

As we exited the church, a limo festooned with violet and white streamers awaited the bride and groom. Candie and Mark climbed in. She lowered the window and waved to her friends gathered on the church step. "It's party time, everyone. Meet you all at Momma Mia's," she shouted to us.

I laughed as the limo pulled away from the curb. Hank opened the door to his Jeep, which was also decked out in matching streamers.

He put his key in the ignition as I got Porkchop settled in the back seat. "I think it is going to be one rollicking party."

"Especially with the Loopy Ladies there."

Hank raised an eyebrow at me.

I reached over and pushed back that lock of brown hair that had fallen over his forehead. Porkchop was already snoozing in the back seat. I think the excitement of being ring bearer had worn him out. "You'd be surprised how crazy a bunch of hookers can act when they're out to celebrate, and Candie and Mark's wedding is something to certainly celebrate."

* * *

I leaned back in my chair at the reception and rubbed my stomach. "I'm stuffed. Susan and Brian outdid themselves today. The penne vodka and lasagna were superb."

"I have to agree. I've never tasted better." Hank lifted a glass of Trails Head to his lips.

My foot nudged the pillow under our table where Porkchop lay chewing on a rawhide bone. Candie had had a special pillow made up for Porkchop—violet, of course, and with his name and today's date 07/07 embroidered on it. "Porkchop did a fabulous job today. Don't you think?"

Hank nodded and reached into the side pocket of his tux.

I frowned and pointed at the brown bag he had pulled out. "What do you have there?"

"Something special I bought for my buddy there."

I laughed as he pulled out a doggie shirt and held it up for me to read.

Police K-9 Unit.

"He's now an official member of the Wings Falls Police." Hank reached down and slipped the shirt over Porkchop's head.

"I hate to mention this after all the wonderful time we've had today, but what is going to happen to Valerie?" I asked, twirling the stem of my wineglass in my fingers.

Hank placed his glass on the table. "She'll stand trial for the murder of Tommy Ray, and her peers will determine her fate."

I traced a circle on the white tablecloth with my fingernail. "And Bret Hargrove? What will happen to him?"

Hank frowned. "That's in the State's hands. We don't get involved in their cases. But he's out on bail. Where he found the money to post it, I have no idea."

"Do you think he'll go to jail?" I asked.

Hank shook his head. "My guess—no. This is his first offense, so I believe the judge will give him probation and possibly community work."

"It's sad what greed can do to a person. At least Mark won the primary on Tuesday, and right now he's running unopposed. If he wins in November—and I know he will—Wings Falls will stay in good hands. Darlene weighs heavy on my mind, too. I wonder what will happen to her and the baby."

"There might be a little good news on that front. While going through Tommy Ray's diary, we discovered an entry where he mentioned that he took out a life insurance policy and made Darlene the beneficiary."

I let out a deep breath. "Thank heavens for small favors. I guess Tommy Ray did have a conscience after all when it came to Darlene and his child."

Hank pulled me closer and nuzzled my hair. "Let's not talk about this anymore and just enjoy the rest of the day."

I agreed. "Oh, look, Candie and Mark are going to cut the cake." I pointed towards a three-tier masterpiece that Franny Goodway had constructed. Creamy frosted layers were covered in white and lavender roses. A traditional bride and groom resided on the top layer.

Susan Mayfield stood next to the cake and clapped her hands. "Attention please. The bride and groom are going to cut this beautiful cake Franny baked."

Applause filled Momma Mia's. I glanced at the table where Franny sat. Pink tinged her dark skin.

Candie and Mark made their way through the tables to the cake, holding hands. "Stand up and take a bow," Candie said to Franny.

Franny blushed even more as she stood and gave a small wave.

Candie took our Memaw Parker's wedding knife into her hands. It twinkled in the restaurant's lights. Mark placed his over hers.

"That's a beautiful knife, " Hank said.

"Yes, it was our grandmother's. She used it on her wedding day, and then both Candie's mom and mine used it on theirs. Sort of a family tradition." I thought of my mother and how she treasured that knife.

Hank squeezed my hand. "I like that tradition."

I blinked my eyes. *What did he mean by that?*

Laughter filled the restaurant. I looked towards the cake and saw Candie mushing a piece into Mark's mouth. I couldn't help laughing, too. "They make a great couple, don't they?"

Hank nodded. "Yes, but I can think of another great couple."

I raised my eyebrows. "Who?"

"Us." He reached into the inside pocket of his jacket and pulled out a small jewelry box and handed it to me.

My heart pounded in my chest. "What is this?"

Hank pointed to the small square box. "Only way to find out is to open it up."

With trembling fingers, I lifted the box's lid. Inside, nestled on a piece of blue satin, rested a gold heart. My fingers shook so much I thought I'd drop it as I lifted it out of the box. I looked into Hank's crystal-blue eyes. "Oh my, this is so beautiful."

He pointed to the delicate heart. "Turn it over."

Puzzled, I did as he instructed. *MTYLTT HANK* was engraved on the back of the heart.

"What does this mean?"

Hank took the heart from me and turned me so he could latch it around my neck. "That I love you—More Than Yesterday, Less Than Tomorrow."

Tears streamed down my face as I turned back to face him. "You do?"

Hank drew me to him and whispered into my ear, "Of course I do. I knew you were special from the first moment we met."

Porkchop stood on his hind legs and barked as if to add his bark of approval.

"What's got you crying like a baby?"

Startled, I looked up and saw Gladys and Frank standing next to our table. I fingered the necklace Hank had placed around my neck. "Hank told me he loves me."

Gladys threw back her head and laughed. Her purple curls bounced along with her laughter. "Of course, he does, you ninny. Anyone could see that, right, pookie bear?"

Frank dutifully nodded.

ABOUT THE AUTHOR

Syrl Ann Kazlo, a retired teacher, lives in upstate New York with her husband and two very lively dachshunds. Kibbles and Death is the first book in her Samantha Davies Mystery series, featuring Samantha Davies and her lovable dachshund, Porkchop. When not writing Syrl is busy hooking—rug hooking that is—reading, and enjoying her family. She is a member of Sisters in Crime and the Mavens of Mayhem.

Learn more about S.A. Kazlo at:
www.sakazlo.com

Made in United States
Cleveland, OH
24 November 2024

10861002R00120